VENTURE CAPITALIST

Book 2

Promise

This is a work of fiction. Names, characters, places and incidents
are a production of the author's imagination. Locations and public
names are sometimes used for atmospheric purposes. Any
resemblance to actual people, living or dead, or to businesses,
companies, events, institutions or locations is completely
coincidental.

Venture Capitalist: Promise/Ainsley St Claire   1ʳᵗ edition

AINSLEY ST CLAIRE

VENTURE CAPITALIST

Book 2
Promise

A Novel

SARA

J TALK TO SEVERAL CLIENTS as I wander our fall picnic, 'Carnival' the theme this year. It's a fun day—until I see him. I knew in the back of my mind that he might be here, but I was hoping that after our break-up Henry would want to stay as far away from me as I want to stay away from him.

Henry's almost otherworldly in his chiseled strength, and from a distance, I can truly see how gorgeous he is. His light brown hair with natural blond highlights has grown since the last time I saw him. His blue eyes still look as if they see right through me. Sometimes with Henry, I used to feel so connected to him and so familiar that I was able to forget how absolutely devastating he is in the looks department.

All the color must drain from my face when he sees me and walks over. "Hey, Sara."

"Why are you here, Henry?"

Staring me up and down like he's buying a dress for his wife, he says, "I'm here to see you, princess." He grasps me by the arm and leads me behind a tent, where we're out of sight.

No one plays my body as well as Henry, and I hate the way it responds to him—my breathing quickens, my nipples pebble and my panties quickly become wet. That is until my brain fully engages, and I remember why we're no longer together. "Henry, where's Claudia?"

Not taking his eyes off me, he points to the throng of people. "She's over there somewhere with the kids. I had to see you."

I glance around frantically. "Henry, this isn't the time or the place."

"But you aren't returning my calls or texts. I miss you, and I need you," he tells me as he rubs his hard cock against my mound while he tries to reach under the skirt of my sundress.

Trying hard to keep my concentration, I say with more confidence than I feel, "I haven't returned your calls because there's nothing more to say. You have a beautiful family, and I don't want to be a mistress." I turn to walk away.

Grabbing me by the arm, he pulls me to his chest. "I love kissing these lips," he says quietly.

He kisses me, taking my mouth as if it belongs to him. My body deceives me, throbbing to feel every inch of him. He distracts me from my fortitude and the haze lifts. Finally, my senses come to me and I push him away to break the kiss.

He smiles at me. "I'll call you later." And he walks away.

I wipe my mouth with the back of my hand, mad at myself for allowing him to get to me. I watch him leave, secretly wanting to reach for him and tell him to stay, but I know that isn't fair to his family or to me. If he isn't going to think of them, at least I will.

Glancing around the carnival, I'm in awe. Everywhere I look it's wall-to-wall employees, clients and their families, here for the annual Sullivan Healy & Newhouse, or SHN, fall picnic. We're the most sought-after venture capital firm in the Bay Area.

To show our strength in the market, our chief operations officer and fellow partner at SHN, Emerson Winthrop, and her team organized this spectacular event for over five thousand people. And what an event it is.

I see Emerson and walk up to her. "Are you hiding?"

She laughs. "Is it obvious?"

"No. I was only teasing."

She puts her arm around my shoulder. "I can't believe so many people are here."

Turning to stare at her, I tell her, "Your team did an incredible job. I know Mason wanted to show the technology community that, despite the recent rough spots, we're strong, and you've done it. Did you see the line of people working their way in?"

With so much excitement, she exclaims, "I know! I hope the food trucks have enough food for everyone."

We begin walking and greet people as we wander through the crowd. I'm awestruck at all the fun people are having. It's wonderful to see so many we work with outside of their offices or boardrooms with their families as they interact, network and enjoy the warm fall day.

A short, dark-haired woman approaches me. "Sara?"

I recognize her but can't remember her name or her start-up we funded and helped to sell. How embarrassing. "Why, hello!"

"You guys have done an incredible job with this event. I can definitely see why these events are legendary. How are Mason, Dillon and Cameron?"

Mason, Dillon and Cameron are the three founding partners at SHN. They began funding start-ups together as a hobby and a way to share some of our luck, giving seed money to projects we liked as a side gig to their regular jobs. When four of their investments were bought for millions of dollars each, they were addicted to the gamble and the high of identifying a winner when investing in an exciting idea.

"They're doing great. Have you seen them? They should be around here somewhere."

"I'm trying to talk to each of you this afternoon. I'm so grateful to all of you. Without your support in my little fashion app, I'd still be working as an accountant, for a big firm dreaming of fashion and hoping to make my rent."

Of course! Cindy Chou. I remember her. Her company was an early investment SHN made, having developed an app during an elective class at Stanford. I remember Cameron being amazed at how simple it was, but it would give all the fashion houses multiple ways to get their clothes out to potential buyers. We helped her sell to each of the fashion houses, then worked our way to the cosmetic companies and finally to the department stores. She's more than a billionaire now.

"Cindy, I don't think you're giving yourself enough credit. You were the one with the great idea. We were just able to help you get it to market."

Glowing, she coos, "I can't thank you all enough. And thank you for inviting me to this party. So many cute single guys."

Really? How is it that I see only married men with their families? "Well, good luck. Let me know if there's anyone I can introduce you to. We single girls have to stick together," I share with her in a conspiratorial tone.

As I walk away, I catch glimpses of our employees and the four other partners.

Cameron is standing with a short, bald man I don't recognize, and it appears as if he needs rescuing. I walk over. "Hey, Cameron."

With a look of relief, he gestures to the man he's talking to and says, "Sara, I'd like you to meet Gary Barns. He has a clever idea for us to consider. Very technical."

I extend my hand. "Gary, so nice to meet you. I'm SHN's in-house attorney. We'd love to see your proposal. You can forward it to our office, and I'll get it to the right people to review." Removing a business card from my pocket, I hand it to him. "My contact information is right there. Feel free to e-mail that off."

"Thank you. I don't have it down on paper yet," he sputters.

Of course you don't.

"No problem. Send it when you do. We get about a thousand requests a week. This allows us to catalog them into our offices and track them so no one can accuse us of stealing an idea. It protects you as well as us. Feel free to check out our website for what we'll need to see from you with your proposal." And before he can say anything else, I turn and lead Cameron away.

"I need to carry my business cards around with me so I can do and say the same thing," Cameron mumbles under his breath. "Gary had me cornered"—he looks down at his watch—"almost forty minutes."

"You were looking rather stranded. Glad I could help. We should know almost everyone here. Hopefully he wasn't a party-crasher."

"No, I think I saw him with someone. But who knows?"

Glancing around and seeing people everywhere, I tell him, "I think I'm going to try the food trucks. Any suggestions?"

"I don't think you can go wrong with any of them. Good luck, and thanks again for the rescue."

I line up at a food truck, and as I debate ordering the shrimp or the carnitas tacos, I feel a tap on my shoulder. Turning, I see Mason. "Hey. Have you tried the tacos? Any recommendations?" I ask.

"I had the fish and they were fantastic. Try one of each and let me know." Leaning in he says softly, "Can you believe all these people? And they all seem to be having a good time."

Turning to him, "You seem surprised."

Mason begins to stammer, when Dillon walks up and says, "Hey. Try the shrimp tacos. They're awesome."

Dillon leans in and barely above a whisper says, "If Perkins Klein thinks they can undermine us, this party shows them we have a lot of people in The Valley who support us."

Perkins Klein has recently been trying to sabotage our business and steal it away. We probably went a bit overboard with the carnival to show people we were viable and strong, but seeing all the excitement, I think it was worth it.

TREY

$\mathcal{I}$ DIDN'T ASK to be born into American royalty, and what's worse, I didn't ask to be born into Silicon Valley royalty. Everywhere I go, people know who I am. They know my name is Charles Michael Arnault III, or Trey. Being famous for being famous—or having a pretty face—isn't enough. I run Sandy Systems, a Fortune 20 company that my parents started, but I still want to make my own mark in the world.

I'm a man who cares about people, a man who has ambitions of my own as opposed to riding the jet stream of my family. I'm regularly approached by the paparazzi, members of the media, or people who've never met me but think they know me. I dislike that they feel they can ask me anything and expect I will happily answer. The answers to the most frequently asked personal questions are as follows: Yes. No. We're merely good friends. None of your business. Honest, she's my cousin from Montana. I've worn both. Maybe someday, but not outside of the Bay Area. Thank you.

I'm out with my buddies at a trendy club in the Tenderloin district. It's dark, the loud music beats to a dance mix, and three of my friends and I have secured a private corner of the club, though girls still seek us out. We get it, we're spoiled. Unfortunately I'm always on high alert. Now that everyone has a camera, everything can show up in the tabloids, so I have to be cautious.

A beautiful blonde, wearing a skintight micro dress and stilettos with cleavage and enough shake that her double Ds are most likely real, shimmies up to me and says, "Hey there, handsome."

"Hello."

"I'm Heather," she says as she leans in and kisses me on the cheek. Immediately her hand goes to my crotch, and she strokes me. It doesn't take much and she has me hard. "Shall we go back to your place?" she asks, putting a finger seductively into her mouth.

I wish this was the first time, but unfortunately this happens a lot. Most women are interested in my bank account, what I can do for them, or getting themselves some publicity. *TMZ* features me about once a month, and I can't stand it. I need to be careful. I have stockholders—and, more importantly, my parents—who cringe every time I show up in the tabloids.

I slow us down a bit, preferring we talk. "Tell me about yourself, Heather."

Seemingly frustrated that I'm not marching her out to my condo, she sits down as she lets out a breath of boredom. "I live here in The City, and I work for a financial company downtown."

"What do you like to do when you aren't at your job?"

Restless in her seat, she purrs, "You mean when I'm not giving spectacular blowjobs?"

Good grief. I force a smile. "Yes."

With a big grin, she sits back, twists her finger in her hair and seductively licks her lips. "I volunteer at a homeless shelter, and I like to take sunset strolls along the beach."

"Really? Which shelter?"

"Oh you know, the one on 3rd Street."

Through my various commitments, we do a lot of work with the many homeless shelters throughout town, and I'm very familiar with where she's talking about. "Delancey? Or is it Sanctuary?"

She runs her finger up and down my chest. "I'd love to see where your happy-trail line goes."

"My happy-trail line?" I know exactly what she means, but she's even more aggressive than the usual women I meet.

Giggling, she coos, "Yes, silly. You know, the line of hair that starts below your belly button and leads to somewhere exciting."

I've got her number. She's one of those who wants the notoriety of sleeping with me.

I give up. She isn't interested in me personally. They never want to talk about when my cousin and I visited the earthquake disaster zone in Port-au-Prince, Haiti. Or when I was sixteen and spent the summer working as a wrangler in Wyoming. They want fame, fortune and notoriety. Not me.

I try several times to start a conversation, then hint at having her move on since I'm not going to take her home or go home with her, but she's relentless.

"Can we take a selfie?"

"My panties are so wet. You should see."

"I love this song. It makes me horny."

My friends are distracted by women they've met, so I politely excuse myself from her relentless attack, explaining that I need to go to the bathroom. She follows me right to the door. I wonder if she was planning to come in and join me.

Club bathrooms are so gross, but I hide for a few moments, stalling as long as I can and hoping it's long enough.

Heather is still waiting for me when I emerge from the bathroom.

"I'm sorry. I need to go," I tell her.

She appears crestfallen as she pulls a card from her pocket. "Oh. Okay. Here's my number. I'd love to see you some time."

I smile, not wanting to hurt her feelings, and say, "Thanks."

I call a Lyft and head out of the club, turning the corner as I wait for the ride-share to arrive. I try not to make eye contact with the people who pass me on the street as I text my twin sister.

Me: Hey. What are you up to?

CeCe: I'm out with the girls. You already done for the night?

Me: Yes. Want to hang out?

CeCe: We're over at Quince. Come on over.

Me: Should be there within fifteen minutes.

THREE

SARA

S ITTING IN OUR Monday morning partners meeting, we're all sharing stories of clients and the success of the carnival, but I can't stay focused. I keep thinking of Henry and what he does for me. I cried over the weekend thinking about him. We dated for only six months, and we broke up a little over a month ago when I learned he was married.

I've concluded that he doesn't want me, he only wants sex. I'm angry at myself for being so naïve to not figure it out sooner, but also angry at him for all the lies. I'm sad that I still think of him and want something we'll never have. I wasted time with Henry. San Francisco is not single-female friendly, and if my job didn't require me here, I'd be gone. I hear there are single straight men in Alaska.

As I try to get my head in the game, Mason says, "Well, I think it's time to let you all know that we have a verbal agreement with Smithright Software."

To take precautions, the partners secretly chose, researched and wrote bids for three companies, all under the radar while we had our firm concentrating on bids that we thought were less than stellar but would be fed to the competitor. It's another sigh of relief to know we won another start-up, and we're all anxious. "Great news!" is heard all around.

"Sara, I'll get you the details, and you can run through the contracts," Mason continues, then turns to Emerson. "We discussed a laundry list of activities that your team will need to get accomplished."

Emerson nods. "I've already identified someone to work on-site, and we can move forward with recruiting a finance person to aid them in the reporting issues that Dillon found during the audit process."

"Good thinking," Dillon says, grinning at her.

Since our creation as a company, we had a rule of not dating in the workplace— particularly within the partners. Dillon and Emerson clicked better than most. As they each struggled with life-altering challenges, they leaned on each other heavily, and their strong friendship developed into a wonderful relationship. With the other partners' blessings, Dillon and Emerson recently got engaged, and we're all happy for them.

Cameron, our technology partner, chimes in. "It appears that Perkins Klein will pull in the three duds we allowed to be slipped to them, but we need to ferret out our mole. While I have no problem working in a vacuum and doing the work quietly, I feel we're spending a lot of money in salaries to not be chasing this with our entire team."

We all nod, and Dillon says, "While I was on my sabbatical, you did a background check on each employee and didn't find anything. What do we think should be next?"

I speak up. "Emerson and Mason, Tom over at PeopleMover

confirmed our espionage suspicions when he gave you our re-search that Perkins Klein presented to them. We need to de-termine who has access to everything. We also need to be sure we're marking things confidential." I turn to Cameron. "Can we determine who accesses what files and who might be checking out things they aren't supposed to be looking at?"

"Absolutely. Everything an employee touches has a digital footprint."

"Great. Do we feel comfortable opening up our research team?" Mason asks.

"I think so," Dillon responds. "My team is constantly review-ing and evaluating proposals." He glances at an Excel spreadsheet he has with him. "Right now we have better than six hundred proposals we're sifting through. How about we have them focus on those companies, particularly those in the Perkins Klein port-folio, that already have angel or first-round funding."

"That sounds good."

"Cameron, if you could review those companies and check out their technology and viability, that would set us up for our next few prospects," Dillon continues.

"Sounds good," Cameron replies.

"Great. And Dillon, you're heading to New York to ring the bell with Tom to celebrate PeopleMover going public this week, right?" Mason asks.

"Yes, we leave Thursday in his private jet. Being there will be exciting."

"Any thought on where they'll land by the end of the first day?"

"I'm guessing that should be around one hundred million dollars for the company bottom line," Dillon tells us.

I whistle. "Nice!"

"Well, I think we should all celebrate this weekend," Mason says. "Not only do we have Dillon and Emerson's engagement party, but this is our biggest win to date. Speaking of which, when we first formed SHN, we talked about an advisory board. Dillon has suggested that since we have an in, we approach Charles Arnault, Jr. to determine if he would like to be on our advisory board. What does everyone think?"

"I love the idea," Cameron replies. "He knows technology, business, and finance. If he'd be willing to do it, it would be of great value to us."

I watch the group, and everyone seems to be on board with the idea. "Has anyone approached him?" I ask.

"No. I thought since they're hosting the engagement party on Sunday afternoon, we might be able to speak with him after the party. It would mean we all need to stick around."

"I've known Charles since I was a freshman at Stanford," Emerson shares. "He's always fair, open, and honest. When you all approached me, he knew you and knew you well. Without his approval, I never would've sold my company to you. I think he would be very supportive."

Mason turns to me. "I'd like to hear from both Dillon and Sara on this."

"I suggested it, so obviously I'm for it," Dillon starts. "But I've gotten to know him these past few months. He's tied to many companies here in The Valley. He's also seen a lot and brings a perspective of experience we don't have and probably need. I don't have any problem asking him. I think the party would be a great way to open the conversation to gauge his interest."

"I agree," I reply.

Looking at the group, Mason says, "Great. I like the idea. Let's see what he says. I think his perspective on the espionage would be interesting."

Emerson sighs. "And to think we almost lost PeopleMover to Perkins Klein."

Dillon puts his arm around her. "Only because you and Mason saved it."

Mason and I shake our heads as Emerson adds, glancing at Dillon, "No, it's because Tom Sutterland had a level of ethics and loyalty to you, Dillon."

"Okay, you two," Cameron pipes up. "Get a room if you're going to start getting busy."

Emerson turns crimson and we all agree that this is going to be a good week.

As we're walking out of the meeting, Emerson asks, "Sara, do you have a minute?"

"Of course," I tell her.

"Any chance I can convince you to walk down to Starbucks with me?"

I'm a bit taken aback, hoping nothing is wrong, "Sure, is everything all right?"

"Absolutely. I'd like to ask you something."

"Let me grab my coat and my wallet."

"You only need your coat. I'm buying."

We have a Starbucks in our building, but to stretch our legs—and sometimes for privacy—we walk the three blocks to another one. Emerson has this amazing glow about her, and she seems happy. I was worried when Dillon asked to come back, but only if he could have a relationship with Emerson. I wasn't sure if the relationship was going to create problems for the team, but I love them both and can't imagine SHN without them.

I don't have many friends. I'm not super outgoing, I work twelve-hour days, seven days a week, and my idea of a fun time is often curling up with a good book. Emerson is the closest thing I have to a close friend, but outside of work and the occasional glass of wine after work, we don't do much together. However, we are more than partners. We've shared a lot of ourselves, and I adore both Emerson and Dillon. I'm glad we're taking this time to hang out for a bit.

After we have our coffee in hand and sit down a moment, Emerson says, "Dillon and I were wondering if you would be willing to be in our wedding as a bridesmaid."

I'm completely stunned. "I'd be honored. But I've never been a bridesmaid before. What do I need to do?"

"Well, you'll most likely have to rein in my best friend, CeCe, but beyond that, you guys will all go out and pick out a dress. My only request is that they should all be the same color and fabric, but maybe different cuts so they flatter your figure. And maybe you can wear them again."

"That's easy."

Conspiratorially, Emerson says, "You would think so. There will be five of you. CeCe, my friends Greer and Hadlee, and Dillon's sister Siobhan. I think you met her at Dillon's father's funeral."

"Yes, I remember her. Isn't she pregnant?"

"She'll have the baby in the next few weeks, and we have a little over a year to get it together. I'll admit, I feel as if I'm getting a late start on this. We have time, but people sure do get worked up about wedding planning, and work has been too busy lately to deal with it all."

"I hear you."

"I've asked Tina to be my wedding planner."

"Great thinking. Tina will put on an amazing wedding, if the fall carnival's anything to go by."

"She has a budget in mind that's probably more than I want to spend—she has so many plans and is going crazy—but it's nice to have her narrowing down choices for me."

I'm stunned at how things have progressed with her planning, but it occurs to me that she hasn't told me *where* they plan to marry. "Do you think you're going to marry here in San Francisco?"

"Part of me wants to, since all our friends are here. But the other part of me wants my family priest to marry us back in Denver. Tina is going to approach him about coming out, and then we'll have a better idea of our options."

Reaching across the table, I grasp her hand and give her an assuring squeeze. "I'm excited. Thank you for including me. That's sweet."

"It was never a question for either of us. You've been a wonderful friend to both of us. When I talked about it with Dillon, he was relieved. He was hoping I'd ask you."

We stand to walk back to the office, and I lean in to give her a big hug, "This is wonderful."

TREY

*I*T'S ANOTHER FRIDAY NIGHT, and I'm out with the guys. We've hit a different spot down in Palo Alto. Emerson has her big engagement party on Sunday afternoon, and all sorts of other activities are going on this weekend, so I'll be staying with my parents.

"I'm excited to see her brother Michael. Shortly after our freshman year started at Cal, Emerson and CeCe, who were roommates at Stanford, showed up to visit us. They arranged a dinner, and I was told Michael, who was also at Cal, would be joining us. I'd seen him around campus at Berkeley. He played football, and one of the girls I had a crush on was hanging out with him. Michael and I became great friends, and after our dinner we began to hang out. When Michael moved into an apartment in town, we decided to live together. He's the brother I never had.

He dated the girl I had a crush on the entire time and eventually married her. Alicia was the girl we all fell in love with. She's smart as a whip, but she's also always positive and could cure anyone of the blues. I was in their wedding almost five years ago. They have three kids now and live in Denver.

Bringing myself back to the present, I realize the guys have been talking, and I have no idea what they're saying. A cute redhead with a decent figure, her dress showing off some beautiful large tits, has been making eyes with me. I signal her to join me, and she seems to glide as she walks over.

"Hi. I'm Mindy."

"Nice to meet you, Mindy. I'm Trey. Would you like to dance?"

Rubbing her soft breast against my arm, she whispers, "I know exactly who you are, and I'd love to."

Not again.

Taking her by the hand, we walk to the middle of the dance floor and, despite the pulsating beat of the music, she turns away from me and grinds her ass on my cock. I immediately get hard, and as she lifts her arms into the air, I stand back.

She beckons me to come closer, but I just smile at her and keep my distance.

The song changes, giving her the opportunity to lean in and brush her lips against my sensitive spot on my neck. Her kisses move seductively up my neck, nibbling as she goes, then whispers in my ear as she caresses her nipple. "Would you like to come back to my hotel room with me?" She's not even fazed by the public display.

I carefully pull myself away and begin to make my exit. "I'm going to need to go."

"You have to leave already? I was hoping we might get a chance to spend some time together horizontally," she says with a wicked smile.

I don't think so. I force a smile. "Very tempting."

She scrambles to her phone. "Can we exchange numbers? I'd

love to see you again."

Trying to be polite, I stretch the truth as I explain, "Unfortunately I don't keep the same phone for very long. I'd hate to give you a number that will change in a few days."

"Oh, okay. Well," she tells me as she whips out a card from her bra, "Here's my number. If you ever want to spend some time horizontal, please give me a call."

Taking her card, I put it in my breast pocket. "You have the most beautiful brown eyes that I could get lost in. Thank you for the dances." Then I turn and almost run out the door. I notice my buddy, give him the nod that says, "Catch ya later," and I exit into the cool evening air.

I settle in the back seat of my car service and direct him to my folks' house north of the club. Glancing out the window, I decide that I refuse to be trapped by the past—or by expectations that come with being an Arnault. I watch as the thick traffic moves slowly. I've had the random one-night stand, but I tend to be a serial monogamist. My last girlfriend lasted six years, though I know my mom and sister didn't like her. She was an actress who seemed to like me for the publicity, nothing more.

I just want someone to love me for me.

"DUDE, YOU'RE HERE!" I say to Michael as he crosses the room and gives me a hug.

"Absolutely. My little sister is getting married, but I'm going to make sure there's a getaway car in case she needs it."

I stuff the last bite of my bagel in my mouth and drink a big gulp of my tepid coffee. I put my right hand on his shoulder, and with a hint of mischievousness, I share, "I don't know, man. I like Dillon as much as I like you."

"Can't stand him, huh?" we hear Alicia pipe up. "Give me a hug, you giant playboy!"

Her blonde hair is pulled back into a ponytail that leaves her neck long and sexy. She's in a light pink peasant blouse, my favorite color on her, and an amazingly tight pair of jeans. You'd never guess she's the mother of three kids. "Playboy? I'm not a playboy."

She smiles and gives me a big hug. "I see you on the cover of those tabloid magazines and even catch *TMZ* when they do a tease about you."

"Don't believe it. It's all fake." She kisses me chastely on my cheek and holds on tight.

"You know I'm waiting for you to realize the Michael is a giant nerd and you need to come live here in San Francisco with me."

Alicia laughs. "I don't think you'd enjoy the kids. They can be a bit challenging right now."

"Well, if they're anything like Michael here, I can manage them." We all laugh, enjoying the company of old friends. Glancing around, I ask, "So, what's the plan?"

"I think the wedding planner arranged for the families and bridal party to go golfing today."

"Great. I can get my ass kicked by your sister." I tell Michael ruefully.

"I got used to that years ago, man."

Alicia continues, "Those of us who don't play golf are headed into The City to shop at Union Square."

Michael groans and attempts to remind her, "We don't have tons of room in our suitcases. Please remember that when you buy a wardrobe for the boys and yourself."

Alicia elbows him in the stomach and smiles. "They can ship it home."

Gazing at his wife skeptically, he turns to me. "All right then, let's go."

"Be back before dinner, boys!" Alicia yells behind us.

TREY

*T*HE ENGAGEMENT PARTY at my folks' house for Emerson and Dillon is a blast. The Winthrop clan is truly family. They didn't grow up in the world that CeCe and I did, but they've never been in awe or treated us as anything other than normal people. We've never known if someone liked us for us or if they liked us for the fame and fortune. With the Winthrop clan, it was never a question.

It was fun playing golf and catching up with Michael this afternoon, and I wish I could spend more time with him, but since this is my parents' home, I figure I need to try to talk to everyone. I work my way around the party and particularly enjoy meeting Dillon's mom, his sister, her husband and their baby boy.

As I glance around, I notice the most amazing woman I've ever seen. Her flowing dirty blonde hair has this soft curl that's sexy as hell; I want to run my fingers through it. She has stunning blue-green eyes and legs that appear to go on forever. I want to meet this vixen who's talking to my sister.

I want to play it casual, so I saunter up to CeCe and say as cool as I can muster, "Hey, sis."

"Oh, hey," she greets me, then continues her conversation with this woman. She doesn't stop her conversation to introduce me, and I just stand there, completely taken by this woman as they go on about bridesmaids' dresses.

CeCe finally notices me still standing there and turns to me. "Do you need me?"

"No. I thought you might introduce me to your friend."

"Oh. Trey, this is Sara. She's friends with Dillon and Emerson and is in the wedding party."

I extend my hand, and she gives me the most brilliant smile. "So nice to meet you."

In a low and sexy voice, she tilts her head slightly and says, "Likewise."

I'm embarrassed by how hard I am right now. She's a pure vision. Unlike me, she's dressed unpretentiously and fashionably in a simple green dress. I tug on the collar of my shirt, a new level of discomfort filling me. It's like she can see right through me. I don't think I've ever felt like this before.

CeCe stares at me expectantly, and I'm at a loss for words. "I'll see you around," I barely manage to get out, then turn and walk away quickly.

I can't believe I screwed that up royally.

What a jerk I must've sounded like. Good grief. Nicely done, Trey!

At least I know I'll see her again.

Positioning myself in the corner of the room, I watch Sara. She's animated, and a few of the men flirt with her. When Dillon wanders over and asks what I'm up to, I carefully ask him about Sara.

"She and Emerson are the two female partners. Sara's our lawyer."

"Oh, so she's smart, too."

"Brilliant, actually. Have you met her?"

"Oh yes, CeCe introduced me. I'm only curious."

Laughing, Dillon tells me, "I don't think she's your type."

I'm stunned by this. "What do you mean?"

"She's a serious girl. I don't think she sleeps around."

I don't know why that wouldn't be my type, but I stutter, "G-g-good to know."

Emerson walks up and says, "Hey, Trey. Are you having a nice time?" She brings me into a tight hug.

I kiss her on the cheek. "I am, thanks. I always like hanging out with your brothers."

Turning to Dillon, she says, "I need to drag you away. My parents' best friends just arrived, and I'd like to introduce you to them."

They walk away, and I see Sara standing alone at the bar, looking around. This is my opportunity. Taking a deep breath, I walk up and ask, "Can I get you a drink?"

She turns to me and flashes that smile again, making my stomach turn and my heart beat faster. "Actually, I was hoping to find a glass for some water. I have to drive home in a little bit, and I've already had my one drink I allow myself when I'm driving."

I'm impressed that she's good about drinking and driving. "I can get you a glass. We have tons of juices and sodas if you prefer that."

"Thanks, but water's easy."

"Water it is." I pour her a glass, adding a few ice cubes and a lemon wedge. "Are you having a nice time tonight?"

"I am. Your parents host a beautiful party. It's great to meet so many of Dillon's and Emerson's family and friends. Forgive me for being so presumptuous, but how did you get so lucky to be part of the wedding party?"

I love a woman who isn't shy about asking questions. "Emerson chose so many of you ladies that I think Dillon asked everyone he knew, and after they all said no, then he asked me."

She laughs, the most beautiful sound I think I've ever heard, and says, "I somehow doubt that."

"CeCe and Emerson were roommates at Stanford, and Michael, Emerson's brother, and I were both attending Cal. They introduced us and the four of us were tight. Over the years, I think she thought of me as her fifth brother. What about you?"

"I work with both Dillon and Emerson."

"SHN has over seventy-five employees. Is everyone in the wedding?"

She blushes a brilliant shade of red, and my heart beats even faster. "No. Just the partners."

"That's right, CeCe did say you were a partner."

"No, actually. She only told you I was in the wedding party."

"Ouch! You caught me." She smiles, her eyes twinkling. "I asked Dillon about you. I made such an idiot of myself when CeCe introduced us, and I needed to find out more about you."

She appears surprised and asks, "What else did you learn?"

"That you're smart and I'm not good enough for you."

She stands straight, seeming ready to pounce. "He said that?"

"Not in those words. He's very protective of you." Attempting to change the subject, I ask, "Other than work, what else do you do?"

"Other than work? That's a thing? We've taken twenty-three companies public in the last year and sold almost forty others. I don't have a lot of time beyond work right now. What about you?"

"I do some volunteer work, and I run the company my parents started."

Most will steer the conversation to my parents' company. The interested people ask me about my volunteer work. I want to jump up and down when she asks, "What kind of volunteer work?"

My shoulders relax and I smile. "I do a lot with homeless shelters for at-risk teens."

"You're kidding. I know the Catholic Charities Shelter, but I haven't been involved with them in over a decade. Father O'Connor ran it then. Is he still involved?"

I'm stunned. "Yes, Father O'Connor still runs the shelter. You really did volunteer there. I'm impressed."

"Well, not really. But he was a nice guy. Really had a great way of reaching out to kids and helping keep them out of prostitution and drugs."

"If you ever want to come with me, I hope you'll call."

We spend the next forty-five minutes talking about various shelters around San Francisco and getting to know one another. I'm floored when she tells me she likes to play tourist and do the tours around the Bay Area. "I know it's a bit kitschy, but it's fun and often educational."

As the crowd dissipates, Cameron walks up and talks to us for a moment, then says to Sara, "Are you ready?"

She nods and turns to me. "It was amazing talking to you. I think we're paired in the wedding party, so you'll be stuck with me a lot."

I want to jump up and down as if I've scored a touchdown. "I look forward to it. Hope to see you soon, and let me know if you want to go with me to Catholic Charities Shelter."

"I will." And she walks away with a small wave and a glorious smile. I can't take my eyes off her, watching as all the SHN partners retire to my dad's office.

Normally I'd take this as my excuse to leave, but instead I talk to my sister and her friends, plus a few others, stalling so I can find out what's going on. I want to see Sara one last time. An hour later they finally exit the office, my dad shaking hands with Mason. Seems like they've made some kind of deal.

Then I see her. I catch Sara's eye, and we smile at one another. It's enough to keep me going for another week.

SARA

CHARLES POURS THE SIX OF US a glass of his favorite cognac, and we all sit around the fire in his home office.

Mason starts the conversation. "Charles, when we started SHN, we knew we would get to the point where we would need someone to, as Emerson says, 'help us see the forest for the trees.' We need someone with your expertise to help us grow to the next level. We were wondering if you would be interested in being an advisor to us. We're having some issues and would like your experience and knowledge to help guide us through our challenges."

Emerson adds, "It's a paid position, Mr. Arnault."

Charles chuckles. "I've shared with Dillon how impressed I've been with SHN and the direction of your company. You all seem to have a unique perspective that has served you quite well. I think if you were to allow me to also be an investor, I'd consider being an advisor to you under one condition."

We're all celebrating, but no one seems to want to ask him his terms for fear of the answer, so I take the plunge. "Mr. Arnault, what is your condition?"

There is a palpable silence before he replies. "Well, maybe two conditions. First, you need to call me Charles and second, we have dinner here at our house every Sunday night for the next few months. Granted, there will be times when some of you won't be able to make it, but I think meeting regularly to discuss what's going on and the challenges you're facing would be a great idea, and we wouldn't be overheard by someone."

Dillon harrumphs. "That's it?" He gazes around the group as we all nod, then says, "That works for us."

"Okay then. I understand you have some immediate concerns, so tell me what's going on," Charles implores.

Mason begins by revealing our concerns about the mole and how we've countered it. Cameron shares a client revealed that we were struggling with Dillon's leave of absence. And the client gave us back a copy of our internal research that had been given to him as proof of our struggles.

Charles sits back and asks pointed questions but mostly listens. "So, you think Perkins Klein has someone in your organization?"

Emerson quietly says, "We believe so, yes."

Nodding, he turns to Cameron. "How are you tracking your digital footprints?"

This sets off a conversation that's heavily technology-driven and right over my head. But from what I can gather, Cameron is going to set up a program that will track and report what people are doing on their computers, and next week we'll see what he finds. Emerson will bring her laptop with access to our human resources information system, and we'll be able to cross-check a few things.

For our meeting next week, Charles will get in touch with an investigator who specializes in business espionage to talk to us after dinner. He also asks Dillon to bring the most recent list of potential investments for discussion.

Mason then tells him about our plan to feed Perkins Klein our duds.

"That's a good idea." He holds up his glass and, staring at the amber liquid, adds, "I have a few friends I might be able to use to lure them in. Let me think about it this week."

We all casually exit the meeting, noting a few stragglers still at the party. Cameron, Dillon and I move over to the food table to snack a little bit and process what happened.

"I'm excited that he agreed to advise us," Cameron shares.

"I know," Dillon replies. "Without any knowledge, he jumped right in and had solutions and even some ideas. This is going to be the right thing for us to grow to the next level."

Finishing the carrot I've popped in my mouth, I add, "I'm stunned at how fast this is going. Maybe with Charles's help, we'll ferret out our mole fairly quickly."

SARA

$\mathcal{A}$s usual, I'm the first to arrive at the office. I don't live far, and honestly I don't have much of a life. I turn all the lights on and enjoy the quiet. At this time of the morning it's bright, and you can see across the entire office. The partners all have glass offices and the desks in the middle of the open warehouse space all have low cubicles.

As I settle into my office and mentally prepare for my day, I see I have a message from a private investigator I hired last year to help find my biological mother. I'd like to meet her. I have so many questions. It has nothing to do with my foster parents, Jim and Carol, who have been amazing and my rock. I'm just hoping my biological mother knows who my father is, and I want to look into the eyes of someone who shares my genetic material.

I need to attend the partners meeting, but I want to know now. Quickly I call him. "Hi, Phil. Any news?"

"Well, I've located her. Her parents have quite a bit of money, and they seem to be hiding her. I was able to determine that after she left you, she went home for a short time and finished high school, and then they sent her on a gap year trip to Europe, but I don't have anything beyond that. No passport hits, and no hits on her social security number. She pays taxes on a trust, but as far as I'm able to find out, she's not using any of the money, but that doesn't tell us anything. Then something happened, and we found her through her lawyer. She's up in the Seattle area, married with a few kids."

Stunned to think that I may have a few half-siblings, I ask, "Have you seen her?"

"I haven't talked to her, but I've made a visual identification. You look a lot like her. She uses Catherine instead of Cathy, which is understandable, and seems to be using a new social security number."

"That seems odd. How did she get that?"

"We can't be sure, but we know it's in her name. I'll e-mail you her contact information, and you can figure out how you want to move forward."

"Thanks, Phil."

The e-mail pops up along with a photo of her. Her name is Catherine Ellington, and she does look like me. In the picture, she's wearing black pants and a red sweater, her blonde hair is piled high in a chignon and she has a very serious façade. Now that I know where she is, I want to reach out to her. I want so much to show up unannounced, but I need to ask her if she'll see me. I don't want to think about why, after keeping me for three years, she suddenly left me and rejected me. I have people who love and cherish me, but I want to get to know my biological mother and, if I'm lucky, my biological father.

The one-hour meeting feels like it takes over four hours. I'm anxious to get out and when we finally break, I walk immediately back to my office, close the glass door and sit down to write her the note I've mentally composed over the years.

I take out a piece of my personal stationery from my desk, a simple embossed card with my initials.

Dear Catherine,

My name is Sara Elizabeth White. When I was three years old, I was left with Father Tom at St. Agnes Catholic Church in San Francisco, California. I believe you may be my mother. I'm not seeking money. I'm an attorney and partner in a venture capital firm in San Francisco. I'd like to meet you and ask a few questions about you and my biological father. I'd be happy to come to you in Seattle. I know this is a lot, but I'd love to thank you for making the ultimate sacrifice. You can reach me at swhite@shn.com, or you may call me at 415-555-1212.

Sara

I walk directly to the post office and stand at the mailbox, nervous about her response. Opening the lid to drop my letter in, I close it again, over and over, unable to bring myself to let it go. I've thought about how reaching out to her may very well open the door to a relationship with my biological mother. What if she doesn't want me? What will I do? Then I think, what if she wants to meet me? I've always had the what-ifs, but now I'll know, and somehow that's scarier than not knowing.

Finally, a gentleman behind me says, "Excuse me," as he

reaches around me and places an envelope in the box.

His comment startles me from my thoughts. "Oh. Sorry." And I drop my letter in after his.

I walk back to the office, picking up a coffee for me and a chai tea latte for Emerson along the way.

Once in the office, I hand Emerson her chai. "Thank you. How did you know this was exactly what I needed?"

"I needed the walk and the caffeine, so I figured you might, too. Any interest in meeting up for drinks after work, say eight-ish?"

"Dillon and I were talking about going for a run, but I think after my crazy day I could use a glass of wine. Do you want it to be only us girls, or do we dare invite the guys?"

"The more the merrier. I was thinking of going to that new wine bar across the street, unless you had something else in mind?"

"Oh that sounds perfect. I hear they have wonderful fried calamari. I'll send a text to everyone. Last one to the elevator at eight buys?"

I laugh. "I'll be there at seven forty-five."

THE SOMA WINE BAR carries over one thousand bottles of wine and appetizers. Mason was last to the elevator, so he's stuck with the first round.

Examining the menu, Mason says, "I'm putting a limit on no more than a fifty-dollar glass of wine." He stares directly at Cameron. "That means stay away from the 1992 Screaming Eagle. A thousand dollars for a glass of wine is out of my budget."

Cameron lets out a big belly laugh. "You know me so well."

The waiter arrives, and we all give our wine orders, as well as six different appetizers. Making small talk before our food and wine arrive, we catch up on the wedding plans. Dillon leans over to the guys and says, "I've learned to just say yes. Really it isn't Emerson who cares. Tina is the ball-buster."

"The event planner from our carnival?" Cameron questions.

"Yes, she's our wedding planner, and she's on a mission," Emerson explains. "You'd think this was the royal wedding. We're looking at churches in the Colorado mountains. There's a beautiful one that my family priest is suggesting, and it might be a fun destination wedding. We're flying to Colorado this weekend with Tina to examine the venues she has in mind. Wish us luck."

"But if there's an emergency, please let me know," Dillon practically pleads. "I'm happy to let Emerson take over so I can handle what needs to be done."

Emerson gives him a sideways death stare. "Not if you know what's good for you. Remember, I wanted to essentially elope— only the five of us, a few friends and our family. Now we're inviting over a thousand people."

After the food and drinks arrive, we talk in hushed tones, mostly about what's going on with us in our areas. We're careful not to disclose anything, but it's cathartic to talk about it with one another. We do chat about adding Charles to our group and what we think he can bring to our mole issue, and we're all enthusiastic, agreeing that Charles really brings a large breadth of experience.

I ask Dillon, "Okay, now that you're back and you've had the chance to consider what's going on, how do you think Perkins Klein is getting our inside information?"

Dillon took a six-month sabbatical a few months ago, and since he's been back, the espionage seems to have lessened. Gazing at his clasped hands, he says, "I do think it's someone internally, but I also think Perkins Klein used my sabbatical as a means to sway some of our more vulnerable accounts. It's the internal person I can't figure out."

Mason shakes his head. "We can't figure it out either. We've gone through a list of those we think it may be, but we don't even agree on that."

"Very few even cross over from each of our lists. Hopefully Charles's guy can help," Cameron says.

"Do you think now that Dillon's back, the mole's going to be too scared to do anything?" I ask.

"We can only hope," Mason replies.

SARA

As I lie in bed, I run through the party on Sunday. I talked to two of Dillon's friends from college, one of whom asked for my number, but I fibbed and told him I was seeing someone. I don't want the complication, and I'm still smarting over my breakup with Henry.

On the other hand, CeCe's brother Trey was interesting. I'm sure I caught him watching me throughout the night, and our conversation was easy. Though I couldn't tell him that I was a runaway at Catholic Charities. It's too much to explain.

It may be wishful thinking on my part, but the two-hundred-megawatt smile he gave me at the end of the night made my stomach flip and my panties wet. Unfortunately, I'm not really his type. He dates high-profile women—actresses, socialites, any women who are famous. Guys like him seem to like girls who are low maintenance in the relationship department, putting up with the lack of privacy thanks to the press. I'm low maintenance in a lot of areas, but not when it comes to dating. I want to see my boyfriend often.

Thinking about Trey, I glide both hands down my breasts, over my hips and back to my stomach, then trace one cautious hand down my wide-open slit, sending one finger inside. As I arch back, I think of his smile and drift softly off as a new, more intense expression comes over his features.

I rock my hips rhythmically against my fingers, having no trouble bringing my already-swollen clit to a state of frenzy. I'm so unbelievably tense with pleasure that my entire pussy is spread wide and open, but I bring my knees even closer to my torso to open even farther. I continue circling my clit as fast as I can manage, breathing jagged and shuddering with effort, but avoiding coming.

I want this to be a mind-blowing orgasm. Pulling at my tender nipples, I think of Trey's beautiful lips and what I wish they were doing to my pussy, his tongue lapping up the juices running down my legs and coating my fingers. My breathing increases, my nipples pebble, and with one final thought, I explode.

Yes, it was a fine party. With the weekly visits and the wedding, maybe I'll be able to see Trey again and can work on my fantasy.

WHEN I DAYDREAM, I wish I had someone who would join me on vacation. Someone to cuddle with and laugh at my silly jokes. I thought I had that with Henry, and I was so hurt when I learned he was married.

He's a cheater. Once a cheater, always a cheater. No, thank you.

My cell phone rings and I answer with a cheerful "Hey, CeCe."

"Hi. Would you have any interest in joining the girls and me for drinks and dinner, and possibly dancing, on Saturday night?"

I think about what I have in my closet and hesitate.

CeCe jumps in. "Don't cancel any dates for us. We can do this anytime."

"Dates?" I laugh. "I'd love to. I was just doing a mental check-list of what's in my closet and think it's a great excuse to go shopping."

"Sounds perfect. We'll probably go to either Boulevard or Butler and the Chef. After, we may hit the Boom Boom Room. Greer loves to go dancing in the Castro, but we don't have to do that if you don't want to. Dinner is the best part."

"I can't wait. See you Saturday."

After we disconnect, I put a quick call in to my personal shopper at Nordstrom. "Hey, Jennifer. I'm in need of a nice out-fit for going out with some girlfriends on Saturday." I share with her the restaurants we're talking about and how dressy I'm looking to be.

"You have such a perfect figure. I have a few ideas. Would you have time to come in, or I can bring it to your office. Which-ever you prefer."

"It's a crazy week. Can you come here in the late afternoon?"

"I can move a few things around. How about this afternoon, say four?"

"Looking forward to it."

SARA

*J*ENNIFER ARRIVES and is shown the private back conference room, the only room in our offices where you can flip
a switch and all the glass walls become opaque.

Jennifer is dressed impeccably. I'm sure it's Armani, tailored
to her tiny figure, and her hair is in a tight chignon. Giving me a
nice hug, she stands back and eyes me carefully. "Sara, you have
the most amazing figure. You're too beautiful to be wearing
black. It's your safety color. I want to see you in colors that ac-
centuate your beautiful blue-green eyes." Turning to her rack of
clothes, she reaches for a dress. "I love this light blue Marc Jac-
obs. I know it's sleeveless, but with a wrap, you'll be warm
enough. The color matches your eyes."

I slip out of my suit and try the dress on, loving the scoop
neckline and empire waist. The beaded fringe embellishments
are stunning, and with a hint of gold and silver, it leaves the options open for jewelry. Looking me over carefully, she hands me
a gold wrap on one side and silver on the other, then shows me a
beautiful pair of silver Badgley Mishka embellished sandals.

I twirl around, feeling pretty. "I love it," I gush.

Smiling, she urges me to consider the other items she's brought. As I undress, she removes the most beautiful Calvin Klein light pink silk dress, sleeveless with a halter neckline and a full skirt. It's sexy and makes me feel desirable. I imagine for a moment what it would be like to have Trey lift the skirt and do naughty things to me while I'm wearing this dress. I look in the mirror on Jennifer's cart as she adjusts the tie in the back. "Oh, Jennifer, this looks amazing."

Still adjusting the dress to be sure it doesn't pucker at my breast, she says, "I thought it would bring out the subtle pink in your skin. It's very becoming on you."

I take one last glance at myself before removing the dress. Standing in my thong and no bra again, I watch as Jennifer takes a Giorgio Armani floral-jacquard dress from its bag alongside a black pair of Calvin Klein velvet sandals. The right foot has jeweled embellishments across the toes, and the left has them around the ankle. Complementing and sexy as hell.

Again, I stare at myself in the mirror, noting that the high neck and cap sleeves are perfect for business-related events, but the knee-length hem shows off enough leg that I seem sexy.

"I love it," I tell her as I swish the skirt around and admire how the embellishments reflect the light.

Smiling, she begins to unwrap another dress. "This is my favorite for you." She carefully removes a medium gray silk Narciso Rodriguez sleeveless cowl-neck seamed handkerchief dress. I slip it over my head, the bias-cut, figure-skimming silhouette hugging every one of my curves. It's simple yet elegant. I step into a silver Jimmy Choo sandal that adds three inches to my height and turn, admiring myself in the mirror.

"I can't decide." Watching myself and seeing the advantages of each dress, I peek at her and whisper, "They're all amazing."

"Well, I've also brought lingerie to match each dress, as well as jewelry." She displays each dress side by side, the accompanying LaPerla, Aubade, Chantelle and Coco de Mer lingerie, and beautiful, simple pieces of jewelry.

I wish this was an easy decision. I've tried all four outfits she brought and can't decide which one I prefer. I rationalize that with all the parties in my future, I'll wear them all eventually, but spending this kind of money is hard for me.

San Francisco and the Bay Area are full of a lot of very wealthy people. Some live it out loud and are in the paper or regularly interviewed on television, living their lifestyle to the fullest, but that isn't me. It's no secret that I'm a billionaire, but I work hard to stay below the radar. I spoil my foster parents when they allow me, but that's about the extent of it.

Sometimes I look at my bank statements and investment portfolio and I pinch myself. But it didn't happen by chance. I've worked my ass off for SHN. I've only been with the company for five years, but I was worth over a million dollars within the first one. And as the company was successful, my bank account grew and grew quickly because, as the first non-founding partner, my percentage of money earned by the firm was generous. Admittedly more than generous—I often earned millions each deal.

I am the quintessential Silicon Valley success story, but my unassuming lifestyle ensures I remain out of the press, which is exactly how I want it. A lot of people work hard and don't see this level of success, so I'm careful because I've lived on the streets, and I don't want to do that again.

"Jennifer, everything is stunning, and I can't make up my mind. I have several parties and dinners coming up." I run my fingers through my hair and finally say, "I'll take it all."

Rarely have I seen Jennifer surprised, but her eyes grow wide before she gives me a big hug. "Come by the store. We also have some nice casual clothes that you'll look stunning in. I'd like to get you in colors other than black."

I agree, and she waves goodbye.

I CHOOSE THE GRAY SILK Narciso Rodriguez handkerchief dress for dinner with the girls. My hair has a nice 'just had sex' look, which is very easy for me to accomplish with all the natural curl in my hair and its stubbornness to being straight. I got a pedicure and manicure during the day and spoiled myself with a makeover at Sephora. This is such a luxury.

Joining the girls at Boulevard for dinner, for once I actually feel like I belong. We all laugh and giggle the night away.

Hadlee turns to me and asks, "Sara, are you dating anyone?"

"I was," I reply wistfully. "But between both of us having crazy work hours, it didn't work out. Mostly because he was married."

"What a douchebag!" CeCe seethes.

I sigh. "Tell me about it. I didn't even find out until we'd been together for six months. I see him through work occasionally, which makes me uneasy."

"It goes to show how women in this city allow themselves to be treated because eligible straight men are so rare. Good for you for having the self-respect to tell him to shove off." Greer pats my arm.

CeCe declares, "We're brilliant, beautiful and independent

women. While we don't need men, w—"

Greer turns to Hadlee. "Oh no. Here she goes."

Peering at the group, she insists, "Sara needs to hear this. An independent woman needs a good friend, a good bottle of liquor, and if she wants companionship, she should buy a dog. If she wants sex, buy a good vibrator."

We all break out laughing. At the table next to us is a couple who seem like they're on an awkward first date. She's chuckling along, and he's eyeing us with disgust.

As the laughter dies down, CeCe leans in and asks, "You do have a good vibrator, don't you?"

I must be beet red as I stammer, "Ye-n-n—"

"Don't embarrass her, CeCe. She doesn't know us well enough," Greer warns her.

"As long as we don't use them together, I'm fine. I just wasn't prepared for that question." Giggling, I share, "I do have one, only I'm not sure where it is right now."

"CeCe has a connection," Hadlee assures me. "She'll take you shopping. It's high-end, and you'll definitely find the right toy."

Fanning myself, I chuckle. "You girls are a lot of fun. Thank you so much for inviting me along."

The conversation turns to a much tamer topic of work. Or so I thought. I'm surprised to learn that Greer was working for one of our clients, helping to prepare to take them public. She's smooth and competent in an area I don't completely understand.

"The head of marketing took a SnapPic of his dick and sent it to half the company," she sneers. "We're for sale. What the fuck was he thinking?"

"Isn't he the guy who keeps talking about a pivot?" CeCe giggles.

Stunned, I ask, "Well, was it a Gherkin or a Cornichon?"

At that point we're so loud, the manager comes over to speak to us.

"We're so sorry for disrupting all the other patrons," CeCe apologizes. "We'll be quieter. We've learned our good friend Sara"—she motions to me—"broke up with her boyfriend who hid the fact that he was married for six months."

Turning to me, the manager says, "Honey, I recently learned my boyfriend is married, too. I'm sending you all a round of drinks. Enjoy, but maybe not so loud?"

The bill for dinner was over two hundred and fifty dollars each, and for once my frugal ways don't mind. I had a nice time, and it was fun.

As we walk out, CeCe asks, "Are you heading to dinner with my parents tomorrow night?"

"I sure am."

"I'm going, too. Can I give you a ride?"

"That would be perfect. I'm a bit directionally challenged, particularly in your parents' neighborhood."

"Great. I'll pick you up about four thirty."

"I'll text you my address. See you then."

As I ride home in the cab, I notice I missed a text message. It's Henry.

Henry: You look stunning tonight in that gray dress. Can I
     come over tonight and peel you out of it, then lick
     you until you come all over my tongue?

My heart races, but rather than respond, I start to think. I didn't see him. How does he know what I'm wearing? His inability to comprehend my lack of interest is beginning to really wear on my nerves.

With a big sigh, I erase the message and try to put him out of my mind. I had a fun night, and I'm not going to let him ruin it.

I WAKE EARLY and do about three hours of work before I start to prepare for my dinner at the Arnaults'. I want to appear casual yet sexy enough to appeal—at least in my mind—to Trey. I think I changed twenty times trying to choose the right outfit. Finally I go with a tight-fitting pair of jeans, a cute pink floral-print blouse with bell sleeves and a pair of light pink Tory Birch ballet flats.

I decide on a natural curl in my hair and minimal makeup.

My cell phone pings at four thirty, and I run out the door. CeCe gives me a big hug, and we talk nonstop all the way out of the city to her parents' house. As we pull into the gated property, the Spanish-style home is deceiving in its size. From the front, it seems like a large home, but once you get inside, you realize it's huge.

A pack of dogs greets us in the foyer, and I get a bit nervous. Seeing my trepidation, CeCe calls to her mom, "Can you please get the dogs?" Her mom and a woman, who I assume is the housekeeper, come racing out of the back of the house and get the dogs moved to another room. CeCe gives me a reassuring squeeze and says, "The dogs can frighten me sometimes, too."

I smile at her, grateful for the encouragement. As we cross the threshold into the house, I spot him. Trey. My heart skips a beat and my pulse quickens. He's handsome in his blue and white knit Ralph Lauren shirt, khaki pants and boat shoes. It's as if he stepped out of a Ralph Lauren print advertisement. My heart flutters when he smiles at me.

Cameron asks me a few questions about a work deal he wants to discuss with Charles tonight, and before I can even get a drink, we're in deep conversation. I'm trying to track Trey, but when I glance in his direction, he's no longer standing in my sight line. I can't help but be disappointed.

Suddenly, Trey is at my elbow and says to Cameron, "Do you mind if I steal her away?"

Cameron laughs. "No, not at all. We're talking about work. It can wait."

Trey walks me over to the bar. "You don't have a drink. What can I make you? We have a bit of most liquors and mixers." Conspiratorially, he adds, "Before you say 'a glass of wine,' I will tell you that we'll drink wine with dinner. This is a pre-dinner drink."

Trey is good at putting me at ease. I can see why people flock to him. "Okay then, how about a Moscow Mule?"

"Oh, that's easy." Pulling out a nice large glass from above the mini freezer behind the bar, he muddles sugar and fresh mint. "How was your week?"

"Busy. And yours?"

He continues pouring the contents of his mix into the glass, then adds the ginger beer and a brand of vodka I'm not familiar with. "Mine was also busy. I run my dad's company these days, and while it's one of the oldest companies in The Valley, our stockholders still expect great returns on Wall Street."

We fall into effortless conversation until everyone arrives and it's loud and full of activity. The housekeeper rings a bell and instructs us to have a seat at the dining room table. As we make our way in, I feel Trey's hand on my elbow as he guides me to a seat, then takes the one beside me. My heart races because he wants to sit with me, and my stomach flip-flops. I'm not sure I'll be able to eat a thing with all the heat he radiates.

Dinner conversation bounces from politics, to football, to gossip in The Valley. I'm often too distracted by Trey's cologne to pay attention to the conversation, but we have a wonderful time enjoying each other's company.

Trey turns to me. "So Sara, what do you do outside of SHN and volunteering at teen homeless shelters?"

I sit back in my chair and glance around, but no one is paying attention to us. "I don't volunteer these days. I don't have much free time outside of work. SHN eats up most of my days. What about you?"

"Ah, a workaholic. I used to be that way when I first took over Sandy Systems, but outside of work, I ride my road bike. I love Muir Woods."

"Oh, Muir Woods is a favorite of mine. It's so green and lush." Turning to face him fully, I say, "If I remember correctly, you volunteered after the earthquake in Haiti. Do you speak French?"

"I do, but only well enough to get me into trouble. I'm impressed. Most people don't remember that I did that."

I cringe internally. *I've shown him that I researched him. Why would I do that? In for a penny, in for a pound, I suppose.* "What was it like being there?"

His eyes light up and he becomes very animated. I'm not sure if he talks for an hour or for only fifteen seconds, too mesmerized by all that he shares. "Haiti is a beautiful country. It's so disappointing that the corruption is so high. My cousin and I arrived three days after the quake with the Red Cross. I was stunned when we saw people digging and pulling people out of the rubble, still alive at almost thirty days after the quake. The people had nothing, but they would give up their own food because we came to help."

In shock, I ask, "Did you let them?"

"No way. They were starving, and we wanted them to eat. The mothers would pass up food for themselves so their kids would have extra. It was heartbreaking."

Looking at the group around the table, I see everyone is listening to Trey share his stories of Haiti. His mother, Margo, says, "We were so worried about him and Jed being in Haiti. He tried to check in with us regularly, but we were jaded by the news coverage, which of course was all negative."

"Trey, you should share the pictures from your trip with everyone." Turning to us, Emerson says, "He really captured the beauty of the island. He's such a talented photographer."

As dinner breaks up, the partners head off to Charles's office. Trey joins us, and when we arrive, another man is already there waiting.

We all sit down, and as Charles serves us his cognac, he makes introductions, "This is Jim Pearson. He's the best private investigator in The Valley and is great at sniffing out moles." As I take my first sip of the deep dark liquid, it rolls over my tongue, and I'm sure it tastes better this week than it did last. "And I've asked Trey here to join us. He runs Sandy Systems and has some great experience in this area from when Pineapple Systems decided they were going to steal some technology from us." Trey sits on the arm of my Queen Anne chair and nods to everyone.

Jim is a former San Francisco police officer and FBI agent, leaving Dillon and Mason visibly impressed. He shares with us what we can expect this week, and he tells me that he'll be in contact with Cameron and Emerson to work through what we've done so far.

As he leaves, we walk through our four successes and the list of upcoming possibilities. Charles has about a dozen that he wants to have our team start doing research on. He knows there are some duds in the group, but he also knows several of the founders of the others and will make calls to run interference.

We talk about what's on the horizon to go public, which I've been thinking about for a while, and I throw out to the group, "I was at dinner last night with Greer Ford. She was telling me about some of the work she did with PeopleMover and with Tsung Software. She thought some of the work she was doing was going to make a difference in stock pricing." I turn to look at Dillon. "You're the finance guy here. Would you agree?"

"Without a doubt. Greer works magic."

"Well, she mentioned that her contract with her current company is coming to an end, and that she was going to hit a beach in Brazil and start searching for a job when she was ready to return. What would you all think about bringing her on as another partner? Her work has a solid return on investment, and she has experience with that big Microsoft purchase, too."

Mason glances at Emerson. "She's your friend. What do you think? This would be a different kind of relationship for you two."

Emerson nods. "Working with her isn't any concern. My only thought is that I'm not sure she wants to be tied down."

Charles speaks up at that point. "I think having an internal marketing person who can speak to Wall Street and to investors is great. Of course, I've known Greer all her life, but I do think she would bring value, and I think we could talk her into it."

Cameron nods. "She took Tsung Software, who have a difficult software for technical people to understand, and broke it down. Their sales are through the roof now. Not to mention she helped rebrand SillySally for Henry Sinclair last year. I think we need to talk to her and see where her head's at."

Everyone agrees.

"Before we head out, I learned that Perkins Klein's first dud company is showing some of the issues that Emerson actually pointed out with their leadership team," Dillon shares. "We may be seeing their first investment go south."

Mason turns to Charles and Trey. "Do we want to rub a bit of salt in those wounds and make a few calls to the papers and wire services, pointing out why their investments are poor?"

Trey defers to his dad to take the question, who says, "I think we sit back. The financial trades will pick it up, and they're smart enough to figure out they overpaid and didn't vet correctly."

Again, everyone agrees. We set our to-do list for the coming week and agree to meet up again next week.

Trey has spent most of the night sitting and talking with me. I'm not sure I want tonight to end. As we walk outside, his hand brushes against mine and sends electric jolts to my core.

"I rode with your sister," I share quietly. I want so much for him to kiss me, but he's never really made any moves, so I'm not sure what he's thinking.

He nods. "Too bad. I'm happy to give you a ride home if you don't want to wait for CeCe."

I turn, and we can hear CeCe yelling her goodbyes to someone. "Well, I imagine it would raise a few eyebrows, particularly since I hear her coming."

"Probably." As we part, he asks me quietly, "Can I drop you an e-mail? Maybe we can make some plans for lunch this week."

I know having lunch with him could expose my crush on him, and we've only hung out over a giant group dinner, but I nod and agree.

TREY

I'M EXCITED. Sara has agreed to meet me for lunch. I was nervous when I asked her, considering it's been a long time since I've met anyone interesting, let alone someone interesting enough to date. I can't even remember the last time I was nervous to ask someone out. What is this woman doing to me?

Something draws her to me. She's incredibly sexy, and I could lose myself in her blue-green eyes for some time. I have this mysterious pull to her, and I want to get to know her.

We've been eyeing a small start-up in Seattle, and the company is being a bit persnickety. They would do well, but I get the feeling something is up. During my morning of meetings, I reach out to Sara.

TO: Sara White
FROM: Charles M Arnault III
SUBJECT: Question

What day would you be available for lunch? I'll clear my calendar for you. I think we can meet at a fun place in Chinatown. It's a bit of a dive, and we're guaranteed to be the only non-Chinese in the place, but the food is outstanding.

TO: Charles M Arnault III
FROM: Sara White
SUBJECT: RE: Question

I can make Wednesday or Thursday work, but don't clear anything for me. I can always push back to next week if that's better. Chinese sounds right up my alley.

I'm thrilled. I have meetings and appointments every day during lunch, but I don't care. I'll change them so I can meet Sara. I don't want to freak her out, so I know I have to take it slow; there's a certain amount of notoriety that comes with dating me, and I like this girl.

TO: Sara White
FROM: Charles M Arnault III
SUBJECT: RE: RE: Question

Let's meet on Wednesday. How does noon work?

SARA

J CAN'T HELP BUT BE EXCITED about our lunch. I know
he isn't married, and we have such a great connection. That's
a start in the right direction. And he's exactly the kind of guy I
fall for: strong, alpha, confident and without a doubt handsome—
he was *People Magazine's* Sexiest Man Alive a few years ago. But
he touches both my professional life and my personal life, so
that's also a reason to be cautious. I jumped in with both feet
with Henry, so I need to be careful this time around. I can't take
a heartbreak like Henry again.

TO: Charles M Arnault III
FROM: Sara White
SUBJECT: RE: RE: RE: Question

See you then!

Thankfully the week passes quickly, though I can hardly
sleep. I've planned my wardrobe down to the color of nail polish

on my toes. To protect my heart, and to hold back from wishful thinking, I tell myself that this very well may be a business lunch. He's definitely cute, though. And those broad shoulders and chiseled good looks give me hope. My internal debate runs from being very professional to down-and-dirty sex. Of course, the problem is those are usually one-night stands, but we'll see each other again, and that would be uncomfortable. I'm not his type anyway, since I'm no actress or socialite, so it's only wishful thinking.

I walk into the office, and of course, Mason's hair is on fire about an upcoming sale of one of our smaller investments. Sales are much easier than all the SEC filings I do to take a company public, but they still have a thousand moving pieces, and Mason wants to go over them to make sure I didn't miss anything. I never do, but he's always anxious.

"Mason, I have lunch plans today with Trey Arnault. I can't be late."

"Is this something I should join you on?"

"I don't think so," I tell him, choosing my words carefully. "I think he's trying to find out what we're up to with his dad from a legal perspective."

"Well, let me know how it goes. If his dad is getting nervous, I want to address it."

"Absolutely. I'll keep you posted."

I work for a few more hours, losing track of time before Mason pops his head into my office. "I thought you were having lunch with Trey Arnault today?"

I glance at my watch. "Oh shit! I need to be in Chinatown in five minutes." I grab my bag and run out of the building to hail a cab.

I check my makeup and determine I'm a lost cause, but still apply a fresh coat of lipstick. *At least I'll have kissable lips to tempt him with.*

TREY

I'VE THOUGHT ABOUT SARA almost every day since we met. I'm positive she's attracted to me; I've seen her pupils quickly dilate when we talk to one another.

I didn't believe Wednesday would ever get here. I have a stuffy meeting with some of our investors, so I wear a medium gray suit with a white shirt with French cuffs, and cufflinks that my great-great-grandfather immigrated to the US with. It was one of the few pieces with any value he brought with him into the New World from France. I'm also wearing my lucky red tie, crazy striped socks and a pair of Gucci loafers. My hair is slicked back with gel, and while usually I'd go with a few days of stubble to make me sexier, today I'm clean-shaven.

I beat her to the restaurant and find a table by the window so I can watch her emerge from the cab. She's a vision in a black pencil skirt with a very seductive slit up the side and a pair of platform heels. I can never remember the brands, but they have a red sole, and her makeup is subtle. She checks her reflection and licks her lips, and I get hard immediately.

She's precisely on time as the hostess points her in my direction. I stand and give her a hug. She's soft in all the right places, and I'm 99 percent positive her soft breasts are real. Once we separate, she sits down and stares at me.

"Is there anything you don't eat?" I ask.

She smiles demurely at me. "I think I'll try anything once."

My cock immediately gets hard as a lead pipe. "That's a good start."

She blushes and quickly corrects herself. "I mean, I'm open to eating whatever you have."

I raise my eyebrows at her.

Her blush extends from her cheeks, down her neck and I'm sure all the way to her toes. "I'm sorry." With a big sigh, she repeats, "I'm sorry."

"Don't be sorry. You're quite beautiful, and the prospect of anything is quite appealing. Thank you for agreeing to meet me for lunch."

"Of course. I figure you have some questions about the relationship we're building with your father. I'm happy to answer what I can."

I'm shocked at her interpretation of my invitation. "No, not at all. I was hoping to get to know you a bit better."

"Me?"

I let out a deep belly laugh. "Yes, you!"

"But why?"

I love that she has no idea how beautiful and sexy she is. "You're smart, funny, sexy as hell, and I think you're positively gorgeous."

Her eyes widen. "I swear there is nothing nefarious going on with your dad. We're not after anything other than some of his experience and guidance. We offered to pay him for his time, but he asked to invest."

I peek at her and remind myself to slow down. I don't want to scare her off. "He's shared everything with me. Really, this is about me wanting to get to know you better. Honest." I can see the doubt on her face, but I continue. "Where are you from?"

"I grew up here, in San Francisco."

"Really? What school did you attend?"

"I graduated from Independence."

Independence is a rough public school known more for gang issues and violence. "I'm impressed. That's a tough school."

She smiles slightly. "I tried to stay under the radar."

"Where did you go to college?"

"My foster family knew someone at Santa Clara, and they were kind enough to give me a full ride."

"Foster family? What happened to your parents?"

"My mom left me with a priest when I was three years old, and I have no idea about my biological father."

I raise an eyebrow. "Wow. I had no idea."

"I was luckier than most. I went from foster family to foster family until I was thirteen years old and landed with an older couple who were never able to have kids. They wanted to adopt me, but my mother wouldn't release her parental rights."

"Why not?"

"I don't know. I always hoped it was because one day she wanted to come back for me. But she never did."

Before I can stop myself, I sputter, "That's awful!"

She smiles at me. "The courts wouldn't allow it, but we had our own impromptu arrangement."

"Do you keep in touch with them today?"

"I do. They're very good to me. Jim and Carol are essentially my parents."

"Why do you call them by their names?

"It's complicated. I came to live with them when I was older, and I always thought my biological mother was coming back. But since I was never adopted, I figured that by not calling them Mom and Dad, if I were removed from their home, it would make the break easier for all of us." She tilts her head and looks me in the eye. "You had a very different upbringing than I did."

"Yes, I did. I grew up with my parents. But it was no picnic having the press camped out at everything we did. My dad tried hard to shield us, but I seemed to go out of my way to get their attention."

She laughs. "I do seem to remember when you were in high school, you had a blowout party at your parents' and people came from all over Northern California. You had something like five thousand people at your house."

I laugh with her. "Well, it was on the lawn. I at least knew better than to allow anyone inside. Honestly, I don't know what I was thinking. My parents were well aware after it made the news and tabloids, of course, and my dad went crazy. He shipped me off to military school after that."

"Oh no! But it didn't seem to stop the press."

"It did for a short time, but once CeCe and I hit our twenty-first birthday, we were given our trusts, which made us interesting to the media."

"Somehow they don't have any interest in CeCe."

"No, she's a bit boring for the press, but I also work hard to make sure they stay focused on me and not her so she can have a life." I decide it's worth it to tell her why. "When we were twelve, they called her fat, and she tried to stop eating. My parents were worried she was developing an eating disorder. She went into therapy, so I made it my job to be outrageous so they would leave her alone."

SARA

I'M SURPRISED AT HOW FUNNY, smart and self depre-cating Trey can be. I glance at my watch and am shocked to see we've been here for two and a half hours.

"You can ride a horse?" I ask, surprised.

"Yes. When I was sixteen, I worked as a wrangler at a ranch in Wyoming. Can you ride a horse?"

I laugh. "I grew up a city girl, so I was taking either the bus or train on my own since I was nine. I'm lucky I can drive." Sitting back in my chair, I think about it, then say, "I'm not even sure I've seen a horse up close. I've seen them in pastures as you drive out to Yosemite, but I can't recall ever standing next to one, and I'm sure I've never ridden one."

"I can't believe you've never even seen one up close. But it's great growing up in a big city. I loved the independence that public transportation gave us. CeCe and I also ran around and had a great time. I loved the seals on Pier 39."

"Oh, me, too. Can you believe they moved and no one knows why?"

"I can't help but think the obvious is the lack of food, but I used to be a swimmer and there's no way I'd get my body in the Bay waters."

"Ugh. I agree. But despite the traffic, the cost of living and all the crazies who come here, I love this city."

"I do, too. I can't imagine living anywhere else."

He's charming and hot as hell. When I look at the time, I jump up and apologize. "I'm sorry but I need to go. I'm already late for a meeting at my office."

He peeks at his watch. "I've completely missed mine." Laughing, he adds, "Can we do this maybe on Saturday night?"

I get my wallet out to give him some money for lunch, but he holds up his hand. "I asked you to lunch. Please let me pay for it."

I'm pleasantly surprised. That means this lunch was a date.

He walks me outside and offers me a ride back in his car, but I decline and hail a cab. I turn to him, stand on my tiptoes and kiss him softly on the cheek. "I'd love to go out with you on Saturday night."

I race into the office, and thankfully it seems no one has noticed I'm late. What a relief that I don't have to explain myself to anyone. I know I'm a partner, but with all the deals we have in process, I don't want anyone to question my commitment; I've worked too hard to prove that I belong here.

Despite the uneasiness of my being out for a long period of time, I sit back and think about our lunch. Trey was so easy to be with. We grew up in two different worlds, but it's surprising to think about how much we have in common. I don't want to appear too anxious, but I'm excited about the thought of something with him, and I haven't been excited about anyone like this in a long time. It wasn't even like this with Henry at the beginning.

I send a note off to Trey.

TO: Charles M Arnault III
FROM: Sara White
SUBJECT: Thank you for lunch

I had a nice time, and I look forward to seeing you on Saturday. Let me know when and where, and I'll be there.

As I click Send, my admin steps in and reminds me of my meeting with Mason and a client in the boardroom. On my way, I detour for a cup of coffee in the break room and meet up with Mason, who's doing the same thing.

"Well, I had an interesting conversation with Greer," he starts. "She's considering joining us and will be at Sunday's dinner to discuss the specifics of what we need."

"That's great news. I really think she'd be an asset to our team."

"I'll talk with Charles to find out how to manage the financial requirements of adding another partner." We both have our coffee and begin walking to the boardroom when Mason asks, "How was your lunch with Trey?"

"It was very nice, thank you."

Staring at me, he inquires, "What did he need?"

Oh crap. Right. I told him it was probably business because I wasn't 100 percent sure. Without giving up too much from a personal lunch, I fib, "I was right, he wanted to find out our intentions with his dad. I think he wouldn't mind being part of our advisory board."

"I like that idea. I'll talk to Charles."

It takes a while for me to get back to my desk. It's always hard to keep up when I have a personal appointment or client meeting, and having both today set me back with everything going on here, and our recent acquisitions.

Throughout the day, my mind wanders to my lunch date, and I think of Trey often. I know I'll need to head home soon, but I just can't seem to focus to get my work accomplished for the day.

My cell phone pings, indicating a text, and takes me out of my daydream.

Henry: Hey, beautiful.

I glance at it but don't respond.

Henry: Come play with me.

Still, I don't respond.

Henry: Pretty please?

He sends over a picture of his erect penis with a caption: We miss you.

I take a big breath and remind myself to stay strong. If he wasn't a big client, I'd tell him to fuck off, but I don't want any of our drama to leak over to our professional life.

My office phone rings, breaking my trance, and I hear Annabel over the speaker. "Henry with SillySally on the phone to speak with you."

"Did he tell you what he needed?"

"No, sorry, he didn't."

Taking a big breath, I tell her, "I'm on a deadline. Can you see if Mason or Dillon can answer his question?"

Surprise evident in her voice, she says, "Oh! Sure, I can do that."

I've told Henry a dozen times that I'm not interested in anything other than a professional relationship. He has a beautiful wife and three darling children. Why would I want to be on the outside, looking in on that relationship?

chapter

FOURTEEN

TREY

Me: Hey, gorgeous! How's your day going? I was wondering if you'd like to hang out with me at lunch.

Sara: Hmm... I can meet you for lunch today.

Me: I don't usually have to work this hard to hang out with someone over lunch.

Sara: I'd hate for you to "hang out" for nothing. ;)

Me: OK, now I'm not so sure. You seem like trouble, and I promised myself I wouldn't date bad girls anymore.

Sara: Sweetheart, you're hilarious...

Me: It's too bad you're such a dork.

Sara: Oh, I'm the dork? I've seen pictures of you on TMZ. I didn't realize a guy who wears a Star Wars T-shirt is allowed to cast judgment on someone else.

Me: Hey, don't knock the shirt. The shirt gets the ladies' interest. Then it's the Star Wars sheets that seal the deal.

Sara: Wait! You mean you have Star Wars sheets? That absolutely seals the deal for me. I can't wait to hang out with you.

Me: Great. What time?

Sara: 1?

Me: Mexican, Italian or Indian?

Sara: Something that won't make me want to crawl under my desk and take a nap afterward.

Me: How about Joe's Pizza in the North Beach neighbor-hood? It's a bit of a hole-in-the-wall, but the food is excellent.

Sara: See you then.

I sit back in my chair and reread the exchange. I love our banter, and it thrills me to no end. I'm excited that we're going out for lunch again. I know it's low pressure, but it also gives me the opportunity to win her over without the stress. Plus I want to see what she'd like to do tomorrow night.

This time she's beat me to the restaurant. As I walk in, she smiles, and my heart skips a few beats. She stands, almost trip-ping over her bag next to the chair, but I manage to hold her steady before we embrace.

"You look positively beautiful."

She blushes the most stunning shade of pink. "Thank you." She glances up at the waiter, who pours us each a glass of water.

After the waiter shares the specials, I lean across the table. "You've glanced at the menu, any ideas?"

"Pizza works."

"Anything you don't like on your pizza?"

"Fish."

"Okay, that's easy." I turn to the waiter. "We'll have a large Gangster pizza." She smiles big. "You like?"

"It's exactly what I would've suggested."

"Really? We must've been made for one another." I bounce my eyebrows up and down like Groucho Marx.

A spark of mischievousness, she says, "Probably. But it would never work."

I laugh so loud, people at the neighboring table stop and gawk. "You're probably right. You're just too short for me." She laughs. "I need my women to be at least six-foot-six."

Our banter continues through our meal, which we manage to keep around an hour and a half. As I wait for the check, I ask, "What do you want to do tomorrow night?"

Appearing astonished, she says, "Oh. I thought I got demoted from dinner to lunch. You still want to meet up tomorrow night?"

My stomach drops. *I need to make sure she understands how interested I really am.* "Demoted? Never. Not with those legs." I want to ravish her right now. Right this very minute.

"I did turn down all those other men who asked me out, so I suppose we should," she tells me with a salacious smile that confirms she's teasing me.

"Let's plan for eight o'clock."

She nods, and I walk her to the curb and call her a Lyft. She faces me, and I can see she's nervous. As the car arrives, she walks forward and presses her body against mine before kissing me softly on the lips. The electric current between us reaches directly to my groin. Her lips are so soft and supple.

Since there's always the possibility of prying eyes, I'm careful to not explore like I want to, but I want much more. *Something to save for another time.*

I run the back of my hand over her cheek. "That was incredible."

She beams with a smile that reaches her eyes, and I add with regret, "See you tomorrow?"

She nods and whispers, "I can't wait."

Our fingers interlaced, we walk away from one another before we break our touch.

Despite being late for my two o'clock meeting, I stay to watch her car drive away before I walk back to the office, thinking of all the things I want to do with Sara. I haven't seen anything to dislike about her.

I don't want a one-night stand. I want to explore a relationship with her.

FIFTEEN

SARA

Henry: Hey. I need to see you today. Company business. 3
   p.m.? SillySally offices. Don't be late.

Sara: What's the issue, so I can be prepared? Do you want
   Mason to join?

Henry: No, it's a legal issue. Just you is fine.

Sara: I'm only available for professional reasons. Nothing
   personal.

Henry: This is professional.

Sara: Henry, if it isn't, you're going to force me to reach
   out to Claudia.

Henry: Get here when you can.

I don't want to see Henry.

The wall clock in my office ticks like the timer on a bomb. I
can't stop it, reverse it or slow it down. Each tick drags me forward, helpless and nervous to endure time with a valued client
and someone who wants more of me than he's willing to give in
return. I can no more avoid this meeting than I can avoid the

beating of my own heart as it pounds with futility against my rib cage. All I can do is let Mason know where I'm going.

Walking into his office, I tell him, "Hey. Do you know what's going on at SillySally? I got a text from Henry Sinclair asking for time with me this afternoon."

He glances up from his stack of papers and gives me a quizzical look. "No clue. Should I go with you?"

"I asked him, and he said it was a legal issue and you weren't needed. Honestly, I'm not sure."

"Okay. I'm buried today, but I'll clear my calendar to go with you if you think it's necessary."

I don't want to take him off track over Henry having a meltdown. However, I know if I were to show up with Mason, Henry might get a clue to move on. I can't decide.

Looking at Mason's desk cluttered with proposals and statements, I finally say, "No, don't worry about it. I can handle Henry."

He goes back to his paperwork, then asks, "How was your lunch?"

"My lunch?"

"Yes. I saw you ran out for lunch today. I figured you had a date."

"Oh. No, no date. I ran an errand."

"Sorry. I was hoping you had a real reason to leave the office at lunchtime."

Smiling at him, I say, "I wish. I'll keep you posted on what Henry needs at SillySally." Turning, I walk out of his office.

I know I lied to Mason, but I'm not sure what Trey and I are doing, or that I want to share. I'm confused, if I'm being honest.

We definitely have excellent chemistry, and from what I can tell, he doesn't fool around—the tabloids last clocked a serious relationship at six years when he dated the actress. But while they capture him with various women, I'm not sure what he's looking for. I'm not getting any younger, and even though I can feel the fire and chemistry we have, what if he likes long-term relationships that don't lead to any commitment? I'm not sure I'd survive six years with him just to have him break it off with me.

I PICK UP MY LEATHER CASE and call for another ride to South San Francisco out to SillySally. When I arrive, the receptionist says, "Ms. White, Mr. Sinclair is expecting you. Please follow me."

We walk back to Henry's office in the back corner. Sitting in what was once Candlestick Park, we're on the water, and I watch the barges cruise down the bay. I lose my train of thought as my eyes move over the various boats across the water, the one directly in front of us catching my attention until the receptionist knocks, opens Henry's door and ushers me in. "Would you like something to drink?"

"A water, please."

Henry's office is quintessentially him. It's in a state of half-organized clutter. His overbearing mahogany desk takes up the biggest part of the room, his MacBook Pro and two black screens with the color fonts indicating software development. He has several stacks of paperwork strewn across his desk, pens of various colors and highlighters jammed in a cup. Behind Henry is a floor-to-ceiling bookshelf, books leaning against one another and in different directions, but I can't help but think they're for show. And then there's Henry trying to pretend he didn't hear the knock on his door, appearing surprised as if we magically appeared out of thin air.

He stands and says, "Thanks, Elizabeth. I have a bottle of water here in my fridge." Turning to me once she leaves, he holds out his arms and steps in for an embrace. "My lovely. You look amazing." His embrace is a bit long, and he moves his mouth close to mine while his hand caresses my ass. He gently plucks a lock of hair from my collarbone. And then he touches my skin.

Pushing Henry back, I say, "Henry, I was extremely clear. I came here for professional reasons. You said you had a legal question."

He stands back, and sighs. "I'm sorry." Running his hands through his hair, he seems to be struggling with something.

Before I give in to the urge to kick him square in the balls, I sit in the side chair across from his desk and ask, "Henry, is everything okay?"

"Of course it is. Our stock split for the sixth time today, and you know that makes me horny."

I stand abruptly. "Henry, I'm very happy for you, but I think you need to call your wife if you're horny. I want to be incredibly clear. Do not reach out to me for any reason other than professional. And the next time you touch me, be prepared to lose a finger and need a surgeon to remove the testicle I'm going to kick so hard it's lodged in your lungs. Do you understand me?"

"I understand." But then he says, "I'm going to ask Claudia for a divorce. I promise. I can't imagine my life without you."

I sigh heavily. "Henry, you're married. I'm sorry, but I'm not interested anymore. I've met someone."

"What do you mean you met someone?"

"It means I've moved on, and I don't want you in my personal life any longer."

"I don't care if you sleep with him. We can slip in a few moments every so often. Baby, you rev my engine better than anyone. And the way you suck my cock is like no one else. I need you. Please don't leave me out in the cold."

I move to the other side of the room to create some distance. I don't want to ruin our work relationship, so I tell him, "Henry, you know I care for you. I'll always care for you, but I don't want you in the way you need me to."

"Do you love this other guy?"

"It doesn't matter. Please, we can only be friends professionally. I'm not interested in anything else with you. And if you persist, not only will I need to take it up with Claudia, but I will with Mason, Dillon and Cameron as well. You have to leave me alone on a personal level."

I sit across the coffee table from him, and he releases a big sigh. "I get that, but you have to know I can't afford to divorce Claudia, but I'll do it for you. We aren't intimate. And I love you. I need you, and God knows I want you."

It occurs to me that something else is going on and he isn't telling me what it is. "Is there even something legally going on with SillySally?"

"Just that I'm horny and I was hoping you would take care of me. I have dreams of bending you over the corner of this couch and ramming my cock into your wet pussy."

I pin him with a warning stare before pulling out my phone and calling for a Lyft. Giving him a look of pity, I snap, "I have a busy afternoon, and I need to get back to the office. Congratulations on the sixth split," I throw over my shoulder.

As I walk out of the building to meet my ride, I think of Trey. Tall, dark and handsome, he's a little bit of a walking cliché, but my heart still races and my panties become wet at just the thought of him.

I'm not sure where he and I are going, but I think I'd like to find out.

As I get in my ride for the twenty-five-minute drive back to the office, I want to text Trey, but I'm sure he's busy, and I don't want to turn him off because I'm anxious. Instead, I review my work e-mail as I daydream about his good looks and the little laugh he does when he thinks I'm funny.

I walk into the office and head into Mason's office. "Henry was excited that they split a sixth time."

Gazing up at me, he says, "I bet he's excited." Picking up his phone, he punches in a number. "Hey, grab Emerson and come here. Sara has good news." Hanging up, he dials again and says virtually the same thing. All four of the other partners arrive and stare at me.

"Henry invited me out to SillySally this afternoon, and he said their stock split a sixth time today."

Dillon stares at Cameron and Mason, then sits down hard in his chair. "Holy shit!"

"Dillon, I believe that would make our original shares worth over six hundred and fifty thousand dollars each, and how many shares do we have?" Mason asks.

Dillon nods. "Before this split we had almost a million shares."

Cameron lets out a giant "Whoop!"

We celebrate for a few minutes, Emerson excusing herself and then returning with a bottle of champagne and five glasses. "Is this reason enough to open this bottle of champagne?"

"Abso-fucking-lutely!" Mason exclaims.

Emerson opens the bottle, pours a glass for each of us, and we toast. "To SillySally, SHN's first official investment."

The team spends the afternoon hanging out and basking in our good fortune. Mason calls Henry and congratulates him, inviting him over to join us.

Henry arrives quickly and shakes hands with the guys, then gives Emerson and me hugs, kissing me on the cheek. Mason lifts his eyes in surprise and I smile, but I can feel the embarrassment burning my ears. It takes all my willpower to not clock him. I hate that I've learned to be polite.

I return to my office, making the excuse that I need to go back to work and concentrate on the two acquisitions. But before I can think about that, I text Trey.

Me: Thanks for lunch today. I had fun.

Trey: Me, too. When can I see you again?

Me: Aren't we meeting Saturday night?

Me: Plus, if I'm seen too often with you, it might ruin your party boy persona.

Trey: I do have a reputation to protect, but maybe if you tell me three things about yourself that you like to do, we might be able to figure something out.

Me: Hmm... three things? Is this where I'm supposed to tell you I like long walks on the beach? You tell me one.

Trey: Only if you like long walks on the beach. But how about enjoying an afternoon wandering a museum and hangout together?

Me: I do like to walk the beach, but up at Stinson where you can search for petrified sand dollars. But I adore the de Young Museum.

Trey: I didn't know you could find petrified sand dollars at Stinson. That would be cool. What about heading up into St Helena and enjoying a day of wine tasting? With a driver, of course.

Me: That sounds fun. You do come with an extra set of eyes at times, so a nice night in sounds low-key and enjoyable.

Trey: That's a little forward. :) Low-key is always preferred. I'm used to the prying eyes, but you aren't.

Me: Snort! Is that why you like the paparazzi following you around?

Trey: According to TMZ, I do like being out. But don't believe everything you read or see. What about renting a paddle boat and taking a picnic out on Stow Lake in Golden Gate Park? We can take in the waterfall and have a bit of privacy.

Me: Wow. Impressive. There's a great hike you can take beyond the Golden Gate and watch the sunset.

Trey: I know we met for lunch today, but what if we were to meet up at Maven tonight and listen to the jazz? They have Sazerac and a sultry vibe, but we can get cozy in the lounge area.

Me: I don't know. We did see each other earlier today.

Trey: I think we came up with seven awesome dates to start us off.

Me: Well, when you put it that way, who could resist?

Trey: Tonight at Mavens?

Me: 10?

Trey: I can't wait. Thank you, Sara.

Eventually, Henry wanders into my office and closes the door behind him. "What can I do for you, Henry?"

"I've always wanted to fuck you from behind in your office, overlooking the Bay Bridge and all the windows in other buildings."

"Leave, Henry. I have work to do."

He laughs. "You used to be so much fun. I remember working late and you getting on your knees for me."

"That was before I knew you were married. It'll never happen again."

"Our destiny is together, naked and enjoying everything each of us has to offer."

It's after seven, and despite having three or four more hours of work, I start gathering my things, preparing to leave. "Our destiny is only business. It will never be personal again. Excuse me, but I have a date tonight. Maybe one of the girls in the office will fuck you, because it isn't going to be me."

My cell phone shoots me an alert from our PR firm. We set up alerts for all our employees' and clients' names so each time one of our names shows up on the internet or news, we're notified. I added Charles after he agreed to advise us, and Trey when he came on board.

Hmmm. I wonder what happened today. I see there are roughly fifty links in the alert. *Must be big.* I click on the first link without realizing it's for *TMZ*. All I see in the picture is an obstructed view of me from when I kissed Trey goodbye after lunch today. My stomach falls as the commentator on the link asks, "Is San Francisco's most eligible bachelor off the market?"

Crap. Shit. Fuck.

TREY

$\mathcal{J}$ JUMP FROM MEETING TO MEETING all afternoon before I finally check my e-mail. Apparently, I got an alert
shortly before two.

"Shit," I say aloud, because I know what it'll be. Opening the
e-mail, I see the photo of Sara kissing me. A sigh of relief goes
through me; it appears much more salacious than it actually
was, but thankfully her face is obstructed.

I need to let her know. Tonight's plans may need to change.

What do I do? Too distracted to focus on work, I pack up and
make my way down to my car in the garage. Once they figure
out it's her, they'll camp out at her home and her office. I need
to protect her from the throngs of people that may come with
that reality if I want to keep her in my life. In the back of my
mind, I knew when she kissed me that something like this might
happen, but the paparazzi haven't been following me lately. I've
been too boring.

Goddammit.

The picture making the tabloids this early in our relationship pisses me off. I was hoping she would fall in love with me

before this crap started happening. I've learned from experience that women tend to run away from me when this shit starts to happen. *Fuck!*

I head home and call CeCe, but she doesn't answer. Just as well, since I think she and Sara are becoming friends, and the last thing I want is for her to inadvertently tell Sara to run away. I pour myself a drink and take in the view from my condo, which faces Alcatraz and the North Bay. I love my place because I can see Berkley, my alma mater, across the bay.

My thoughts are consumed by Sara. I can't let her go. Not yet. We're only getting to know each other and already I feel a deeper connection to her than anyone before.

Sitting in my living room, I watch the sun fall behind the horizon, painting the sky shades of red and pink, and I thank God that this day has come and gone. All the anxiety of the fucking tabloids has come again. All the hurt they cause.

I won't let her go that easily. I want to talk to her face-to-face about this. At least we have plans tonight, but I have to prepare her in case they've figured out who she is.

I text Sara.

Me: Have you seen the tabloids today?
Sara: Apparently I'm almost famous.
Me: I'm sorry.
Sara: Did you have the picture taken?
Me: Absolutely not. I hate them with a passion.
Sara: Then don't worry about it.
Sara: That's unless you'd prefer to forget tonight.

Me: Are you kidding? I still want to see you. I didn't want it to ruin your night.

Sara: Don't worry about me. I'm still not on their radar. I'll meet you there and we'll find a quiet corner, enjoy a drink, listen to some music, and ignore the tabloids.

Me: You can come to my place and we can have a drink here.

Sara: As much as I'd like that, it may not be a good idea. That kiss was electric and I want to slow down, not speed us up.

Me: We'll go at whatever speed you want to go.

Me: Leaving now. Can't wait to see you.

SARA

T WISH I HAD TIME TO GO HOME and take the edge off.
Between the flirting with Trey and Henry's aggressiveness,
my hormones are at a colossal level, and I'm wound tight. I take
a Lyft over to Maven's in the Civic Center and walk in a few
minutes early, heading back to the lounge area they call the
Opium Room and finding a booth in the back.

Me: I'm in the back in the corner. Come and find me...

The waiter appears and is taking my order of a glass of
scotch when Trey arrives.

"How about making it two scotches," Trey tells him. Turning
to me, he asks, "Are you okay with blended scotch? They have
Johnnie Walker Blue here."

He scoots into the booth beside me as I nod. "As long as it's
neat."

"Two glasses of Johnnie Walker Blue neat, please."

"Can you make mine a double?" Work has too many things
going on at once, and Henry not getting the hint has my nerves
frazzled. With a strong drink, I can relax.

My heart is beating fast from being next to Trey. I can't believe I'm sitting with my own Greek god.

"Make them both doubles." Reaching for my hand, he says, "You seem upset."

He can't be interested in all the drama at work. Plus, I prefer to focus on the positive. "We got some good news. SillySally split a sixth time."

"That's huge. How does that affect you? "

"I'm not sure yet, though I was a full partner at the time we invested in SillySally. I'm sure we'll talk about that on Sunday night. You'll be there, right?"

"Of course. But something's bothering you," he persists.

He's so perceptive, but I can manage my crazy work and Henry. He doesn't need to share that burden.

I relax and snuggle in close. "Not anymore since I'm here with you."

Our drinks arrive and we listen to a young jazz group, the music mesmerizing. With his arms around me, I feel safe for the first time outside of Jim and Carol. I trace an imaginary eight on his leg with my fingertip before I take a sip of my drink. It's an indulgence to enjoy a good drink while listening to the sultry voice interpreting a wonderful Ella Fitzgerald tune with a sexy man on a work night. It's relaxing, and while I've always enjoyed jazz music, hearing Trey share what excites him about the music seems to drag me further under his spell.

I stare into his beautiful eyes and feel an immediate connection. I've never experienced such an intense, unexplainable bombardment of sensations all at one time. It's insanely beautiful.

chapter

EIGHTEEN

TREY

H ER TOUCH IS DRIVING ME CRAZY, and I'm as hard as a baseball bat. But she's clearly distracted, and something seems to be bothering her, taking her mind away from our night out. She insists it isn't the *TMZ* photo, and it can't be money since she probably has more than I do—which is really saying something. Money doesn't seem to affect her, anyway, which is a good sign for me.

I rest my chin on the top of her head, placing my hand over hers that's driving me crazy. "I'm trying really hard to abstain here, but you're not making this easy on me."

With a provocative gaze, she murmurs, "I'm sorry."

Giving her hand a comforting squeeze, I take a deep breath, exhale and say, "Don't be sorry. You're driving me crazy, and I like it."

She visibly relaxes, and I enjoy the feel of her body pressed close to mine. She snuggles in, and we enjoy our drinks and the seductive sounds coming from the band.

I take in the slope of her neck, the way her breasts move with each breath she takes. I want to explore her, succumb to this urge to take her into the bathroom and have my way with her, but I have too much respect for her, and I know I want more than a quickie in the bathroom.

After about an hour and a half of good music, a second round of doubles and two tall glasses of ice water, we pay our tab and I escort her toward the door, telling her, "My car service is waiting. Can I give you a ride home?"

I can see the conflict on her face before she says, "You don't know how much I want that. But that may not be a good idea."

Turning to gaze at her, I confirm, "I have no doubt there will be a few cameras pointed as we exit, and I don't want you to be in tomorrow's tabloids. May I kiss you here, just a chaste one?"

I watch with bated breath as her full lips quirk up into a seductive grin. She stops mere inches away from my face, and suddenly I wonder what it would feel like to press my lips against hers. My mouth grows parched at the thought, and I still my movements while licking my lips. She nods and I lean in, giving her a kiss that is demure and yet leaves us both wanting more.

She whispers, "Please don't break me," against my lips before pulling away.

Break her? I think she'll break me.

"Tomorrow is Friday. Would you feel comfortable coming over to my house? We can have a nice dinner and relax without the worry of landing in the supermarket tabloids. Very low-key and quiet."

She thinks about it a few moments, then takes a big breath and, without glancing at me, softly says, "I have a better idea that may give us some more freedom and a lot of privacy. My foster parents have a place up in Stinson. It's a beach house in a small gated community. Nothing fancy like you may be used to, but it might keep the paparazzi away. How about we pack a bag and go up there for the weekend? There are a few bedrooms, so there's no pressure. We can pick up some groceries and wander the beach and relax, and then we can come back either late Saturday afternoon or Sunday."

Get out of town, only the two of us? That sounds like a perfect way to get to know her. Very low pressure, and it might even be fun. I can tell it was hard for her to ask, but I want to take some of the pressure off her, so I joke, "As long as you want me for my mind and not just my body."

She laughs. "Can't I want both?"

Staring at her intently, I tell her, "You can absolutely have both. When can I pick you up tomorrow?"

No one seems to notice me in our dark corner, so I lean in close and slowly bring my lips to hers. Hers are soft and pliant as she pushes herself against me. I want to deepen the kiss, but I can't risk it showing up in the tabloids.

Pulling away, I tell her, "Seems like every time we kiss, I lose all reason."

"Have a good evening. I'm excited about our getaway."

"Me, too. How does three sound?"

"Perfect. See you then."

I CAN HARDLY SLEEP, too keyed up about our weekend. She made it clear that there are multiple bedrooms, and I'll only take this as fast as she wants to go. I pack a bag, hoping she wants to stay until Sunday. The idea of being alone and exploring everything she has to offer thrills me, and I want more from her.

Finally, just before three, I surprise my staff when I walk out of the office and wish them a nice weekend.

I text Sara and let her know I'm waiting outside her building. It takes a few minutes before she walks out in a suit. I jump out of the car to help her load her things, and then we're off. The Friday afternoon traffic is busy, but we don't notice, chatting away as we head out of town. We stop for groceries outside of Sausalito, then trek over the mountain through Mount Tamalpais State Park and drive into the Northern California beach town.

The entire drive, we have a relaxed conversation. I love that Sara has her opinions and she shares them freely. I've been raised to rarely have an opinion as it might offend someone, and it's refreshing to feel comfortable enough to share mine. We disagree on a few things, but when pressed, she can formulate a convincing argument, and when my belief doesn't change, she doesn't hold it against me. As we talk, I realize that in these simple exchanges, she knows me better than anyone outside of my family, and we've only known each other a short time.

Driving through the two-block town, she directs me into the neighborhood to her foster family's home. It's a classic Cape Cod-style house on the beach with plenty of land to keep the neighbors and other prying eyes at bay.

After we carry everything inside, she gives me a tour and shows me a room where I can put my things. I load my closet with beachwear—T-shirts, sweatshirts, khaki cargo pants and jeans.

Hearing pans banging and music blaring, I investigate and find the kitchen, where I watch her for a moment as she chops peppers and shallots.

AINSLEY ST CLAIRE

"Can I help?" I ask when she's between vegetables.

"It isn't a fancy meal, but we should be able to eat before eight. Can you open a bottle of wine?" She points me to a bottle next to two glasses.

"Of course." I watch her move around the kitchen with ease. "Tell me what you know about your biological mother."

"I don't have much memory of my mother. I know she was a runaway and sixteen when I was born, just a child herself. She was nineteen and I was three when she left me at a Catholic church in San Francisco. The law allows for mothers to leave children at churches without criminal prosecution. The priest had been counseling her, so we have some information. It's through the priest that we learned her family wasn't interested in a bastard child. My biological mother was sent the paperwork from the state to release her parental rights, but she never returned them, so I was stuck in the foster system. I was difficult on good days and ultimately lived in thirteen foster homes over the next ten years. I never spent an entire year with one family until I landed with Jim and Carol."

"Wow. That must've been difficult. Tell me about your foster parents."

"I was placed with them at thirteen. They could never have kids of their own. Jim is a civil engineer and Carol's an elementary school teacher. I knew I could wind up taking the same path my mother did, and I struggled with that. Jim and Carol were patient with me and my foolishness." She eyes me, and I give her an encouraging smile before reaching for her hand and caress her knuckles.

"One night, I snuck out and came home high, and Jim was

waiting up for me," she continues. "He made it clear that I was welcome to stay, but I needed to follow his rules, and they would respect me as long as I respected them."

"What did you think of that?" I ask as I reach for the bottle of wine and top her glass off.

"I won't kid you, part of me didn't care about what he said. I went to bed and was angry that he wanted to put rules in my life, since in the past, those kinds of rules only got me in the cross hairs of people I didn't want to notice me. But Jim never ogled me like a piece of meat. His hands never 'accidentally' touched me. I realized that was the first time I could ever re-member feeling safe."

I can see she's uncomfortable, but I only look at her and hold her hand.

"The next morning, Carol took me shopping for some nice clothes and shared that she was hoping we could all make this work. Then she offered to help me find my mother, if that was what I wanted."

She withdraws her hand from mine to wipe a tear away, then pinches the skin between her thumb and index finger. I reach again for her hand and place it between both of mind, whisper-ing, "You don't have to go on if you don't want to."

She smiles at me through her tears. "No. You need to hear this." She takes a deep breath. "I realized then that Jim and Carol weren't in the foster system to collect checks like so many others. They were hoping to fill their hearts."

I lean in and wipe her tears, then cup her cheek.

"My life changed that very day. It was a pivotal moment, and for that I'm forever grateful to Jim and Carol. We started the search for my mom, and Carol helped me get caught up at school. They spent much more money on me than the foster system ever gave them, and we grew to love one another."

"Forgive my ignorance, but don't you age out of foster care at eighteen?"

She nods. "Yes, and they helped me achieve a full-ride scholarship to Santa Clara University. But it wasn't always easy. Whenever things started to go well, I'd rebel, but Jim, Carol, and a therapist helped me funnel my anger into academics. But the day I left for Santa Clara, they sent me off with a suitcase full of clothes and a backpack full of school supplies, and over a congratulatory dinner, they presented me with a check. They never cared about the money they received for fostering, putting every check they received in a savings account that they gave to me when I graduated. The financial cushion that provided was the second time in my life I felt safe."

I'm in true awe of her story. She started with absolutely nothing, an orphan with a runaway mother who left her with a priest. "I'm impressed they did all of that. And you keep in touch with them, too."

"I do. They're my rock when the storms get bad, and my sun and flowers on a beautiful spring day. I'm incredibly grateful that we found each other. Since then, I've tried to spoil them, but they rarely let me buy more than a dinner here and there."

I watch her transition from vulnerable to nervous to fill the quiet. Turning to me, she asks, "Tell me about your family. How do you manage to live any kind of normal life when everything you do is in the tabloids?"

"I guess you get used to it. My family had its challenges. When CeCe got herself in big trouble shoplifting when she was thirteen years old, my mom sat my dad down and explained that he needed to be home more. It took multiple conversations, and CeCe showing up in the tabloids a few more times, before he agreed."

Eyes wide, she asks, "CeCe was in the tabloids? Not you?"

I laugh. "Yes, it was more CeCe at that point. They focused on her appearance and were rough with her. So rough we thought she was going to commit suicide from all the unwanted attention."

"You're kidding. CeCe is so confident and strong. I can't imagine her struggling like that."

"I won't kid you, they're relentless. There were fake stories in the tabloids that some of her 'friends' planted. You see how social she is. She examined her group in high school and determined most of them weren't truly friends. And don't get me started on the mean-girl thing."

"Tell me about it. That's why I hid in high school. What did you do to help her?"

"I decided to take the attention off her and make sure they left her alone. I'd assumed they'd give up on me after a while, but they always seem to be fascinated by my boring life."

She stutters, "W-w-why would the tabloids care about you and CeCe? I mean, I get that you have fame, fortune and amazing good looks, but why would they care?"

"You've asked the million-dollar question. My parents are credited with founding Sandy Systems before CeCe and I were born. Together they networked the computer lab while they were both graduate students at Stanford. My dad was running the computer science lab, and my mom was running the business school's lab. Both were computer science grad students. Computers at the time couldn't 'talk' to one another unless they were in the same room, but my parents changed that. Dad told Mom that he was doing it just to see if he could create something, but it's old lore in The Valley that they did it so they could send love letters to one another.

"They got pregnant with us after trying for several years. Having twins was a real surprise. After CeCe and I were born, my mom attempted to go back to work and leave us with nannies, but it got to be too much. She would tell us we were more fun than work, but I think she was growing tired of the politics at Sandy Systems, and we needed her at home. CeCe is truly the troublemaker in our family. She kept my parents and teachers on their toes."

Smiling at me, she says, "I'm not sure that being young, handsome and rich is boring. You've been seen with all the most beautiful socialites and women in Hollywood. You're the ultimate catch for some women."

"I guess the real question is do *you* think I'm the ultimate catch?

Blushing the most amazing shade of pink, she says, "Of course I do."

That makes my heart race, and I want to sing and dance.

After dinner, we snuggle by the fire. "There isn't a television, and internet is spotty, so our only option is to play games. But we have a nice game closet." Reaching into the closet, she picks up a box a little larger than a deck of cards. "This is my favorite game of my childhood."

"Mille Bornes?"

"Absolutely. It's a car race played with cards in French."

"In French?"

"Well, the cards are in French, but we don't have to speak French. It was always my favorite growing up. It made me want to go to France."

"When did you go?"

"I've never been."

I raise a brow. "You can afford to go now."

She nods. "Oh, I know," she says, blushing, "but I've never had anyone to go with."

I get that. San Francisco isn't always the easiest for single women, and though I'd love to show her the City of Lights and share with her all that I love about Paris, I don't want to overwhelm her and possibly freak her out. "Show me how to play."

She kills me playing Mille Bornes and then Scrabble. At the end of the night, I escort her to her bedroom door, and she leans in and kisses me. My brain lights on fire and warmth spreads throughout my entire body. I'm addicted, unable to bear not being with her, though I can barely breathe when she's around. These kisses are my salvation and my torment. She's the half that makes me whole. Her eyes tell me that we both want more, but we're cautious, taking it slow.

The next morning, we both easily agree to stay until we need to leave to be in Hillsboro on time for dinner Sunday night. I want to devour her. I'm trying to be patient and not jump her, but it's hard.

After a nice cup of coffee, we walk up and down the beachfront, enjoying the waves as they lap along the sand. We walk silently at times and other times we talk, one just as simple as the other. I don't think I've ever felt this relaxed with another person outside of my immediate family.

"Tell me more about why the tabloids are so interested in you and CeCe."

"It's a bit of a long story, so bear with me." She smiles, giving me permission to continue. "My father was raised as the only child of his parents' union. He has eight half-siblings from his father's other marriages—six marriages, actually. His father—my grandfather—was incredibly wealthy. My great-great-grandfather came to the US from France and made his money in the steel industry. After my dad was born, my grandfather moved on to his next wife. My dad, against his father's wishes, came out to Stanford to get a computer science degree and met my mom their freshman year. My dad grew up in the newspapers, but they weren't like they are now. They only wrote about what they were supposed to, no hiding in bushes or combing through their trash."

"Really? They comb through your trash?"

"You'd be surprised where we find them. So, my mom was from a big Montana ranching family. They fell in love, and together they built Sandy Systems when they were in grad school.

"Because my dad wasn't going into the family steel business, my grandfather pulled my dad's trust fund, but they didn't care. Sandy Systems was doing well. My grandfather died after our tenth birthday. When they read his will, he gave specific things to each of his children. My dad got a letter, and CeCe and I got my father's inheritance."

"Wow. That sure would be a turning point in anyone's life."

I squeeze her hand. "My parents raised us with a strong work ethic and taught us to never take it all for granted."

"You do know that's a huge asset, don't you?"

"I do. As my grandmother once told me, having reason to wake up each day and having a purpose are important. I've grown to understand that and find that there's so much truth in that philosophy."

Nodding, she says, "That's how I feel. The money came with a lot of work, but it could also go away."

"We weren't given the companies outright either. Both CeCe and I started on the ground floor of the family businesses. I delivered mail and was often known as Trey Michael—my nickname and my middle name. It allowed me to work under the radar and learn without any preconceived ideas or people thinking I was entitled to anything. Most of my managers didn't know who I actually was, so I worked my way up the corporate ladder."

We return to the house, but before we walk in, she turns and hugs me. "Thank you for sharing all of that. It means a lot to me."

Despite knowing it was safe, it was difficult to share my history with her. It's clear she understands that, and I'm grateful.

It's hard to believe that our day flies by. We didn't do anything in particular, and I relished in the simplicity of it. When it's time to start dinner, she does the prep work while I heat up the grill, open the wine and set the table. I find some candles and light them, and we enjoy our dinner together.

"What a great day," I tell her.

"I'm so glad I could share one of my favorite places on earth with you."

"I can see why you like it, but I also enjoyed spending time with you." I reach across the table for her hand and rub her knuckles with my thumb. "You're not only beautiful and incredibly sexy, but you're also brilliant, funny and easy to be around." I stand and take her by the hand. "Would you like to build a bonfire out on the beach?"

"Let me get the marshmallows, chocolate bars and graham crackers."

We make s'mores by the fire, then sit and take in the heat of it. As the sun goes down, the fire becomes bright and vivid, as though someone has shone a spotlight on it, full of brilliant reds, oranges and faint yellows. We huddle closely, giving us the warmth we need to remain outside on a brisk, cool evening.

I have chocolate all over my fingers from the s'mores. Reaching for my index finger, she places it in her mouth to lick it off. I breathe in heavily, wanting more. Seductively, I ask, "Shall we go inside?"

She nods, and we stand to put the fire out. Sara holds my hand as we head back to the beach house. We don't talk, just walk leisurely and enjoy the contact. I'm content knowing that for the rest of the evening she's all mine. Being near her excites me, and also gives me a serenity I've never known from anyone else. It's like the breaths I take aren't full when she's not with me, like the smiles I smile are incomplete somehow. She creates the warmth in my soul that fills me full of love and keeps the fire burning in my eyes. My eagerness increases as we reach the house and she leads me inside.

SARA

H IS FINGERS INTERLACE WITH MINE as he leans over and kisses me, his lips soft and insistent. He stops to gaze at me as if asking for permission to continue, and I stare at him with desire burning in my eyes. Kissing me again, this time he pushes his tongue past my lips, parting them. My body responds to his and I'm suddenly pliant in his arms, his tongue tangling with mine as his hands move to my hair. He pulls back and stares at me, giving me a half smile like he knows he's going to get what he wants, and then he's kissing me again, deep and passionate, my head spinning with the intensity of it.

I sit in a chair to catch my breath, and he stands before me. I unbuckle his pants and let them fall to the floor, his hard cock tenting in his cotton boxers. It seems almost too big, but I want him.

Taking him in my hand, my fingers don't quite meet on the other side and I wonder how I'll ever manage while also wanting to take every last inch of him in my mouth.

I flick my eyes up at him as I press my tongue flat against his base, slowly dragging it up the full length.

"Jesus," he gasps.

I see pure lust in his eyes, and it turns me on. I trace over the slit at the top and twirl my tongue around the entire head. Then I start again, licking up the front and swirling around the ridge on the underside, teasing him. I run my hand up and down before dipping my head, stretching my jaw as wide as it will go and taking Trey in my mouth. He lets out a deep moan.

I slowly lower my head inch by inch as his fingers dig into the hair at the base of my neck. Knowing I have him so hot makes me want to give him more. With one hand on his throbbing cock, following the motion of my mouth up and down on his slick member, I gently cup his balls with the other. They tighten under my delicate touch.

My main work is done with my mouth, though, and I savor every taste, keeping my lips and tongue firm against him, releasing only to lick him at the tip. Each time my head dips down, I take more of him into my mouth, marveling at how loose my throat has become, that it can take much more than I ever imagined.

"God, Sara," he moans, his fingers fully tangled in my hair as he guides my head at the pace he wants, my mouth stretching wide. I pause and take my mouth off his cock, giving it quick kisses up the side before taking it as deep as I can once more, Trey gently pushing the back of my head to have more of him. His breath comes in gasps as I quicken my pace, my hand still stroking him.

"Don't stop," he gasps, and I wouldn't have even if we were on a plane going down. "Sara, I'm going to come," he says, and knowing my mouth could do this to him makes me moan with him. Soon he explodes and I take all of him, holding him there as cum slides down my throat, his grunts hardly contained. His hand falls from my head to my shoulder, and finally he braces himself on the arm of the chair, panting for air. I slip him out of my mouth.

Once he pulls himself together and tugs his pants back up, he sits on the bench across from me, rubbing his hands over his face and through his hair. "Damn. I'm going to need a minute. I think I went off to another universe for a while there."

"Flatterer," I tell him, but secretly I'm pleased. I've never made a man say my name like that. I move over and sit next to him.

"I'm not kidding," he says.

Very happy with his satisfaction, I lean over to nip at his neck. His breath becomes labored, and I'm sure he's getting hard again.

He leads me by the hand to my room, then sits on the bed facing me with his hands on my hips. He breathes in my scent before covering my midsection in soft kisses.

I'm speechless as I allow him to peel my pants and panties off my body in one fell swoop. Even though I feel incredibly exposed, all my inhibitions have flown out the window. My heart is beating a million miles a minute as I think, *I want this man.* Every sexually deviant thought I've ever had before has resurfaced with a vengeance, and I thank my lucky stars it's Trey who will put out the fire.

The effect of his one hand is profound. My nipples pebble, my breath grows shallow and goose bumps cover my skin. I'm much more turned on than I should be, and it isn't just his hand—it's the way he watches me. I know without a shadow of a doubt that he's as aroused as I am, and that really works for me.

"Open your legs," he demands.

I do as I'm told, and his fingers trace my wet folds, teasing me. I'm almost ready to beg him for more when his fingers dip deep inside me. First one and then another plunge into my wet crease, and I moan my appreciation.

"Soaking wet," he rasps, then removes them as quick as he started. My body aches at the loss. Placing his wet fingers into his mouth, he sucks my juices and I'm further turned on. "And as I expected, so sweet."

"I want more." I raise my hips, and with a groan, his hot, hungry mouth moves down to my core. The blood rushes through me as his movements pick up pace and become more urgent.

He deepens the suction of his mouth with his fingers inside me, rubbing my G-spot. Lights flash before my eyes as a tsunami of pleasure rolls over me, obscuring everything. My climax jolts through my entire body, and I throw my head back and grip his shoulders to keep myself upright as my legs turn to Jell-O.

We lie satiated on the bed, facing one another without saying anything, his hands caressing me from my hips to my shoulders. His erection presses into my stomach, and I lean in to lick his lips before I start to aggressively probe his mouth with my tongue.

He pulls away, and I hear the tear of a foil packet as he sits on the edge of the bed, rolling the condom down his length. Then he's there, the head of his cock pressed against my slit. I'm so wet and turned on that he has no problem sliding inside, but he stretches me tight, filling me like no one ever has before. The sensation is indescribable, and I dig my nails into the sheets below me.

We simultaneously moan in ecstasy as he begins to pull out. My core greedily fights to tighten and clench around his girth, not wanting him to move, going to any length necessary to keep him inside me. He pauses when the very tip of his cock rests just inside my opening. I sigh in relief and savor the feeling when he slides his full length back into the depths of my warm center, his movements slow and controlled as he gives my body what it craves. He lets out a satisfied groan, and we both come again in a glorious moment of ecstasy.

Once our heavy breathing calms, he grins. "That was amazing."

He pulls me in close so we're spooning, and I drift off to sleep feeling satisfied, safe and adored.

TWENTY

TREY

*L*YING IN BED, I think of how our weekend has gone. What a pleasant surprise. I thought when Sara suggested we could visit the beach house, it would be full of sex and debauchery. But when we arrived, she showed me my own room and initially set an expectation of two friends getting to know one another. We had a nice time starting out as friends, and it eventually moved into something more serious. Getting to know a woman outside of the limelight makes such a difference. Finding how beautiful Sara is on the inside as well as the outside has been absolutely amazing.

Sara seems to meet every requirement on my mental checklist of a woman. She's smart, beautiful, and has a dry sense of humor that meshes quite well with mine. I know there's a certain amount of baggage that comes with dating me, so the women who want all the attention aren't usually the ones for me. But even if Sara and I never amount to anything romantically, if we discover we're only shooting stars in the night, fired up and soon to burn out, I'll always have this moment to fill my soul.

Waking with a woman in my bed is new for me, but it feels comfortable and right with her. The heat of our bodies so close together brings the comfort of a warm blanket on a cold morning. I hear her rhythmic breathing and know Sara's still sleeping. Slowly I open my eyes and see the beautiful woman sleeping beside me. The slope of her back is so sexy as she lies on her side facing away from me, the sheets wound around her waist. I can't help but run my fingers over her smooth skin, starting at her shoulders and caressing down her arm to her glorious waist. Leaning in, I begin a trail of kisses down her side, following the path my fingers laid.

She rolls over and gazes at me with a sexy smile, purring, "Good morning."

"Good morning. Did you sleep well?"

"I do tend to sleep better at the beach." She stretches, exposing her breast. The nipple beads, and I lean down and bring it in my mouth, making her moan and push her hips into me. She bites her lip, closing her eyes momentarily before opening them again to watch me, her lips parted. I gently glide my finger across her pussy, so wet and pink and mine—mine to play with, mine to please. I dip my finger into her, and she lets out a moan as I pump inside her before slipping my finger out and giving her clit some much-needed attention. Her face flushes with passion, and I know she's going to start begging me soon for more. I love that she always needs more.

My hands glide from her face down to her shoulders, clasping them tightly before making my way to her breasts, pulling and kneading them as she arches into me. I'm drunk and dizzy from the ferocity of her tongue alone, but combined with her soft chest pressing into mine and her intoxicating smell of orange, jasmine and rose, it takes an ungodly force to make me let go of her.

"You taste so sweet, Sara," I murmur, then plunge my tongue in and out of her mouth again and again. My hands wander to her sweet spot and, pressing my thumb firmly against her bundle of nerves, I begin massaging it in small circles. Her legs shake uncontrollably against my thighs. I want to watch her fall apart.

"Come for me, sweet princess. Ride my fingers, work your hips and take your pleasure."

I can feel her pussy quiver and spasm around my fingers, and I growl as my cock throbs with need. With her mouth parted, her labored breathing comes out in quick puffs while her lips form an O. She coats my fingers with her luxurious juices, creating erotic wet sounds that have me almost spilling my load.

I can't take anymore. I need to feel her from the inside. I roll a condom on my throbbing cock. I growl as I hold on to her hips and slowly guide myself past her opening. The thickness of my cock stretches her core further as I to push myself in inch by slow inch, her muscles exquisitely expanding to accommodate my full length as I fill her.

I let out a satisfied groan once I'm spent, and we collapse to the bed, breathing heavy.

She stares at me and grins. "Who needs a gym when we can do this."

It's our final morning, and I don't want to leave here. We make love slowly and softly before we finally get out of bed.

While I make her the French toast I promised, she runs into town to grab the *New York Times* and the *San Francisco Chronicle*. Savoring our French toast with real maple syrup, we enjoy good coffee and read the paper. It's a perfect Sunday morning.

Glancing at my watch, I see it's getting late, so I begin to clean up. She offers to help but I shoo her away, and she sits close by and watches me closely. When I finish cleaning the end of the dishes and wipe down the counters, she says, "You do know that doing the dishes and cleaning up is a major turn-on for most women."

"Well, we haven't tried the kitchen counter." I bounce my eyebrows suggestively.

She lets out the most melodious laugh that makes me hard just hearing it. I want so much to take her on the counter. Maybe another time.

"I hate that this weekend needs to end." Bringing her into my arms, I kiss her and say regretfully, "If we need to get down to Hillsboro, we'll probably need to head out shortly. Do you want to stop by your place to drop off your things? And if you'd feel more comfortable rolling up to my folks' in your own car, I understand."

Her face falls. "We can do whatever you feel comfortable doing."

She matters to me. Her feelings matter to me. I'm not always the best at communicating that, but I want her to know that I want more. Staring deep into her blue-green eyes, I tell her honestly, "I'd rather stay here with you for the next month, but unfortunately that isn't an option because my dad and the partners of SHN are expecting both of us."

Nodding, she sighs. "I guess you're right."

As we drive over Mount Tamalpais, I reach for her hand. "I want you to know that I want to scream from the rooftops how wonderful you are. But I also don't want to jeopardize your relationship with the partners. When you're ready to tell everyone, I'll be ready too."

She smiles at me. "Thank you. If you're okay with it, I'd like to keep this between us for a while. Only because this is special, and I want to keep it that way."

Squeezing her hand, I assure her, "I think it's special, too."

WE ARRIVE AT MY PARENTS' HOUSE, and I'm distracted by my mother's dogs as we walk in. She has a herd of dogs that seems to grow each time I visit. I stop to greet them, and Sara gives me a wink as she continues on.

We don't seem to be going out of our way to be together, but she's never out of my sight as she talks to each of the partners and my sister. As we sit down, we find what are becoming our regular seats, which means I get to sit next to Sara on my right and CeCe on my left.

As a general rule, I hide my emotions, having learned a long time ago that they were intel I'd rather not hand out freely. But today is different. Sara has awoken something inside of me that has me excited with the anticipation of what we can be and where we're going. The lovesick smile that breaks across my face hasn't been seen for many years, and throughout dinner I both talk and eat faster. I have a good feeling about the weekend; nothing that feels this right could possibly go wrong. It couldn't.

Dinner seems more fun than usual, the partners sharing funny stories about their weekends that seems to further bond them together. When Sara's asked about her weekend, I'm very interested in hearing what she has to say.

"Well, I spent it with a friend up in Stinson Beach at my foster parents' beach house."

"Was it with your mysterious man?" Emerson asks.

Everyone leans in for her answer, and she says, "It was a great weekend. We walked the beach and enjoyed all that Stinson has to offer. Have any of you ever been?"

I'm impressed at how she answers the question but doesn't actually answer it at the same time.

The conversation moves around to what to do in Stinson when CeCe leans in and asks, "Okay, big brother. Spill. What has you so happy?"

Smiling and determined to not to give her any information, I simply say, "I guess it's life."

She scoffs. "Life? I'd ask if it was a girl, but I know better. I saw the picture on *TMZ*. Getting serious?"

"Maybe. I don't know yet," I tell her honestly. I'm not going to talk to CeCe about this until Sara and I know for sure what we are.

"Hmmm. Okay. I know you better than anyone else in this world, so you can tell me later."

I kiss her on the cheek and give her a hug. "I've met someone, and she's perfect for me in almost every way, but I don't want to make a big deal of it yet. I promise I'll keep you posted."

"I love you, and I'm happy for you. When you're ready to tell her, you can tell me."

I laugh because her twin sense is so accurate. "Promise." Standing next to her as we begin to move into Dad's office, I knock my hip into hers and ask, "And what about you?"

"I've got my eye on someone."

"Does he know?"

She blushes. "I'll never tell."

As I DRIVE SARA HOME, I hear her cell phone repeatedly ping, indicating that she keeps getting texts. She isn't answering them, but I can't help but wonder if they're from another man. I'm not usually jealous, but for some reason this time I am.

"You're awfully popular this evening. Is everything okay?"

She glances at me and smiles, but it doesn't reach her eyes. "Yes. It's a friend I can catch up with later. Seems everyone had big weekends."

I realize she's being equally as evasive with me as she was at dinner, but I'm not going to let it bother me. I place my hand on her thigh and quietly share, "I'm not sure I'm ready for the weekend to end."

Staring out the window as the traffic passes us while we drive back into The City, she tells me, "Me neither. It was so much fun being with you. I wish it didn't have to end, but I have a crazy week ahead. What about you?"

My week is overwhelming, with my deal out of Seattle getting shaky, but I really want to see her. "It's a crazy week for me too, but I'd love to see you. Do you have any time?" I ask, trying not to sound too desperate.

"I didn't get much work done this weekend, so I have a few

things to get accomplished that will make for some long days. Can we talk later and figure something out?"

I may be imagining it, but it feels like she's pulling away. And I can't be sure it isn't because of something I've done, or if it's her way of getting back into a work mode. "Of course," I tell her, trying not to show my disappointment. "No pressure. Really."

"I know. I'm sorry, I'm just preoccupied with everything I need to get done. We have a closing this week, plus I have three SEC filings to get finished, and those are very labor intensive."

"You don't have any help?"

"Not really. Our outside counsel can only do so much. I have an admin and I use the receptionist, but as a start-up, it mostly falls to me."

As we pull up to her apartment building, I turn to her and say, "I'll clear my schedule whenever you can make time for me."

She leans in and gives me a slow, passionate kiss. "I'll give you a call. Have a good evening, and sleep well." Her lips brush mine. Not innocently, like a tease—it's hot, fiery and demanding. I want to pull away before I lose myself, but I can't seem to; my senses have been seduced and I can no longer think straight. Her hand wanders to my achingly hard cock and she strokes me through my jeans. "I do want to see you again later this week."

My heart soars as she heads to her building, turning to wave as she opens the door and enters.

SARA

I WANTED TO INVITE TREY up to my place and continue our fun from our weekend, but I just have so much going through my mind right now, to the point that I need to write down a checklist of things I want to get done this week.

Opening the door to my apartment, I'm shocked to see Henry sitting in my living room. "What are you doing here?"

"You gave me a key, remember?"

"What would Claudia say?"

"We have a fictional marriage. She wouldn't care."

"That's bullshit. You've been telling me that, and yet you have an infant son. What do you want from me, Henry?"

"I want you. I want to get between your legs and hear you call my name as I eat your sweet pussy. I want to watch as you take my cock deep down your throat." Running his hand up and down my arm, he tries to pull me closer to him.

My patience running thin, I firmly tell him, "Henry, I've been clear. I don't know how to be clearer that you need to leave me alone. I can't and *won't* get involved with you ever again."

"Baby, we're good together when we're naked. You and I

click." He puts his hand on my breast and tries to kiss me.

Pushing his hand away, I sneer, "Henry, you need to leave. *Now.*"

"We can make this our secret," he pleads. "Your new boyfriend never needs to know. Just like you don't tell Claudia, I won't tell him."

I push him away. Henry is never going to see me as anything but a cheap lay, someone to fuck.

Walking to my front door, I open it and stand there holding the knob, waiting for him to walk over the threshold. "Good night, Henry. Please only call me for professional purposes. And please leave my house key when you leave." He doesn't move to leave, but reaches for my breast again. Almost violently I push his hand away. I don't want this. "Get the *fuck* out, Henry. *And don't.* Come. Back."

He finally walks by, handing me the house key. He's hardly out the door before I slam it behind him.

My hands are shaking. *I can't believe he had the nerve. Why can't he listen?* We had fun when we were together, but when I compare Henry and Trey, several things remind me of how he really wasn't that into me.

Hell, there are so many reasons why we were so wrong together, and more to the point, why he's a waste of my time and energy. For starters, he was never honest with me. I hold back the snort of disbelief regarding all the ways he lied to me. Nor did he or does he respect me.

I sit back and wipe the tears that are beginning to fall. These things make me feel bad about myself, but I can't allow myself to waste any more time on Henry.

I find my fortitude and regroup. It dawns on me that Henry doesn't know one thing about my family, and I'm not sure he even knows my favorite color. I realize that Trey knows more about me from our two days away than Henry knows after six months of dating. I start to feel used when I realize that he only cared about my job regarding what was going on with Mason, Cameron or Dillon. And when things didn't go his way, I'd get the silent treatment and he would shut me out. How old are we?

I'm not sure why I didn't see it until now. I gave my heart freely to Henry and allowed him to break it, getting zero in return. I need to forget Henry and focus on Trey, and whatever it is that we're considering building.

With that behind me, a weight's lifted off my shoulders. Having found my purpose, I'm able to clear my mind and write my to-do list for the week to help quiet my brain and hopefully get some sleep.

Shit. There are over thirty objectives on my list. Each one will take at least two hours. How am I going to fit this all in—and this is only Monday's list? I don't think I'll be able to see Trey this week. That's disappointing, and I feel so overwhelmed it makes me want to cry.

ON MY RIDE TO WORK this morning, I text Trey. Good morning.

   Trey: Good morning. Did you sleep well?
   Me: Yes, after I wrote out the list of all I have to do. You
      don't happen to have about 40 hours today you can
      lend me?

Trey: I wish. Sorry. I'm running out of town this afternoon
and will be back Wednesday. Can we have dinner?

Me: Is everything OK? I'll let you know how my week is
going.

Trey: Hopefully it works for you. I'd love to see you. Have
a great day.

Me: You, too.

Work is already crazy when I get off the elevator, and it isn't
even eight. I can't believe how many people are here. I see Annabel and ask, "What's going on?"

Putting a stack of papers aside, she says, "I just got here myself so I'm not sure."

"Do you know who else is here?"

"I'll wander around and see."

"Oh, that's not necessary. I was only curious."

"I need coffee anyway. I'll informally look around."

Annabel knocks on my door a few minutes later with a cup of
coffee for me. "I picked this up for you. It looks like the acquisitions team has a lead on something."

"Thanks. And thanks for the coffee."

During our Monday morning partners meeting, we discuss
some open issues from the previous night, and then Mason makes
an announcement, "Great news. We were notified today that
Fractional Technologies is accepting our offer."

We all celebrate another win, smiling and giving each other
high fives.

"I'll reach out to Christine to get the contract rolling and make the initial arrangements for a funds transfer for you and Dillon," I tell them. The SHN leadership team has independently approached several prospective companies for SHN to invest with. Meanwhile, the SHN staff has been working on other less desirable companies which are being fed by our mole to Perkins Klein. We have been going out of our way to lose those less desirable companies. "I can't help but wonder how these companies we approached below the radar and behind our employees backs are affecting our morale."

Mason nods. "Sara, I think you're right. We do need a better answer than 'We knew these guys and want to invest.'"

"What does Jim suggest?" Emerson asks.

Cameron glances up. "Jim? The FBI guy?"

"Reaching out to Jim is a good idea," Dillon agrees. "He must have some experience in this area."

"I'll call him and ask," Mason says.

As our meeting breaks up, Emerson asks me, "Busy day today?"

"I have a long list and not enough time. You?"

"The same." She turns to me, and says, "Good luck."

As I wander back to my office, my cell phone pings with a text from CeCe. Hey. Let me know if you can meet me for lunch. We can talk about bridesmaid things if you'd like.

I want to have a girlfriend I can share my love life with, but it could never be CeCe. As Trey's sister, I don't think she'd be objective. Eventually, I text her: We landed our third win below the radar. Time will be tight today. I can meet about 10 tonight, or we can try tomorrow?

CeCe: Tonight would work and be much more fun. How

about we meet at Bourbon and Branch? Tonight's
password is Hill Rock.

Me: Got it. See you about ten. Can't wait.

After spending the day running around completing contracts
and getting a few issues handled, I only manage to cross off five
things on my list. I want to cry, but I don't even have the energy
to do that. I eat a small bite for dinner in the office and head out
in time to meet CeCe. Bourbon and Branch is one of those super-
hip spots that no matter the night, it's packed, and to get in you
need a reservation that comes with a password. It changes
nightly and is usually a small bourbon brand that winds up
being the drink special.

When I arrive, CeCe waves me over. She's surrounded by all
sorts of handsome men, who she makes leave as I reach the table.

"Don't send them away on my account," I tell her.

"Oh, honey, these guys are only good to look at." Leaning in,
she says in a conspiratorial tone, "They really don't have much
going on upstairs. We'd be bored."

I laugh. "I don't know about that."

She nods. "Trust me."

Standing, she kisses me on both cheeks and says, "You always look like a model. Just gorgeous."

"You're very kind." Then I whisper, as if it's top secret, "I
have an incredible personal shopper at Nordstrom, and she
picks out my clothes and tells me what to wear together, even
down to the underwear."

"Really? Do you share her name?"

"Of course! It's Jennifer. She works on commission, so she

doesn't cost anything, but she has a real eye for what I'd like and what looks good on me."

"I think we need to go shopping soon, and you can introduce us."

The waiter arrives and we order two of the drink specials, then gossip about the boys around the bar. We don't really know them, just have fun imagining what their stories are.

She points to a clean-cut blond Greek god, probably six and a half feet tall, leaning against the bar wearing tight-fitting jeans, his legs crossed at the ankles, and his black T-shirt straining against his broad chest and muscular arms. He's hot and oozes sex. "That one there, his name is Steve. He's a fireman with SFFD."

"Oh I like firemen."

"He grew up with three sisters, so he respects women. Currently he's between girlfriends. He loves going down on his girlfriends and always makes sure they're satisfied with two orgasms before he gets his own."

Laughing in hysterics, we actually attract his attention, and he gives us a megawatt smile.

I point to a short, dark-haired balding man with a small potbelly. "Meet Jacob."

"Oh I like Jacob. He's wearing a custom suit. Bring it on," she giggles.

"He's a partner at the largest law firm here in The City, practicing business law. He grew up in San Francisco and went to all the finest schools, along with Harvard undergrad and the University of Chicago Law."

She nudges me with her shoulder and teases, "Aw, I went to business school at the University of Chicago."

I wink at her. "That was for you." We snicker, and I continue. "I went to school with dozens like him. Guys weren't as bad as the girls, but it was competitive."

"Chicago was the same. Thank God that's behind us."

We make up a few more biographies of various men, and even some women. Boy, do I sound catty when I called one woman an easy lay. CeCe doesn't judge me or criticize, just giggles. "Ouch! Meow!"

As I drain my drink and finish my water, CeCe shares, "The girls are getting together on Friday night at One Market around eight. Can you join us?"

Of course I'd love to hang out with her more. "It's a Friday night, but I'll try to tear myself away from the office early. That sounds like a lot of fun."

Trey had mentioned wanting to get together, but he's only asked for time during the week, not the weekend. I'll hold Saturday night for him, and if he can't make that work, it's just as well. I've been buried at work, so I need to spend most of the weekend working anyway.

SARA

J STOP IN THE COMPANY BREAK ROOM and make myself a double Nespresso, then take a seat in my typical chair in Mason's office for the partners meeting. Cameron and I are the first to arrive, and he's obviously anxious, fidgeting and restless as everyone arrives. We all make small talk, and when Mason arrives last, he shuts the door and nods at Cameron, who announces, "It appears Perkins Klein has won one of our projected duds."

"Wow," Emerson exclaims. "What should we expect?"

"Well, the technology has a flaw, which they recognize. They were seeking heavy funding to repair and move on. It's a good concept, but they aren't technically strong enough to pull it over the finish line, and they aren't interested in any outside help."

Dillon explains, "They don't have the team to let go. They want money to keep doing it their way. And in this case, had we gone in, we'd want to have Cameron and some of his team rework the technology."

"I'm not even sure I could do that level of math to make it work," Cameron admits.

Mason asks the group, "Should we have Greer put out a counter public relations campaign to the win, or let it ride itself out?"

Dillon shares, "I like the idea of a counter public relations campaign."

"Me, too," Cameron chimes in.

"What do we gain by doing the public relations campaign?" Emerson asks.

"We do get some vindication, but probably not much more than that," Mason replies.

"It sounds like if we point out that the technology is struggling, and management is lacking, we would be giving them a way to fix it and make a mistake profitable." Glancing around the room, she adds, "Maybe we should celebrate among ourselves and consider the public relations campaign after it implodes. How much did they invest?"

"Over twenty million," Dillon tells us.

Cameron whistles, and we all agree that it may not have been a wise investment for Perkins Klein's portfolio. Cameron asks, "Dillon, in examining their portfolio, how confident are you in their position?"

"Funny you should ask. I've been crunching those numbers, and I have to believe if they lose out with the seven companies we've planted them with, they're going to be in bad shape."

Mason turns to me. "Sara, what do you think?"

"I guess I'm with Emerson on this, and I'm grateful that Dillon is managing our portfolio rather than David Klein. Of course, if the portfolio had a double-D chest and looked amazing in a thong, he might be paying better attention."

That gets quite a few laughs from the team before our meeting breaks up and we all head back to our respective offices, where I sit down to work on three SEC filings and two intent letters.

Up pings a notification in my e-mail. I don't usually pay attention to the notices, but this one catches my eye. Catherine is responding to my letter. My nerves are frayed to the quick, unsure if I want to see what she has to say. In my building anxiety, I've constructed elaborate rationalizations for why everything would turn out all right, but the nagging voice in the back of my mind speaks of nothing but doom ahead. Her response is swift and cutting.

TO: Sara White
FROM: Catherine Ellington
SUBJECT: Your letter

Sara,

You have nothing to do with me. What I did 30 years ago is my affair, nothing to do with you or anyone else. I've started a new life. No one knows about my past, and that's the way I want it to be. I do not want to see you or hear from you again.

Catherine

I'm devastated. How can she be so callous? What does she mean it has nothing to do with me? It was *me* she left behind—it *absolutely* has something to do with me. No words can describe the hurt I feel.

Lonely, starved of warmth, I stare out my window into the Bay and watch the barges and sailboats. I'm drowning in sorrow, yet I reach for a spark of strength from within that pushes me to stay strong for a moment longer. Then the tears fall, along with cries and sobs. *What have I done to deserve this rejection?*

Cast out by my mother again, feeling three years old once more with nowhere to call home, yet the Bay and the barges are steady as they move goods from port to port. Somehow it gives me comfort, allowing me to see myself and recognize the hurt for what it is.

I can hear the sounds of an active office—everyone going about their duties and lives—tickling the tip of my ear, keeping me company.

Chastened but not deterred, I e-mail her back in an attempt to "sell" her on meeting me.

TO: Catherine Ellington
FROM: Sara White
SUBJECT: Your letter

Dear Catherine,

I certainly understand your reluctance to meet with me. I'm not trying to upset your home life. I'm hoping for information on my biological father and some history about my family. I'm happy to come to you and we meet over coffee, or if you prefer, we can talk via e-mail. Please?

Sara

I press Send before I talk myself out of it. I'm hoping she's still online and will reconsider meeting me.

It takes a few minutes of stalling, but I finally go back to work. Each time my e-mail notification sounds, I jump, desperate for a reply, but it's never from her.

TREY

EVER SINCE OUR WEEKEND, I've been thinking a lot about Sara. I know I'll see her each Sunday, but I'd love to see her again before that. I text her with a simple Hey.

She doesn't respond, though there could be a thousand reasons why. I didn't reach out to her, waiting all week to hear from her instead. I try to put it out of my mind that she's been silent all week, but it's hard; I want to see her, or at least talk to her. I haven't spoken to my sister this week either, so I figure I might be able to talk to someone who at least replies.

I call CeCe. "Hey, baby sister. What's up?"

"Not too much, busy with Emerson's wedding," she says, stifling a yawn.

Trying to not give away my feelings for Sara, I ask, "It's mostly people from SHN and family in the wedding, isn't it?" I cringe. *Talk about being desperate to get information from my sister.*

"You're in the wedding party," she explains, as if I'm slow and don't realize I don't work for SHN.

"True, but I cross a little of both."

"In your dreams," she snarks.

I'm stung by her directness. "Be nice."

A hint of tenderness appears when her tone changes from light-hearted banter to caring and compassionate. "What's wrong?"

I decide to tell her enough that she can help me rationalize what I might've done wrong and maybe help me fix it. "I've met someone who's rocked my world, but I have a feeling she doesn't feel the same."

"How is that possible?"

I love that CeCe always sees the best in me. "You do know that we have a bit of notoriety, don't you?"

"Sure, but it isn't like that's a secret when *you* date someone. Don't the idiots on motorcycles carrying cameras give you away?"

I run my fingers through my hair. "Thankfully, she never experienced that."

"Then how did she find out?

"She was in the *TMZ* photo, but I think she would rather not deal with it."

CeCe, with her typical directness, says, "Then dump her. You're amazing. We can't control the chaos that surrounds us."

Frustrated that CeCe thinks I should walk away from this amazing woman, I need to tell her how much I like this girl. "It's not that easy. I think she may be *the one.*"

"You? *You're* thinking of settling down? You aren't even serious about her." She's quiet a few moments before she finally says, "Are you?"

"Yep. I think I want to settle down with this one."

"You think? Why don't you know?"

"We had a great weekend away, and I really feel that we connected on a level I've never connected with anyone before. But when we got back, she essentially ghosted me. She won't talk to me. I've called, e-mailed and texted, but all I get are crickets."

"I love you, big brother. You're perfect in every way." With a playful push, she urges, "Go after her!"

I knew CeCe would know what to say to encourage me and make me feel better.

After hanging up, I pour myself a gin and tonic from the bar in my office, then sit back in my chair and watch the hundreds of cars crossing the double-decker Bay Bridge. I'm lucky to have a great relationship with my sister. So often it seemed it was us against the world. I also wish I knew a decent guy for her to date. CeCe deserves a great guy who will allow her to be strong and confident on the outside, while understanding that she's insecure and fragile on the inside.

Sara's much like my sister. I know I can't make her like me, but certainly I'm going to try.

I wish I knew how to fix this, how to make my life less interesting for the tabloids. If I were less interesting, maybe they'd leave me alone. Maybe Sara would want to spend time with me.

I text her again. Any interest in a quick drink after work? Nothing.

I don't want to go home, nor do I want to work late, so I send out a group text to a bunch of my buddies. Anyone up for meeting tonight?

In seconds I get a round of yeses, and we agree on a place and a time.

I run home to change out of my suit and into something more

appropriate—jeans, a black T-shirt and a pair of Cole Hahn black leather ankle boots.

I'm the first to arrive and find a booth in the corner, ordering a bottle of Johnnie Walker Black for the table and six glasses.

While I wait, I watch all the activity in the bar. It's a bit of a pickup joint, but it's dark and I enjoy watching my friends try to score girls.

A young Asian woman smiles at me and I smile back as she walks over. "Hi! I'm Tanya." She has long black hair and barely comes to my chest she's so petite. She's a bit bubblier than I normally date, but she's the opposite of Sara and an excellent diversion.

"Nice to meet you, Tanya. Call me Charlie."

Cocking her head to the side, she glances up at me, one eyebrow quirked. "You seem familiar."

Not wanting to have a deep conversation with her, I say, "I do? I get that a lot."

She giggles and keeps touching her hair. "So, tell me about yourself."

"I'm not that interesting. Why don't you tell me about yourself instead."

She smiles and laughs. "I work for a venture capital company."

That piques my interest. "Really? Which one?"

"Perkins Klein."

I need to be careful. She doesn't know I advise SHN, so maybe I can collect some insider information if she's in the mood to share. "Really? What do you do for them?"

"Research mostly," she says with confidence.

"I think I've heard of Perkins Klein. What does someone in

research do for a venture capital company?"

"I evaluate prospective companies and determine if they'd be a wise investment for our funds. I work on the financial side and assess companies, checking their expenses and projecting their profitability."

"Wow. That's huge." Trying to charm her, I say softly, "You're obviously very important."

Holding up her finger and thumb to show about an inch, she says, "Maybe a little."

"Well, come closer and tell me all about it."

The waitress's timing is perfect, arriving with my bottle of scotch and six glasses. I offer Tanya one, then, trying not to be too obvious, say, "Tell me about what your company does."

She lights up. "We're the best venture capital company in The Valley. We invest in small and mid-sized companies." She continues talking for almost ten minutes straight, sharing with me the size of her team and their names and backgrounds. I nod in the appropriate places, and she breaks down her role in the company very specifically. While probably not inner circle, she most likely knows all about every deal.

Curious, I ask, "How do you decide who to invest in?"

"Our founders are super connected. We get better than a thousand requests a day."

"A day?" *Well, color me surprised.*

She nods. "It's crazy. Somehow Terry and Bob pick these winners. It's their money and they've been doing this for many years. They have the cars, houses all over the world and jets to prove they know what they're doing."

She mentions a few companies Perkins Klein is targeting. I

recognize some that we've discussed in our Sunday night meetings, but also a few I'm fairly certain are existing clients of SHN. I'm going to need to e-mail my dad and Mason when I get home and share what I learn.

She's really a nice girl. As I start to talk about leaving, I thank her for a nice evening. "You're a wonderful listener," she gushes.

"You're very kind."

"I hope whoever broke your heart realizes she's made a mistake before some other girl steals it out from under her."

Wow. I didn't realize I was so transparent. "You're incredibly astute, has anyone ever told you that?"

She smiles, gives me a hug and says, "Good night."

SARA

I'M WRAPPED UP IN THE COVERS, my insomnia at an all-time high, when I hear a ping from my cell phone in the other room. Glancing at the clock, I see it's after eleven. *Who is texting me this late?* I debate if I'm going to find out, but finally my curiosity wins.

Shuffling in my sweatpants, sweatshirt and big wool socks, I walk into my home office as it pings a second time. It's Trey: How are you? and then I miss you.

Truthfully, I miss him, too. The sex was amazing, and he's a great guy, but I have chaos at work and the mess with Catherine. I do feel a pang of guilt for ghosting him, but how could he ever love me if my own mother doesn't?

WHEN I GET HOME FROM WORK, Henry's sitting outside my apartment.

"Why are you here?" I ask.

"Because I need to see you."

Exasperated, I implore, "What can I do to help?"

He appears dejected and actually nervous. "I need time with Mason and Dillon."

With a big sigh, I push my key into the door lock. "You could've made those arrangements yourself. Why do you need me to set up a meeting?"

"Because I wanted to tell you first." I turn to stare at him and wait, until finally he tells me, "Jennifer has resigned."

"Your executive vice president?" I clarify, confused as to why it matters.

"Yes," he squeaks out.

"Why?"

Then it hits me why I need to know.

"She feels that she's ready for a new adventure."

"Is that all?" I push knowing there has to be more.

He stares at me, then quietly shares, "Well, we may have been involved."

"So that's the reason you wanted to tell me, because you were having another affair?" In that moment, I realize I don't care. I might have a few months ago, maybe even a few weeks ago, but we never had a real relationship, at least in my mind. I finally understand that now.

"No!" he exclaims. "You know I'm in love with you. It wasn't always working the late nights. It's you. It's always been you."

"Don't worry, Henry. I'm not going to rat you out with SHN. You're fine. Go home."

"I can stay if you'd like," he growls, winking.

"No, thanks. I'll reach out to Mason and Dillon and let them know about Jennifer."

He kisses me on the cheek and walks away—whistling, no less.

How could I ever have liked that asshole?

IT'S ANOTHER LATE NIGHT and I'm still in the office. Hearing a noise, I walk out just as Annabel stops by my office. We both jump at the sight of the other.

"Hey," I greet her, surprised she's still in the office.

"You're still here?" she asks, seeming equally surprised—and possibly a bit tipsy.

"I am. Why are you still here?"

"I was hoping to talk to Mason."

"Is everything okay?"

She shyly shares, "Yes, I like to end my day talking to him."

It suddenly dawns on me. "Sounds like someone has a crush."

She nods. "Maybe a small one. I met a girlfriend for drinks, and she encouraged me to come back and talk to him to see if we can go out. But despite my asking him out for drinks and making sure he knows I'm interested and single, he hasn't done anything about it."

"Annabel, you do realize that because he's your boss, he's probably doing his very best to keep it professional?" Her face falls, and I try to soften the blow. "But that doesn't mean he doesn't like you. It just means he can't do anything about it right now."

"Oh, I guess I never thought about it that way. He's cute, and I love the way he cares about each of the employees."

I smile at her. "I agree. He puts everyone ahead of himself."

"Well, it doesn't appear that he'll be back tonight, so I'm going to head home. Good night."

"Good night, Annabel. See you in the morning."

As I PREPARE to shut down for the night, an e-mail pops up from Catherine.

TO: Sara White
FROM: Catherine Ellington
SUBJECT: Meeting

Sara,

Please resist all contact moving forward. I'm happily married to your biological father, and together we have four children—not five. None of them know you exist, nor will they ever know. You were a mistake of a young couple. If you can't leave me alone, I'll be forced to contact my lawyer and get a restraining order. I owe you nothing. Leave my family and me alone.

Catherine

I'm stunned. I have four actual siblings, not half. Devastation doesn't even begin to describe how I'm feeling.

TREY

$\mathcal{M}$Y PHONE IS RINGING.

"What the hell?" I glance at the bedside clock: after 10:00 a.m. Caller ID shows it's my mom.

"Hi, Mom."

"I'm sorry I woke you, sweetheart. I waited until after ten to call."

"That's okay. I need to get up anyway. What's up?"

"Your dad and I were wondering if you were going to be at Sunday night dinner tonight."

"I don't know."

I hear her relay that to my dad, and the next thing I know he says to me over the phone, "Trey, you're an advisor and they need you, too. We need your input on a few things today. Do you think you can make it?"

"I guess I can try."

After climbing out of bed, I get on my touring bike, leave my condo in Pacific Heights and ride it the three miles over the Golden Gate Bridge and back again, then through Golden Gate Park. I'm going to be sore tomorrow, but at least it's a good sore.

I don't want to seem like I'm trying too hard when I dress for dinner, so I choose a nice pair of dark jeans, a gray sweater that rolls up at the bottom, a pair of Cole Haan black leather boots and a black leather biker jacket. I roll my pants up and tuck my sunglasses into my sweater below my chin. I think I look good.

Sara, you can eat your heart out!

I arrive at my parents' house the same time as Mason does. He's a good guy. As I've gotten to know him I've found that he's one of the smartest guys I've ever met. Really the team at SHN are all incredibly smart. If I were to leave Sandy Systems, I'd rally these guys hard to join them. They want to make money, but they invest with a love of technology and a lot of altruism.

"Hey, man," he says as he grasps my hand and pulls me in for a half hug. "So glad you could make it."

"Of course. I'm not sure I have much to contribute, but I'm happy to be here."

"No, we need your input. It's very helpful."

We walk in and I see her sitting with my sister and two of her best friends, and my heart skips a few beats. Sara looks radiant. Her hair has these amazing waves and curls I want to run my fingers through. Her jeans are tight and show off her curves, and her green sweater makes her eyes shine.

"Sara," I say as I nod at her. Addressing my sister as I've done since we were seven, I chide, "Hey, ugly."

The glare she shoots me would kill most men before she stands and hugs Mason. "Mason! So wonderful to see you," she gushes.

I lift my hands in mock surrender and walk to the bar cart. "Anyone need a drink? Mason? Greer? Sara?" I ask before muttering to myself, "I sure do."

During dinner, people share stories of crazy things that happened over the week, switching between stressed-out clients and personal interests. I'm sitting next to Sara once again, and she spends most of dinner talking to CeCe about Emerson and Dillon's wedding.

Turning to me during a lull in their conversation, Sara gives me a dazzling smile and asks, "How are things going with your acquisition in Seattle?"

"It's moving. The owner is very religious and has his concerns about how a large company is going to affect their culture."

Sara nods. "That makes sense. Do they pray at work?"

"Well, yes and no. We understand it to be voluntary, but those who join the company sign waivers because of group prayer."

"Wow. That'll be a huge change if they're purchased."

"It would be. But we also pride ourselves on trying to maintain our acquisitions culture."

"I'm curious, why do they want to sell? Money?"

"Their product can't sustain itself without being purchased by a larger entity."

"Then the prayer issue would exist for everyone."

"That's exactly what we're saying."

"What else is keeping you busy?" she asks.

"I got on my tour bike today and got over the Golden Gate. What about you?"

"My to-do list grows. I feel like every time I cross one thing off, I seem to add five more."

CeCe joins in with "I know what you mean."

Then the girls are back to their chat, and I turn to Dillon on the other side of me, talking about college basketball and the NFL draft.

As dinner winds down, my dad has everyone move to the study, and my mom and the housekeeper begin the process of cleaning up after dinner.

Greer starts us off. "I was alerted this afternoon by our PR firm that SillySally is being hit with a substantial sexual harassment suit. Apparently, Henry Sinclair and his EVP of Finance, Jennifer Wallace, had an ongoing affair for many years, and she alleges a few big bombs.

"How does this affect us?" Cameron asks.

Dillon grimaces. "We'll see a drop in their stock prices."

"Unfortunately it may be worse than that. Rumor has it that Jennifer may be naming SHN in the lawsuit," Greer says.

"Do you know why?" I ask.

Greer nods. "Apparently, she says we knew about the harassment and permitted it. I don't have to tell you what this kind of publicity does to companies in this climate."

The room erupts with everyone talking at once, and my dad lifts his hand to get everyone's attention. "One at a time, please." The room quiets, and he turns to Mason. "What do you know about this?"

"Jennifer was always professional and easy to work with. I only knew she quit when Henry told Sara," Mason replies.

Everyone turns and stares at her, and she says, "Henry, Jennifer, Dillon and I worked closely with the offering. He alerted me last week that she'd quit. I wondered if he was hiding something, but he didn't say anything else when I pressed."

We go back to all talking at once, comparing stories of our interactions with Jennifer. I see Sara's brow crease as she begins to put something together. Glancing around the room, she settles on me and I see tears well up in her eyes. In a shy voice, she tells us, "I think this may be the time to let you all know that I had an affair with Henry."

The room immediately quiets, and the surprise on everyone's face is noticeable. "Sara, can you elaborate?" Cameron asks softly.

Wringing her hands, she quietly shares, "Please let me start with the fact that we dated for nearly six months and I never knew Henry was married. I saw him most days, and we often spent the night together. He had a growing company that he'd founded, and he traveled a lot. Or so I thought. We don't go out of our way to share our personal lives, so when Cameron, in passing, mentioned Henry's wife, I was stunned. I asked Henry about it, and he immediately came clean. He kept telling me he loved me and he was leaving her, but she was newly pregnant."

"Sara, I understand you're embarrassed, but please tell us the G-rated version of how the affair started, where you may have had intercourse, and when you broke up," Emerson requests.

Sara looks like she's going to cry. "We'd been working long hours on the SillySally offering. Often with Jennifer, but it was always on the up and up. We were talking daily, and we started flirting. It was very innocent. He made me feel attractive, and I hadn't had that in a long time. I don't have a life outside of the office, and it was nice to have someone make me feel beautiful." Sara begins weeping, and my heart aches for her. Emerson rubs her back, and she's eventually able to continue. "Then in February, before the offering, he made a move. We had sex in his office the first time."

Dillon quietly says, "Sara, please don't cry."

"How did he make the move?" Emerson asks.

"As I said, we flirted. He'd tell me he liked something I was wearing, or stare a few minutes too long at my chest, but that happens in the workplace."

Mason snaps to attention. "It shouldn't."

Greer pats his hand. "You're 100 percent right, but it does happen."

Emerson turns to Sara, who's now quietly sobbing, and prods, "Then what happened?"

Cameron hands Sara a tissue, and she wipes her tears. "We were sitting in his office across from each other at his desk. He had a question about one of the spreadsheets, and I got up and was leaning over his desk. He cupped my breast, then leaned in and we began kissing. It was consensual, and I was a willing participant. I had no idea he was married. I had no idea about his relationship with Jennifer. I thought we were exclusive, and when I found out we weren't, I broke it off with him."

I'm angry listening to this. This asshole was married and thought he could make Sara feel like less of a woman. What really pisses me off is that he made her cry.

My dad asks, "Did he and Jennifer flirt or ever be inappropriate while you were together?"

Shaking her head, she cries, "No. Never."

Emerson quietly asks, "Where did your affair happen? Always in his office?"

"He has an apartment in Cow Hollow. We spent nights and weekends there, or in my apartment. I swear, I didn't know about Claudia."

"Did you know he was involved with Jennifer?" Mason questions.

Sara's head snaps up and she definitively exclaims, "No! Absolutely not."

Emerson holds Sara's hand as she says, "I don't see any risk for us."

"I think we need to distance ourselves from SillySally," Greer suggests. "We need to talk about how we didn't know it was going on. Dillon, what percentage of ownership do we have?"

"Thirty percent, which is worth at last count almost two hundred billion dollars," he responds.

"How much does Henry own?"

"He owns 31 percent."

"I'm assuming the other 39 percent is owned by various sources."

Dillon nods. "Roughly 20 percent is held by employees and the board, including Jennifer, and under 20 percent is traded."

"I reviewed their board, and between Charles and us, we probably have most of the board members' personal phone numbers," Greer tells the group.

"I think that's accurate," Mason agrees.

I nod. "Okay then, I suggest we go to the board, minus Henry, and see if we can garner the votes to have him step down."

I interject, "That's probably the best course of action. Mason or Dillon, if we can get the votes, you'll need to call Henry and let him know. But you can stress to him that he still owns his shares and voting rights on the board. So he isn't losing his company—yet—but he will if he doesn't play nice."

"Meanwhile, once you get it all wrapped up, I'll have a press release ready to go across the wires, telling people he's no longer CEO of SillySally," Greer adds. "It'll save the stock price if we can do it mostly tonight and then release the statement before the market opens tomorrow morning."

We all agree and work our way through the list of board members. Greer sits at her laptop, waiting for the thumbs-up to send her press release across the wires.

It takes less than an hour to track the board down and capture 51 percent of the stock share votes. Then Mason, Dillon, and Charles call Henry. The conversation doesn't go particularly well, but Henry seems to take it in stride.

We set a plan for the week to deal with this issue as well as our mole, and we'll follow up next week.

SARA

$\mathcal{J}$T'S GIRLS' NIGHT OUT, a nice dinner in Pacific Heights. Our Saturday nights out are becoming a regular routine, and I'm really enjoying having a group of friends. We get together as a group, but they've all reached out to me individually as well. For the first time in many years, I feel like I belong, and it really seems to lift my spirits and put a spring in my step.

Hadlee and I had a spa day at Burke Williams. We started our morning with facials, ordered in a wonderful lunch and then received ninety-minute massages. I've really never spoiled myself like this before, and it was glorious.

Greer and I went out into Napa. CeCe wants to play a bit of matchmaker with a vineyard owner, and together we checked him out. We didn't get to see him, but we did have a fantastic day and a fun dinner at Cindy's Backstreet Kitchen. It was wildly decadent and full of fun.

Emerson and I made a point of spending a day together doing some wedding planning. It was an exhausting day, though I can definitely see why people go Bridezilla. She wanted red roses in her bouquet, and they made her order two dozen different shades. In the end, most of them seemed alike, and she took me out for a nice dinner after the ordeal, where we gossiped about work and the boys.

CeCe and I spent a Saturday shopping, and I was able to introduce her to Jennifer at Nordstrom, who now has a big client. She put CeCe in an incredible Eileen Fisher for tonight. I love the light green top and matching silk jacket with black silk pants and beautiful Jimmy Choo sandals. She looks truly amazing.

We've all been trying to make a point of getting out and meeting men. CeCe had a date last night, mixing up our girls' night out, which is how it wound up being tonight instead. But she hasn't mentioned it yet, and I'm curious.

"How was your date with the real estate agent?"

With a heavy sigh, she says, "He knew who I was, and he went into full sales mode. He had actually set up showings at several high-end condos on the market." We all gasp in horror, and she continues, "At first I thought he took me to my Aunt Millie's condo as a way to get laid in a fancy house. He was super flirty, and then I realized he was trying to sell me a new place."

Greer jumps in. "Wait. I've been to your Aunt Millie's. She's selling?"

Chuckling, CeCe tells us, "Her condo on Embassy Row. She's keeping her Marin house and moving there."

"I'm interested in your Aunt Millie's place. Should I call your new boyfriend?" Greer ribs her.

We're laughing so hard that people are turning and staring at us.

"Really?" CeCe asks when she's able to catch a breath.

Greer nods enthusiastically. "Yes!"

CeCe picks up her phone and steps away, and we continue to pick our dates apart. When she returns, she declares, "Tea for all of us at my Aunt Millie's tomorrow at one. We can go to dinner with my parents afterward. Hadlee, that means you're stuck with us for a bit, but at least the view at dinner will be good." CeCe leans in conspiratorially and whispers, "Our good friend Hadlee here"—she does her best Vanna White impression—"has a crush on one of your partners."

Puzzled by this, mostly because I think of all the guys as brothers, I ask, "Which one?"

"Cameron!" Greer answers for her.

I reach across the table and grasp her hand, chuckling. "Honey, I'm so sorry. That boy is trouble with a capital T."

"I know! But I can't help but love those broad shoulders, blue eyes and that curly hair. And oh. My. *God,* those tattoo sleeves are to die for!"

"How can you tell he has curly hair? He's always wearing a stupid baseball cap," Greer grumbles.

I sit back in my chair and grin. "He cleans up well, I promise. You'll see at Emerson and Dillon's wedding."

When I return home, I'm too wired to sleep. I sink into my hot bath and smell the vanilla and rose perfume as it rises in the steam from the tub, smiling to myself. I have a good job, I have money in the bank, I own my condo and, most importantly, I have friends.

But then my mood quickly clouds, thinking about the mail I got from Catherine. I understand it must be difficult to know you have a child out in the world, but to know the child is biologically related to all of your other children and yet shun them is confusing at best. These aren't people who share half my DNA—these are my full-blooded brothers and sisters. I don't want to ruin her life, but I want to meet my father and my siblings.

After my bath, I pour myself a large glass of wine, and I cry. I cry for the loss of my mother, for the loss of my father, and more importantly for the loss of my siblings I've never met.

CeCe calls me first thing in the morning. "I'll be by to pick you up around noon. We'll get Emerson, Hadlee, and Greer and make it to my aunt's by one."

"Great. Can I bring anything?"

"No, I think we'll be okay."

"I'll be outside waiting for you at noon." I'm about to end the call, then quickly ask, "Oh, how formal will your aunt's be?"

"I'm wearing nice pants and a sweater. Greer will be in trendy jeans most likely."

"Thanks. I'm sure I have something I can make work. See you at noon."

I know just the thing.

At noon I step outside wearing black palazzo pants, a light pink sweater, a choker strand of pearls with matching earrings and a nice pair of Calvin Klein low kitten heels as CeCe comes barreling up in her dark blue Mercedes SUV. I have no idea how she's going to park this beast in The City. We pick up everyone and arrive at Aunt Millie's right on time.

The doorman directs CeCe to the visitor spot, and we pile out as he announces our arrival.

As we enter the penthouse apartment, I'm stunned by the floor-to-ceiling windows with a view from the Golden Gate

Bridge to Marin, and from the east windows, I can see the East Bay, Treasure Island and the Bay Bridge. Spectacular. Not many places in San Francisco offer a bridge-to-bridge view.

I'm surprised when Aunt Millie greets us. She doesn't seem too much older than us.

She spreads her arms open wide. "CeCe! Good to see you," she exclaims as she brings CeCe in for a warm embrace.

She walks up and gives each of us a hug. CeCe introduces us, and I learn Aunt Millie isn't actually a "real" aunt but was CeCe's mom's college roommate at Stanford.

"I hope you girls are hungry. I've had the terrace set up for tea. But first, let's take a tour." Locking arms with Greer, Millie says, "I understand you're considering a new place."

Greer smiles at her. "I remember coming here when we were young girls. I'd love it and would take good care of it."

She walks us through the four-thousand-square-foot apartment and points out a few things that will probably need some work, Greer not batting an eye at all the work the already seven-figure condo will cost.

Greer and Millie leave us to work out a deal, and we start our tea. It's the perfect girls' afternoon.

Three and a half hours later, full of cucumber sandwiches, fresh scones and jam made from the strawberries from Millie's garden, we pile into CeCe's car and head south to Hillsboro.

I'm consistently amazed at the Arnaults' estate, the Spanish-style home and the grounds surrounding it so welcoming. I've begun to think of it as a second home.

The dogs greet us as usual, and CeCe's mom meets us. Turning to Greer, she asks, "Well?"

A big smile crosses her face. "I'll take ownership in about two weeks, and then I'll move in after I complete some renovations. I can't wait!"

"Oh, Greer! I'm excited for you. I love that place, and Millie is happy to have the condo go to someone who will love it as much as she did."

Trey looks so hot in his Levi's, a pair of old-school black Vans sneakers, my favorite Star Wars T-shirt and a leather biker jacket. I miss him. I can smell the sandalwood and leather scent, and it makes my heart race. I haven't responded to any of his e-mails or voice mails since we returned from Stinson, but I'm so busy, and honestly, I wish I could get over my mother's rejection. How can I explain that to him? My mother had five children with the same man, and I'm the only one she doesn't have anything to do with. It's inevitable that he'll reject me, just like she did. Plus, what about the mess with Henry? Why get my heart more broken than it already is?

As I ponder this, Trey walks up to me, running a hand through his hair. "Do you have a minute?"

I know I should be an adult and have the conversation, but I'm not sure I can explain to him why I've essentially ignored him. Eventually I nod, and he leads me to the backyard.

"How've you been?" I ask.

"Okay, I guess, and you?" Before I can answer, he says, "I thought we had an amazing weekend up in Stinson. What happened?"

"We did. But Trey, you need to understand, my life is SHN. I've worked hard to be an important part of my company."

"Sara, I'm not asking you to walk away from SHN. But you also can't spend every minute there. Why can't you make room for me? I feel as if you're my greatest loss. Not talking to you every day leaves a gaping hole in my life. You're gone, but yet you're still here. It may have only been a weekend to you, but the loss impacts every part of my being. Not only can I not think straight, but I find myself running on automatic pilot. I miss you. I know my life isn't easy, but please, can't we try?"

Oh God. Why do I screw everything up?

I don't know how to explain what a clusterfuck my life is. How do I explain that there aren't enough hours in the day for me to work, even if I worked twenty hours a day, seven days a week? How do I explain I've learned I have four full siblings I will never get the chance to meet? How do I explain that I miss him, too? How do I explain that I'm a mess?

All I can muster is to say, "I can't right now. I'm sorry." Then I turn and essentially run away, saying my goodbyes to the group and calling a Lyft to drive me back home without staying for dinner or the meeting, tears running down my face like waterfalls.

I'm such a fucking mess.

TREY

ANDY SYSTEMS has been in negotiations to buy Cedar Pine Cypress Technologies based in Seattle. The head of our mergers and acquisitions group, Mickey Johns, is joining me on this trip. Actually, this is his trip and I'm joining him. I'm just the figurehead.

Our flight to Seattle is relatively low-key, and we fly in adjoining seats in first-class. The flight attendant is very attentive and basically ignoring everyone else in the cabin once she recognizes me. "Would you like a drink, Mr. Arnault?"

"Yes, a Woodford neat, please."

When she brings my glass of bourbon, she hands me a napkin with her phone number on it, then places another napkin under my glass and winks at me.

She's cute enough in a plastic sort of way, but I need to keep my head in the game. We should run through our proposal one more time, but I'm not truly interested. My mind keeps drifting to Sara from last night.

Mickey leans over and asks in a low voice, "Is it always that easy for you?"

I'm not sure what he's talking about. "What?"

"Hot girls giving you phone numbers?"

Confused by his question, I finally realize what he means. "Oh, that. I don't know. Do you want her number?"

He holds his hands up as if he's surrendering. "No, I was curious."

Leaning back in my seat, I put my noise-canceling headphones on and listen to nothing. The quiet helps me think.

Last night at my parents' was hard. Watching Sara and pretending we haven't shared intimate moments was extremely difficult. So many things about her have left me intrigued, and I've only scratched the surface. I've been with lots of girls, but not one of them made me feel the way Sara does. But I can't be a passenger in this train wreck of a relationship. It's time for me to take control and make Sara understand what I already know—we belong together.

I didn't mean to make her leave before dinner last night. I just wish I knew why she's snubbed me. I know work for her is busy, but I also know she's making time to hang out with my sister and the girls.

I lean back in my seat and imagine the pretty blonde hovering over my thighs, her eyes locked on mine as she licks her lips.

I need to stop this feeling and move on.

I may not be able to make Sara understand yet, but I'll work on a plan and keep myself distracted while I throw myself into my work.

SARA

MERSON DUCKS HER HEAD INTO MY OFFICE. "Hey. Interested in going out with the partners for drinks after work? Maybe try to leave about seven thirty?"

Looking up, I say, "Sounds great. I could use an excuse to get out of here before eleven."

"Cameron's figuring out where we're going. Let's meet by the elevators."

I bury my head into wrapping up a few items so at least I feel like I'm able to get something accomplished before I spend time with the group.

Cameron pokes his head in my office. "We're going to Trick Dog tonight. Are you familiar with them?"

"No."

"They have ingenious cocktails that are named after various random cool things, and the food is incredible. It's on Potrero Hill, and we'll all Lyft over. I know the owner, and she'll save us a spot in the loft. See you at the elevators in fifteen. Don't be late, I want Mason buying tonight."

I really love my coworkers.

I shut down my computer and, for once, decide that I'm not going to take it home and leave it on my desk.

When I arrive at the elevator, everyone's here except Mason.

"Mason buys the first round," Cameron announces, then yells at the top of his lungs, "Mason! Get your ass out here."

"I'm here. Am I last?"

"The first round is on you," I tell him.

The five of us pile into a Nissan Armada, Emerson and I taking the back. As she climbs over Dillon to get to the back seat, he smacks her on the butt.

"Hey!" she yells at him, laughing.

"I couldn't resist," he smugly says.

We make small talk during the three-minute drive, helping one another out when we arrive. Walking into the bar, Emerson and I spy our reserved table.

I push my way through the crowd to the bar as Cameron catches the eye of the bartender, who knows him by name. He tells her, "We need a Jurassic Fog, a Seasick Hedgehog, a Hick Dialogue, a Frantic Frog and a Picnic Snog." She nods and begins mixing the concoctions as Cameron continues, "My buddy Mason will be buying."

Smiling at Mason, she asks, "Any food with that?" as she points to a menu.

"Yes. Pick five things you recommend that can easily be shared."

"What if you don't like what I pick?" She bats her lashes at Mason.

He smiles. "Oh I'm sure that would never happen." Then he hands her his Black Amex.

"I'll bring your food and drinks over shortly."

He thumbs over his shoulder to our table. "We're over there."

"Gotcha."

As we walk back to the group, I tell him, "Mason! I had no idea you were such a flirt."

"I wasn't flirting."

"Then what do you call it?"

"Being nice and friendly."

"Let's ask the team." I walk up to the group and share the exchange.

"Dude! She's totally hot. You were totally flirting, and she was flirting back. Ask her out," Dillon says.

He blushes. "You guys are putting too much pressure on me."

The bartender arrives with our cocktails. As she places the drinks in the center of the table, it's obvious she's overheard our conversation. Putting her hand on Mason's shoulder she says, "Don't worry. My husband doesn't typically like me dating other men."

Mason turns to her as we all laugh. "My loss."

From there, the conversation goes downhill. We become rowdy and border on obnoxious, but we have a great time together.

My mind regularly drifts to the e-mail from Catherine. I don't know what to say or do. She's already caused so many sleepless nights. I can't let her reject me again.

I need to spend some time on a therapist's couch and work through this.

I've ruined the best relationship I might ever have because of her.

TREY

J TEXT SARA: What's up? A group of us are getting together tonight. Come out.

She doesn't respond.

I don't want to go completely stalker, so I only reach out to her once a week, and I look forward to sitting next to her on Sunday nights at my parents'. It isn't much, but it's something.

I can't stay home another Friday night, so when my buddies invited me out, I agreed to go as long as we didn't go clubbing—I'm getting too old for that.

We've landed at Foreign Cinema tonight. Half the place is a high-end restaurant, the other a bar. It's an old warehouse with beautifully hung violet and cream drapes, which soften the industrial look.

Through the bar and restaurant, a fifty-foot large screen shows an old black-and-white movie, though I don't recognize the actors or the movie. The noise of the crowd drowns out the audio, and the lines at the bar are at least four people deep. The cute girls and gay men attract the attention of the bartenders and get served the fastest.

It's a fun place to see and be seen.

I spot her across the room. She's watching me carefully. Each time I smile, she glances away. I'm not good at flirting these days, what with my heart still attached to Sara, but I can try, at least.

Finally, I watch her float across the room. She's petite, dark-haired—darker than mine—with large brown eyes, and her olive skin glistens almost as if she's wearing glitter.

"Hi. My name's Jill."

"Nice to meet you, Jill. My name's Charlie."

She smiles at me. "Are you sure you don't want me to call you Trey?"

I smile at her, busted. No surprise. "It's Charles Michael Arnault the third, thus the nickname Trey."

She strokes my arm. "I'm fine calling you Charlie. Whatever floats your boat."

"Either works. Tell me, what brings you to San Francisco?"

"I was born here, and I still live here."

"Really? Where did you go to school?"

"Convent of the Sacred Heart School," she tells me proudly.

"Impressive. And what keeps you busy?"

"I'm an interior designer."

Trying to remain interested, I say, "Very creative."

"Everyone knows you run your family business. What do you enjoy doing in your free time?"

"Well, I ride a touring bike to work out. I have a Trek. Do you know touring bikes?" I ask.

"I do. I ride an AWOL. My goal is to do a three-month ride through Vietnam." She plays with her hair and licks her lips suggestively as she stares at me.

"Wow. I don't think I could do that."

"You own the company. You can do whatever you want," she says matter-of-factly.

"Well, that's not exactly true. I report to the board and the shareholders, but I think I'd be too saddlesore to last much more than a few days."

She giggles. "It does take some work."

Our conversation is going great. She's a perfect diversion to my heartbreak, but I need to slip in that I'm seeing someone, so she doesn't get the wrong idea. Stretching the truth, I say, "My girlfriend and I like walking on the beach and traveling. If you could do anything, what would it be?"

She walks her fingers up my arm and kisses me softly on the lips. "I'd like to know what it's like to grow your baby in my stomach."

I must be hearing things. "What did you say?"

"I'm fertile today, and I want to get pregnant with your child."

I jump out of my seat. "I don't think so."

She reaches for my belt buckle. "Oh come on. I think we both know you don't have a girlfriend, and I don't need any support. I think we'd make beautiful babies."

"Definitely not. I'm seeing someone." I start to leave but she grabs my arm.

"You asshole!" she screams. "I've been tracking you for months. I've waited patiently. I had to get rid of that blonde bimbo by selling that picture of you. I saved you! You owe me!"

"Look, I'm not sure why you think I'm your guy, but I have no desire to be your baby daddy."

I keep waiting for her to tell me she's kidding, but instead she's screaming, "I have more pictures and video. You will either do this or I'll release them all!"

I turn and walk out. This doesn't happen in real life. I'm living in a fucking soap opera. Perfect.

I summon a Lyft and head to my folks'. If Jill's been stalking me, she's probably figured out where I live. She's completely psycho. How do I find these girls?

Wait. Apparently they find me.

I give up. I'm committing to no one and being single for the rest of my life.

From the back seat of the car, I call my sister. "Hey, do I have a winner story for you today."

I give her the blow-by-blow with Jill. When I'm done, CeCe is silent a moment, then asks, "Are you making this up?"

"No, I swear!"

"Points for her honesty, I suppose."

"I'm going to Mom and Dad's for the weekend, and I'm giving up on all women. Stick a fork in me. I'm done."

THIRTY

SARA

MERSON AND I walk to Starbucks for a break and some caffeine.

"When do you meet with the attorneys for the depositions?" she asks.

"Tomorrow afternoon. The more this story unfolds, the uglier it becomes. I don't know how I was so blind. I mean, he was having affairs with six of us, plus his wife. How the hell did his dick not fall off?"

"No kidding. Don't you think he must've been faking it with some of the girls?"

"I have no idea. But I think to this point, the attorneys don't find any fault with SHN, so I believe we're going to be dropped from the case."

"Well, that's good news. Is he reaching out to you at all?"

"The lawyers pulled my text records, which showed my lack of response when he reached out to me after we broke up, so that's helped to vindicate me. Plus, when we first broke up, he texted me for a booty call and I told him off. His response was that I was the only one he was intimate with."

"Thank goodness for that." We sit down at a table with our drinks. "I can't believe the publicity this is garnering for him, and thankfully right now they aren't keying in on us."

"Exactly. I'm staying away from my foster parents, and you girls have been great to organize things so we don't attract any unwanted attention. What a fucking mess. I'm embarrassed by this, and forget going on a date!"

"You have too much to offer to be single. It'll happen."

I take a deep pull on my latte and fight back the tears. Changing the subject, I reveal, "I know we have a few deals going with Charles's friends, and I don't know who they are and I'm happily out of the loop, but something weird happened on Saturday, and I don't know if I'm crazy or not." Emerson gazes at me expectantly, urging me to continue with her eyes. "Friday night, when we all went to Trick Dog, I specifically recall closing my computer down. Usually I'd take my laptop home with me, but I didn't want to take it to the bar, and I knew I'd be in the next morning before seven. When I came in, my computer was on. It had run an update, but I didn't think it could do that if it was turned off. Plus, the screen saver hadn't kicked in. There wasn't anyone in the office, but it's been freaking me out a bit. Am I crazy?"

"Have you told Cameron?"

"He wasn't there last night, so I left him a message. I don't want to panic anyone, so I wasn't specific."

"Do you mind if I text him and have him come over here?"

"Sure. I mean, all I really can confirm is that my computer was left in my locked office overnight. I turned it off before I left and when I arrived, it was on."

We hear a ping from Emerson's phone. "He's grabbing Mason and Dillon, too."

"We could've just gone back to the office."

How is it that I've fucked up again? I don't know how I'm ever going to recover from this. I wrote the exit clause in our contracts. My affair with Henry is a terminable offense, and now if I'm the source of the leak, that would do it again.

Why is it that every part of my life is a mess?

We watch the guys cross the street and approach us. Mason gets in line and orders drinks for the guys, while Cameron sets a device on the table and encourages all of us to put our phones next to it. I'm puzzled, but he explains, "This is a cell phone jammer. I got it from Jim. He wants us to turn the Bluetooth off from our phones and"—he turns to me—"we need to run a complete diagnostic on your laptop."

I stare at him. "Cameron, I could be overreacting."

"Tell me what happened," he insists.

Mason arrives and hands out the drinks as I walk them all through what I already shared with Emerson.

Cameron shakes his head. "If you turned your computer off, it shouldn't have turned back on. And even if you had inadvertently not turned it off, all of our computers should go to a screen saver after five minutes of inactivity and power down after four hours of inactivity."

"What do we do?" Mason asks.

"I have a secure phone. I'll step out and give Jim a quick call."

Cameron steps outside and Dillon turns to me. "Do you leave your computer at the office often?"

"No. Hardly ever. I think this is only the second time."

"Sara, don't worry about this," Mason assures me. "This may provide us with a clue on who's involved."

I nod and dab at the tears pooling in the corners of my eyes. Slightly above a whisper, I ask, "I'm the focus of a lawsuit with a man I had an affair with, and now I may be the leak in our office." My hand falls to my mouth and I begin to cry.

"Sara, Jim checked all of us out when he took over. We know you would never be the intentional leak. If they've taken your computer, we have a path to follow. We've been at a standstill for a while, and now we may know what to do for next steps."

Cameron returns and tells all of us, "Jim and members of his team are going to be at the office about five tonight. They're going to replace Sara's computer so she isn't without one, then run diagnostics on everyone's computer." Combing his hands through his hair, he adds, "We may all need to lose our cell phones for a day or so."

"What do I do about Tina?" Emerson says in a panic.

"Well, Jim thinks they may be using our cell phone microphones to spy on us. So moving forward, we need to use a jammer and not bring our cell phones into meetings. Particularly those at Charles's house.

"I hate this," I cry. "I've made such a mess of all of this."

Mason pats my arm. "Don't waste too much time stressing out over this. We've got it under control."

SARA

"YOU MUST BE MAKING THIS UP," Greer says.

I lazily stir my vodka tonic. "I wish I were."

"He was sleeping with *how many* women?" CeCe scoffs. "What is it with men in this city? I bet there are men who are celebrating that he was sleeping with seven women—his wife plus six others."

Hadlee and Greer nod in agreement.

CeCe continues, "We can't become man-haters, but some of them sure make it really hard."

Hadlee laughs. "Maybe you should lower your standards."

"Emerson and I set the same standards, and she found Dillon. I'm sticking to my guns."

I'm confused, so I lean over and say, "Spill it. What are your standards?"

"Oh, that's easy. They must have car insurance and can't live at home."

"I agree that they can't live at home. No mommy issues. Car insurance can be difficult here in The City."

"Nope. Not an excuse. I don't want to be tied to The City. I don't want to be anyone's chauffeur."

"Okay, car insurance is an absolute must." I turn to Hadlee. "How was your date with the program manager?"

She chuckles. "It wasn't as dramatic as yours. Derek was a nice guy. He recently got out of a five-year relationship with another man."

CeCe says, "Why are you dating gay men? In my experience, we don't have the equipment they're looking for."

"I know. I didn't know the relationship was with another man. His parents want grandchildren."

Greer laughs. "Has he ever heard of surrogates?

"I get the impression that they don't know he's gay. He told me they're conservative Christians."

I take Hadlee's hand. "Promise me you aren't thinking of getting involved with him. It seems like you'd be walking into a loveless relationship."

"Sara, don't let Henry's mess keep you away from finding a good guy."

"Oh, don't you worry. It isn't Henry. I have other issues."

"Is it your childhood? You've mentioned foster parents in the past. What about your biological parents?" CeCe asks.

I have the inner debate about sharing my story with my friends, then decide they aren't really my friends if I can't be honest and vulnerable with them. So, I delve into the story of my mom being married to my biological father and that I have four full brothers and sisters living up in Seattle.

Hadlee comes over to me and gives me a big, warm embrace. "Fuck her!"

CeCe joins her. "What a bitch. Remember, they're the ones who are missing out, not you."

"I know." I lift my glass. "To my best friends in the whole world."

When I get home, a little buzzed from the liquor, I decide it's time to finally e-mail Catherine.

Dear Catherine,

I know you don't wish to hear from me; however, since you dropped the bomb that you're married to my biological father and I have four full siblings, you can't imagine my disappointment. I've reached out to you to find out about you and understand why you left me with Father Tom. I'm sorry it's inconvenient that you lied to your family and left me to be raised by the State of California. I know you want to have nothing to do with me, so you get your wish.

Goodbye, Catherine. I won't reach out to you again.

Sara

Before I have any second thoughts or sober up, I send the e-mail. Then I crawl into bed with my clothes on and sob uncontrollably. I cry until the tears no longer fall.

When I wake up the next morning, I'm dehydrated, and I'm tired from the restless sleep.

But the sun is shining. Life will get better. I may not be able to bond with those who are genetically linked with me, but I do have wonderful foster parents.

I decide to call them, needing to hear their voices. "Carol, it's me. Any chance you and Jim are free for lunch today? My treat?"

"Of course. We've missed you, and you work so hard. We can't wait to see you. How about noon?"

"I'll pick you up. I know Jim loves Hamburger Haven, so maybe I should pick you up about eleven and we'll beat the crowds."

"We'll be ready."

"Carol, I love you. Thank you."

"Is everything all right, Sara?"

"Yes. I'll tell you what's going on when I see you."

"See you shortly."

I take a shower and dress casually in jeans, sneakers and a gray sloppy-necked sweater. My doorbell rings as I'm finishing up, and I have no idea who it could be.

I open the door to a delivery man with two dozen yellow roses overflowing in a beautiful clear glass vase. I'm shocked that anyone would send such a large gesture that I forget there must be a card until I see it sticking out from between two flowers: 'Stay strong. You're an important member of our pack. We love you. Greer, Emerson, Hadlee, and CeCe.'

I'm humbled, honored and grateful. I quickly snap a pic of the flowers and send a group message to the girls: You're all the very best. You've made my day. Thank you for making me part of your pack.

Each of them sends additional words of encouragement and lots of hugs and kisses.

I pick Jim and Carol up, and we make it before the lunch rush. I hear all about a river cruise they're hoping to take next spring in Eastern Europe. I offer to pay for the trip, but by their reactions, you would've thought I'd peed on their cornflakes.

Our lunch arrives, and as they eat, I share with them about locating Catherine and what I've learned.

"I'm angry. Not because she rejected me again, but because she wouldn't sign her parental rights away. We could've been a real family, and she stole that from us, too."

Jim reaches across the table and rubs my arm. "Sweetheart, we are a family. You're our daughter, and we don't need a piece of paper to define that. You know that."

I start crying. "I've never told you how much I appreciated everything you did for me, and it means so much to me."

Carol gets up and sits next to me, putting her arm around me and holding me tight. "We've known, and you make us proud."

"It's Catherine's loss," Jim adds. "Not yours. Imagine what this secret must do to her."

Through my tears, I tell them, "I love you both so much."

TREY

I CAN ONLY SLEEP WHEN EXHAUSTED. My thoughts drag by in slow motion as I slink to a quiet spot and curl up next to the fire. I think only of Sara and what seems like will never be.

Sitting with a tumbler of amber liquid, I watch the fireplace, the gas flames curling and swaying, flicking this way and that. It's nice to feel the warmth on the outside. My drink, burning as I swallow, warms me on the inside.

I miss her.

It's all my fault, and my head swims with regret. My blood feels like molasses as my heart struggles to keep a steady beat, my melancholy mood permeating every corner of my life.

I don't hear my mom enter the room. She sits on the adjacent overstuffed leather chair and reaches for me. "Sweetheart, is everything okay?"

With a deep sigh, I murmur, "Hi, Mom. It isn't right now, but it will be eventually."

"Do you want to talk about it?"

"I don't know."

"Well, I'm probably not able to fix it, but I can certainly listen."

"When you met Dad, you said you knew all about him. What made you stick around? Why didn't you walk away and find some regular guy?"

With a deep breath and a hint of concern in her voice, she says, "Well first, we met in prehistoric days." Ruffling my hair, she continues. "We didn't have crazy people stalking us for photos. Your dad grew up in the press, but it was always positioned press, so the world saw what the family and a public relations firm wanted them to see. But still, people thought they knew him, thought he was their friend. The worst it ever got was when his grandfather's company sold and it caused the stock prices to drop. Someone accosted him while we were at a diner for dinner. It was scary, but your dad handled this irate man so well that he left our dinner table happy and still thought your dad was his friend. I knew right then that I was in love with him."

"I've heard this story. I'm tired of people who like me because they think they know me or that I can do something for them. I'm sad that the woman I love wants nothing to do with my life."

"People will come and go from our lives. Try not to discount every new person you meet as someone who wants something from you."

"I need to be better with that. This girl seemed to like me for me. Then this picture hit the tabloids, and she seemed to be okay with it, but shortly after, she disappeared."

"Honey, there's always the possibility that her disappearance stems from something totally unrelated to you."

"I've seen her since and she ignores me."

"Well, maybe the next time you see her, you can talk to her about it?"

"I've already tried."

"The son I raised would keep trying until she bent to his will. Where did he go?"

The dogs jump up and run to the front hall, barking and creating a ruckus. CeCe's arrived. I know who it is without her even saying a word.

"Dork?" she yells. "Where have you been? Why are you hiding here at Mom and Dad's?"

"I'm not hiding," I say indignantly.

"Really? You aren't even responding to my texts. Your buddy Tim tracked me down to make sure you were okay."

"He wants the gossip on crazy Jill. And there's nothing to share."

In a soft and caring tone, she asks, "Tell me about this girl who seems to have broken your heart."

"Nothing to tell. We had a few dates and had a great time. She was photographed—by crazy Jill, no less—and then she just disappeared on me."

"You told me you went out with her after the TMZ photo. Are you sure that's why she's MIA?"

I sigh. "I don't know."

Mom stands. "I'm going to bed. See you both in the morning?"

CeCe gives her a big hug. "We'll be here. Good night, Mom."

I lift my glass and say, "Good night."

CeCe pulls a chair up next to me. "What are we going to do about this woman?"

"I've been sitting here working on a plan."

"Good. Can I do anything to help?"

"No, I think this is something I need to do on my own."

"Dillon, Emerson, Mason and I were going to play a round of golf at Palo Alto Country Club tomorrow morning. Do you want to play for me, and I can join you in the clubhouse for drinks after? I'm not in the mood to get up that early, and my game sucks right now."

I peek at her. The idea of hanging out with Dillon and Mason is appealing. Getting clobbered playing golf, less so, but Emerson never rubs it in. "Sure, I'll go. When is the tee time?"

She leans in and kisses my head. "7:10 a.m."

"Thanks for giving me a good distraction."

PLAYING GOLF was what I needed. Emerson kicked our butts—as expected—and Mason, Dillon and I had fun. We meet in the bar afterward, where CeCe and a friend of hers I've never met join us.

CeCe walks her over. "Emily, this is my brother Trey. Trey, this is Emily. She works with me and oversees the marketing on the Street line."

Emily is pretty, tall and very lithe. Her hair is a trendy gray with a wide violet streak. Dressed casually in tight jeans and a violet sweater that matches her hair, she's wearing a lot of makeup, but then she does work for a cosmetics company.

She extends her hand wrist first. I'm not sure if she's expecting me to kiss or shake her hand. I grasp her fingers from underneath and it feels wrong. "Nice to meet you."

She smiles like a cat with a canary in her mouth and breathlessly says, "Nice to meet you, too."

Nope. She's not the girl for me. I'm swearing off girls who only want sex from me.

The guys and I enjoy a local beer while the girls chat. Emily doesn't participate, just plays with her phone.

As the party breaks up, CeCe mouths to me, "I'm sorry."

I smile at her and mouth back, "I love you." To most people, it may seem like my sister and I don't get along, but in reality, she's my best friend, my rock, and she means everything to me.

I turn to everyone and say, "I'll see you all at my folks' to-morrow afternoon. Emily, it was a pleasure meeting you."

She smiles and bats her lashes. "I hope to see you again."

I watch Dillon and Mason exchange looks, and then I wave goodbye.

c h a p t e r

THIRTY-THREE

SARA

J'M IN DEEP THOUGHT when Annabel calls through the intercom. "Sara, Cindy Chou is on the phone for you. Can you take it?"

"Of course. Did she say what she needs?"

"No, only that it was personal."

Personal? What could that mean? "Thank you, Annabel."

I pick up my line and say, "Hi, Cindy. How are you?"

"I'm great. I'm sure you're curious why I'm calling. I ran into a guy I went to college with at Stanford, and he's super cute and has a really great job. He told me he was hoping to meet someone, and I immediately thought of you."

"Really? Wow. Thanks. What can you tell me about him?"

"He's a doctor, tall with brown hair and brown eyes that are so yummy. He's funny and outgoing."

"Why is he single?"

"He's been building his practice and really doesn't meet women in his business that he can date."

"Okay, that makes sense."

"Can I give him your number?"

"I suppose so. But give him my cell phone number. It's 415-555-1212."

"His name is Kenny Johnson. Let me know how it goes. And I want to be invited to the wedding."

She hangs up and I cringe. Wedding? I don't think so, but it might be fun to go out on some simple dates and enjoy some time with someone who isn't in technology.

I go back to work, and less than thirty minutes later my cell phone rings. I don't know the number and I have a deadline, so I let it go to voice mail. After I get my contract out, I listen to the message and am surprised it's Kenny. Cindy must've really sold me to him. He sounds anxious. I'm not sure if that's good or bad.

I call him back, and he answers on the first ring. "Hi, Sara."

"Oh hi. I was returning your call."

"Cindy told me a lot about you, and I thought we might get together. Would you like to meet for dinner?"

I guess I need to like a guy who jumps right to the point. "I suppose we could. I live in San Francisco. Where do you live?"

"I'm down in Monterey. There's a cute place down here by my house that serves the best calamari."

"Well, that's a little far. How about we consider something in the middle? Maybe San Jose?"

He agrees, and next Saturday night we schedule a place to meet in San Jose.

SATURDAY, I leave with enough time to meet him, though the weekend traffic is really tough and it takes me almost two hours to get to San Jose. When I arrive, he's already there in a big Chevy F-150 that is built up on off-road wheels. We talk a few minutes, and he tells me to follow him to where he wants to go to dinner.

I follow him in my car down the highway toward Monterey, and as each mile passes, I realize he's leading me into Monterey. I left his cell phone number at home and I can't seem to find it in my call history while driving. I should turn around, but every mile we pass, I tell myself, *Well, we've gone this far. It's too late to turn around now.*

I follow him to a house close to Carmel, south of Monterey. He grabs me by the hand once I open my door and leads me to the backyard. People are everywhere, and it seems there's a big barbeque going on.

An older couple comes forward, and the woman pulls him into a big hug. "Kenny! You made it."

He turns to the couple and says, "Mom, Dad, this is Sara. She's the woman I've been telling you about."

Instantly, he's introducing me to a line of people—his mother, father, three brothers, a few cousins and several aunts and uncles. I'm stunned. I'm not sure if these people understand this is our first date.

Joining his brother and cousins to wrestle in the backyard, the aunts and wives of the brothers and cousins join me to sell me on Kenny. I'm so overwhelmed that I'm speechless as I'm peppered with questions.

"How long have you and Kenny been dating?"

"Have you decided if you guys will live in Monterey or in San Francisco?

"Did he tell you about how he's an amazing chiropractor, and he's cornered the market at the demolition derby?"

"Has he asked you to join us in Lake Tahoe next week yet?"

I do the math in my head, and with traffic, it's most likely a three-and-a-half-hour drive back to my place, if the traffic is decent, and it's now after nine. I can't get Kenny's attention, so I make polite excuses and leave.

As I reach my car, Kenny comes running up. "You're leaving already?"

"I am."

He reaches out and pushes my hair out of my face. "Anything I can do to persuade you to stay?"

"You're sweet, but I don't think so. It was nice meeting you." I get in my car and use the GPS to find my way home.

It's after midnight when I pull into my driveway. I'm too tired to be disappointed.

CeCe calls late the next morning. "Well?"

"I met his entire family."

"Entire family? Like parents?"

"And three brothers, cousins, and their spouses. Plus aunts and uncles. It was a family barbeque that he tricked me into going south of Monterey!"

Laughing to the point of snorting, CeCe tells me "Time to go back to the drawing board."

"No. I'm taking a break. I'm done for a while."

"Please don't give up."

"I love you, CeCe, but maybe I'm still licking my wounds about my last love. Let's focus on your dating life."

"Honey, I've long been a lost cause. Care to join me for a ride to my parents' tomorrow?"

SARA

I'M SITTING ON THE FLOOR with one of the Arnaults' dogs in my lap and enjoying the heat of the fire. I stroke the dog's belly, and she's obviously content.

Charles and Jim, the private investigator, are talking about our mole. We're going after a few new companies, with the entire company working toward the same goal. We actually want to win these, and while we're hoping our mole has moved on, we're also prepared for it to go to our competitor.

"Where are you with your research?" Charles asks the group.

"We're about done. Our program manager is collecting it all," Cameron replies.

"We have keystroke monitors on his system," Jim says. "So if he sends it to anyone outside the company or downloads it to a cloud or thumb drive, we'll know."

"When are the presentations?" Charles asks.

"We go on Wednesday," Mason responds.

As the meeting breaks up, Trey holds my hand to help me stand, then asks in a low voice, "How are you?"

I take a deep breath. "I'm good. And you?"

"I miss you."

His revelation catches me off guard, but I can't think about him right now. This thing with work is crazy, and I can't allow him to get too close. If he were to reject me like my mother's done, I don't know if I'd ever recover.

Closing my eyes, I lean back and take in the subtle tones of his cologne, letting my mind slip into how pleasant it would be to spend time with him. All I can think to say is "It's nice to see you." I head toward CeCe's car.

He races after me. "Sara, please. Talk to me."

He pushes me against the car, his tongue tracing the seam of my lips, asking permission to deepen the kiss. I open my mouth. When his soft tongue meets mine, my belly dips. In a split second, the kiss becomes forceful and heated.

We hear CeCe yelling for me and I break away.

Trey growls in my ear, "This is not over."

WEDNESDAY'S PRESENTATION includes the program manager, Steve Bassel, plus Mason, Dillon and Connie from Cameron's team, who's an expert in the technology they're using.

We are watching the clock and beginning to get nervous. It was only supposed to be an hour and it's been almost two. Cameron, Emerson and I all pace. We're like expectant fathers waiting for the birth of our first child.

Annabel stops by my office. "Hey. You have a second?"

I glance up and I don't, but I invite her in to sit down anyway.

"You're here a lot of long hours. I was wondering if you've ever considered hiring help?" she asks.

"Well, of course I have, but we're a complicated business. If I were to add someone to my team, they would most likely be another attorney."

"I understand that, but I'd like to plant a bug in your ear. You share Carrie with Emerson, and both of you could use an admin specifically devoted to you. I know our business and I'm constantly helping Carrie so I was hoping that, if you and the other partners were going to open up a spot on your team, you would consider me."

I'm impressed by her determination and looking out for herself. "Annabel, I think that would be a great idea. I'll run it by the partners."

She stands up and smiles. "Thank you, Sara."

I go in search of the team and rejoin them for the wait. When Cameron's cell phone rings, we all pounce. "How did it go?" he asks, putting the call on speaker.

"It went well," Dillon says through the line. "We spent most of the conversation dissecting the money and ownership percentage. We didn't get any commitments, but we expect to by Friday."

"Mason, what do you think?" I ask.

"Well, they really drilled down on the numbers, and I spoke about some of the benefits we would bring to the table. Cameron, Connie was really good with the technology. She was able to speak very succinctly to their chief technology officer, and together they mapped some places where she could add value. I don't know, I think we may get this one."

"Well good," Cameron replies. "Get on back here and let's celebrate."

Like the remainder of the company, I'm anxious for the team to return to the office, but my to-do list is long, so I throw myself into my work while I wait. My e-mail pings and I quickly check it, hoping for good news. I open the first link and my face falls.

My phone rings. "We've hit the wires and not in a good way. Meet at Charles's at seven," Greer tells me.

This doesn't sound good. My stomach does a few somersaults.

Cameron walks into my office, looking as if he's going to cry. "I can drive if you'd like."

"Sounds good. Do you need a few drinks? We can take my car if you prefer."

"Let me check with Mason. He may join us, and then we'll go in his Range Rover."

"I'm fine either way. Leave in twenty?"

"Sounds good. I'll meet you at the elevator."

Before shutting down my computer, I check the PR alerts, and I cringe. "What the hell?" I page through probably five hundred links. These aren't *TMZ* but business publications—*The Wall Street Journal*, every major newspaper and business journals.

I open the *San Francisco Business Journal*. The article is a complete slam piece. They go after all of us, and our research. They have quotes from the evaluations of Baker Software's team and confidential financial projections. These are Dillon's proprietary plans for financial success, and this is a roadmap for the industry. This information is incredibly hurtful. It leaves us appearing as if we aren't interested in any of our investments' long-term success, only the quick profit.

I scroll through the mainstream publications and find the same information, but they go after Mason, Dillon and Cameron personally, giving it a real gossip flare. Some of what they're saying is outright lies.

Maybe driving is going to be a mistake. I think I need a good drink, too.

Mason insisted on driving, and Dillon and Cameron are with us. "This is a fucking nightmare," Cameron growls.

Dillon is on the phone with Emerson, who's stuck in traffic coming from the East Bay. "Don't do anything stupid. Take your time." He listens for a few moments, then says, "Oh yeah, we're pissed."

"Pissed isn't even half of it," Cameron chimes in loud enough for Emerson to hear.

Dillon turns away from him so he can continue his call. "Yes, I'll make sure we have something for you to eat. None of us has had anything either."

Picking up my phone, I call CeCe. "Hey, we have a company emergency, and Greer has called a meeting at your folks'. All the partners are working their way there now."

"I heard. Trey and I are on our way. We're at the South San Francisco exit on the 101."

"So are we. I'm with Dillon, Mason and Cameron. Emerson's working her way to the Bay Bridge now. Listen, we all ran out and haven't had dinner. We don't want to be difficult for your parents. Can you tell me who delivers to their neighborhood?"

"I've already ordered from a friend's restaurant. It's Indian and amazing."

I smile. "I think we can all make that work."

WE SPEND the evening regrouping. Greer brought our PR firm's account manager with her, and together they're sending out our response, setting up interviews on the morning shows in New

York and contacting news writing sources to have them write counter articles. They also write an e-mail to every employee and client about what's going on, which is also released to the media to show our perspective.

With that behind us, we talk to Jim, our PI. He's beside himself without an answer. We do know Steve didn't send or copy the research, but that's about all we have right now. He needs more time, and we hope by Sunday to have more answers. This kind of publicity will have a significant impact—and not in a good way.

It's almost three o'clock in the morning before we start to break up the meeting. Some of us will head home, but Mason, Cameron and Dillon are going with Greer to our PR firm's office, where they have a studio for all the morning show interviews.

Emerson is kind enough to give me a ride home.

It's going to be a long week.

THIRTY-FIVE

TREY

Tim Lucas: Dude! Where are you? We're getting together
   with Monkey Business at The Chapel tonight. My
   buddy from college works for the band and got us
   tickets and backstage passes. Are you coming?

I glance at the text message and debate. Getting backstage
tickets to one of the world's biggest bands and a small and intimate venue sounds appealing, but I'm not sure I want to go out.

Tim Lucas: Are you in or out? I need to give my buddy a
   number.
Me: Count me in.
Tim Lucas: Cool. We'll meet my buddy when they're warm-
   ing up and we can hang with the band. Be there at 7.
Me: Sounds good. See you tonight.

I take a Lyft over to The Chapel and arrive about ten minutes
early. I ask the ticket taker where I'm supposed to go, and she
directs me to the back door, where I see a bouncer the size of an

NFL offensive lineman. His arms are crossed in front of him, and he watches me carefully as I walk up.

I explain who I am, and he checks his clipboard. I'm on the list. Nice. He hands me a badge that has my name and says "All Access" then allows me to enter the chaos backstage.

I don't see any of my friends, so I hang back and watch as everyone sets up. I've never been backstage before, and it's pretty interesting to see all the activity.

After a while, I spot my friend talking to someone else, and I walk over to join the group.

Tim shakes my hand, then turns to the guy next to him. "Pete, this here is my buddy Trey."

I extend my hand. "Hey, Pete. Thanks for the passes. What a treat."

"No problem," he says. "Enjoy the show. If you don't mind, let the band do their pre-show routine, and after the show you can hang out. I heard Jimmy, the bassist, has whiskey his dad brews. It's good if you like whiskey."

"We do," Tim replies. "What are you up to during the show?"

"I'll do a few things. We're heading on the road and working on our sets, checking out sound and music flow. There's someone from my team at the label who'll be watching how the audience responds. These kinds of shows are for the fan clubs and all the background work. We'll run through some bigger pieces with lighting and choreography at a sound stage in the coming weeks."

"Who would've known so much goes into a show," I say, almost to myself.

"We've got to give the fans value for paying at least a hundred dollars a seat—and that's the cheapest Monkey Business ticket. They go up into the thousands, and that's before the brokers get involved." Pete turns to me. "You seem surprised."

"I am. I didn't think about the music business as anything more than fun. Naïve on my part, for sure."

Pete laughs. "Oh this is a business all right, and we're expected to be profitable. I'm the business manager for the label. They have a band manager, but he doesn't always travel with them, just takes a cut of what they earn. He's more interested in venue contracts and making sure the guys get along. I watch every penny and make sure the band is taken care of to the requirements of their contracts while also ensuring the label makes money. It's definitely a fun business, but it's also a real business."

I feel a tap on my shoulder. Knowing exactly who it is, I turn and hold out an arm. "Pete, I'd like you to meet my sister, CeCe." Glancing around, I see the group joining her and my stomach drops. "And her friends Greer, Hadlee and Sara."

Sara has the same look of dread that I feel. What a mistake it was to date someone in my social circle. Well, not so much a mistake, because I never would've known that I was capable of finding someone I could connect with and be attracted to. I now understand the phrase "Don't pee where you eat." I wish I knew how long it was going take for this ache to lessen.

Pete's eyes light up and a bright smile covers his face. "Nice to meet you, ladies."

"Nice to meet you, Pete," CeCe gushes, clearly smitten.

Pete walks through the same rules he gave us, and then we all stand to the side, catching up and watching the bevy of activity. I chat with Greer and Hadlee, and Tim talks to CeCe and Sara.

I can't believe she's here. I wasn't prepared for this. Despite Monkey Business being one of my favorite bands, I wouldn't have come had I known Sara was going to be here. She's dressed so sexily: tight jeans, a black sweater that hugs all the right places, black boots. Her blonde hair is piled high on her head with sexy tendrils falling delicately around her face. Her lips are a dark red, and I want to kiss that lipstick right off her lips.

I'm a mess.

As the band goes on, Tim walks around with a large bottle of whiskey and a stack of Solo cups, passing out drinks to everyone backstage.

I should've stopped at one. I was buzzed, but I continued to drink, and I don't remember much of the performance. I have a vague recollection of walking out of the venue and walking into a neighboring bar, but after that, it's a complete loss.

I wake to the sun streaming in my window, hitting me in the face. I'm not even sure if it's the next day or if it's been two weeks.

Rolling over to check the time, I see a large glass of water and a bottle of ibuprofen. Sitting up slowly, I think I need to throw up. I prop myself up with a few pillows and lean against my headboard.

Once my stomach settles a minute, I turn to swing my legs to the floor and attempt to sit up. *Please send the jackhammer away!* I finally adjust to the change in equilibrium and stand. I'm dizzy, and my mouth feels like a cat walked over it and shit inside. Ugh.

I find my pants on the floor in my bedroom and attempt to

put them on while standing, but moving my head makes it feel as if it's going to explode. I struggle to sit on the bed, but it's the only way for me to get my pants on without falling over.

Somewhat dressed, I hear a noise from the living room, so I stand and walk slowly to follow it, finding my sister.

"Hey," I mutter.

"Hey, yourself. How are you feeling?"

"Like I was hit by a bus."

"I bet. When you're ready, we need to talk about last night."

"What happened?"

"We've got a problem."

"Do *I* have a problem or do *you and I* have a problem?"

She picks up her iPad. "Here, let me show you."

I cringe. *YouTube? I'm in trouble.* The first of two videos titled "Trey Arnault's Sexcapades" begins to play. It's extremely explicit.

As I watch the video, I notice there's no camera movement, meaning it was stationary. There's also some infrared camera work, so there's a weird green glow to the couple on the screen. It takes a few seconds for me to remember that it's the one-night stand from a few years ago. In the first video, you can see me go down on her and her porn star orgasm, and then she goes down on me with some weird grunts and groans. I know I don't make those sounds. I'm sure of it. There's more weird grunting and groaning during the sex act, and he calls her Elly. Her name was not Elly, it was... Michelle.

The second video is a repeat of the first.

I run my hands through my hair. *Fuck!*

Unfortunately, CeCe shows me they're all highlighted by

TMZ. They've clearly been voiced over, because I know I don't say the things that are being said in the videos. They're graphic and ugly.

My emotions overwhelm me: disappointment, sadness, regret, anguish and grief. Crazy Jill told me if I didn't impregnate her, she was going to release a bunch of pictures and videos. I know it was her, and she's going to pay for this. I have a lot of very expensive lawyers, and I wasn't the only one to hear her threats. But the immediate will have a ripple effect well beyond a *YouTube* video.

Turning to CeCe, my eyes wide, I ask, "Has Dad seen this?"

She glances at me with sadness, and before she tells me, I know. "Unfortunately, so has the rest of the board."

"Un-fucking-believable!" I take a deep breath and drag my hands down my face. "You know it was that bitch Jill."

"I think so, too. That isn't even your voice. I've explained it to Dad, but he and the board are still upset."

"I'll call him in a bit. I need the Advil to kick in, and then I need a solution. Fuck! Just when it seems like I might've been able to swing Sara back into my corner, too."

A FEW HOURS LATER, I've figured out what I'm going to do. I've called my lawyer and explained what happened and share everything I wrote down from my night with Jill. We put his firm's investigator on to find her. I then sit down and call my dad. My mom answers first, telling me she loves me but is disappointed in my behavior. She asks me to come home, and I explain I'll try in a few days.

My dad gets on the phone, and I've rarely heard him so angry. "Dammit, Trey! We raised you better than this. What made you think you could record these kinds of videos and not think they would eventually be broadcast? This is completely unacceptable for the CEO of our company."

"Dad, first, I did not record these videos. These were recorded by the girl—"

"Why would any girl risk her reputation by releasing a video?"

"For the notoriety, obviously," my mom interjects. At least someone's on my side in this fiasco.

"Please, Mom, Dad, let me finish. These are years old, I promise. Second, that's not my voice in those videos. A woman approached me a few weeks ago in a bar. We hit it off, and I thought we had a lot in common. Then she flips a switch and is talking about her being fertile and me making a baby with her that night. She said she had video and was going to share it. Dad, I've already contacted my attorney, and we're working with an investigator."

"Jesus! She came right out and said she was fertile and wanted to make a baby with you?" my dad asks, surprise evident in his tone.

"It was worse than that. She admitted to following me for weeks and for selling the last photo to *TMZ*. I figured because we hadn't heard from her since that day that she was all talk."

"Your mother wants to know if you used protection when you had sex with these women."

"Really? Of course I did. I may not have known that I was being recorded, but I do know that I don't want to be a parent with some strange woman who's only interested in me for a monthly check. Dad, talk to the board and let me know what they want. I know this doesn't seem worthy of a CEO, and whatever the board deems as an appropriate punishment, I'll take it. If they feel I should step down, then I'll resign.

"I'm meeting Greer at the house before the SHN meeting tonight and will ask who she recommends I contact to counter all this. Normally I'd ask her to do it, but she seems a bit busy fighting this mess with SHN."

"Relax. We're not happy, but we need to address this in the press. Greer's already given me a name. I sent it over to your e-mail a few minutes ago. Reach out to them, and don't worry about the SHN meeting tonight."

Part of me is relieved that I'm not expected at tonight's meeting. I don't think I could stand Sara's disappointment. No wonder she doesn't want to date me.

My life is a fucking mess. Fuck!

TREY

I'M ANGRY that my privacy has yet again been violated. This kind of crap has happened to me my entire life, but this time seems the most intrusive.

Videos? Is nothing sacred? Who thinks making a sex tape is going to make them famous?

I'm positive Jill is behind this. She's totally crazy. I'm not sure I'll ever understand why she would talk any woman into making a video, let alone why she posted them and what she expects to accomplish. If we find her and can help her understand what she did and how it has adversely affected so many, maybe she'll be truly sorry and take steps to apologize. I mean, does she think this will make me say, "Wow! You've really scared me. Now I want to make babies with you"? I don't see any upside to this. What the fuck was she thinking?

My mind drifts from Jill to Sara. What do I do about her? How can I convince her that these videos are years old and not who I am anymore?

My phone rings and breaks my train of thought. Seeing it's my sister, I answer with "Hey, ugly."

"Old man, what's up?"

"Just sittin' here and hangin' out."

"Are you medicating with alcohol?"

"Not really. I've had one beer. I figure if I don't stop now, I may never stop."

"I hear ya. We're getting too old to deal with hangovers anyway."

"I keep thinking about what it would be like to move far away, change my name and find a nice girl who doesn't care about money or notoriety and is just looking for a nice guy."

"I suppose you can do that. Yeah. Sure. I'd miss you."

"You might be the only one."

"I doubt that. Have you thought about using an online dating app?"

"I used to use Tinder all the time."

"Okay, dumbass, that's a hookup site, not a dating app. Maybe you need to get to know them before you sleep with them? How about something like matchme.com? The girls and I are all doing it. None of us has met anyone decent yet, but you might actually meet a nice girl."

"I'm not sure I'm ready. Plus I don't want to meet Hadlee or Greer. I know them already."

"Whatever. You're still hung up on the skank who broke your heart."

"She isn't a skank." Taking a deep breath, I say wistfully, "She's actually awesome. This crap and having *TMZ* follow us everywhere we go just sucks."

"I know. Trey, I love you. I always have despite the mullet in eighth grade and the fact that you're now a porn star." Her voice turns endearing. "You deserve an amazing woman, and I hope you find her soon."

"Me, too." There are a few seconds of silence, and then I say, "I love you, too. Have a good night. I have meetings with the PR firm tomorrow morning. They have a long list of things for me, and probably you. I'll keep you posted."

"Whatever you need."

I turn my music up. I'm listening to AC/DC's "Back in Black" loud, and it makes me feel a little better. I have a meeting with the PR firm in the morning, and from the e-mails, I see they'll be keeping me busy. I sure hope they're able to help save our acquisition.

THE PR FIRM is putting me through my paces. They were successful in getting me on a few women-centric talk shows, and they set up a *People Magazine* cover. I guess they'll have an extensive article that discusses my notoriety, but also highlights all the work CeCe and I do for our community and for women in general, including women charities. Hopefully it'll also cover the shock of having women secretly record my sex life and having it dubbed over. But I'll leave all that to the PR professionals to sort out.

I need to get out of town and hide somewhere. I have paparazzi hanging out near my home and work, and CeCe has them, too. This will pass once someone else does something stupid, but until it does, I'm the flavor of the month.

I'm embarrassed that everyone around me is affected by this shit. Banging my hand on the table, I yell, "Dammit!"

SARA

W HENEVER I SEE A TEASE on *TMZ* about Trey, I'll read it or watch it. They've captured him riding his bike, out to dinner with friends, occasionally with a famous actress or musician but never the same woman twice. I'm stunned when they tease a sex video of him.

I admit, I find it and watch it on the internet. I'm certain he didn't know he was being recorded. It makes me miss him even more than usual.

He can't seem to walk out of his place or do anything without a horde of photographers capturing his every move. It's been three days since the announcement and yet he's still the daily tease.

I debate reaching out to him and finally give in, texting: Hey. I know I've been out of touch for a while, but I wanted to tell you how sorry I am for all the publicity. I've been thinking of you. If you want to talk, please know I'm here, and if you don't, I understand. XXOO Sara.

He almost immediately texts me back.

Trey: Thank you. I didn't know they were recording. But I assure you, they're several years old, and they do a voice-over in several instances.

Me: I can tell. You never look directly at the camera, yet she does. I'm truly sorry.

Trey: I didn't catch that I never look at the camera. Wow. Thanks. I'm sorry you had to see the videos, but I'm glad we're still friends.

Me: Of course we are! I'd offer meeting up for a drink, but I have a feeling it would make it worse.

Trey: It would—not for me but for you.

Trey: Would it upset you to know that I miss you?

Me: I miss you, too.

Trey: I'd like to see you, but right now the paparazzi are camped on my doorstep. I need to get away, and you do not want this mess.

I'm crazy about him. I can tell he's hurting. A good friend would help when their friend is in need. And Trey is in need of a good friend.

Me: Do you want to try to escape the frenzy and meet up in Stinson? We can use Jim and Carol's place. Very proper but private. Promise.

Trey: I'd love that. Are you sure? It's a perfect hideout.

Me: Then let's go.

I quickly call Jim and Carol and ask if I can go up with a friend to the beach house for a week. They tell me to have a great time.

Me: I checked with Jim and Carol. It's yours for the week if you'd like.

Trey: Thank you. I can't tell you how much this means
to me.

Trey: You're going to meet me in Stinson, right?

That's a positive sign.

Me: I can't wait. I'll call the front gate and give them a
fake name for you. What do we call you?

Trey: My personal favorite is John McClane.

Me: As in Die Hard?

Trey: Yep. You're good.

Me: Then John McClane it is. The code to get in the front
door is 9753#. Go when you're ready.

Trey: I'll head out in the morning, and when you're done
with your day tomorrow, come on up.

Me: There are a few things in the morning for me to take
care of. I'll try to head out of The City by noon.

Trey: That means 3. I'll stop and get food and will bring
wine with me.

Me: OK. Let me know if I can bring anything.

Trey: Make sure you make it over before dark.

Me: Promise.

Trey: Sara, thank you for this.

I'm glad I can be a good friend and offer him a chance to breathe a minute outside of the cameras. Even if they follow him into Stinson, they'd have a really tough time getting beyond the gate. This will be good for him.

And I'm kidding myself if I think I'm not excited to spend time with him.

I take a deep breath, remembering his sandalwood smell, and my heart races.

TREY

HEADING UP TO STINSON is a perfect getaway. My friends, the board of directors at our company, our stockholders and my family—particularly my parents—are all upset.

I know I've not always been super careful, but recently I've wanted to stay below the radar. I'm ready to settle down, and no woman wants the mess that comes with me and a sex tape.

These days, with everyone having a cell phone, there are cameras everywhere. I get my picture taken almost everywhere I go. As I leave San Francisco, the motorcycle that was following me seems to have dropped off, but I've picked up a dark car that's staying close.

I hope they're up for a long ride.

To check their determination, I might even make a few stops. It's sad, really, that I find fun in irritating them. I know some people throw food and things like rocks at them; for the most part, I ignore and find more passive-aggressive ways to annoy them.

Stopping by Whole Foods, I buy enough food for a week so we have a lot of options. I packed a case of my favorite pinot noir from the Willamette Valley in Oregon. I talked to my parents and told them I was heading to a friend's out of town to work and get away, and they've been supportive.

Checking the rearview mirror once I'm back on the road, I still see the dark car following me. The car's occupant didn't come into Whole Foods, but I *was* stopped by a housewife asking me for a photograph. As I start the trek over the mountain that will take me to the seaside town, a level of anxiety starts to weigh on me and what it means to have the press at every turn.

A week ago, these vultures were nowhere to be seen. As the rain pitter-patters on my windshield, I feel as if I should be running somewhere that doesn't affect Sara. What was I thinking to agree to this? Still, I drive onward, over winding roads amid the green pines that scrape the clouds.

As I enter Stinson and drive through town, those following me will be challenged to find a place to stay here. There's a small hotel, but it's closed until summer. Most homes are either seasonal rentals or occupied by the owners. I drive up to the gate and give the guard my name, then explain that I think there's a car following me, stressing, "They're not with me. Do not let them convince you otherwise."

"I know who you are, Mr. Arnault," the guard assures me. "I understand. If I might suggest, at the split in the road, you should take the right side. It leads you to the inlet and may put them off from trolling the waterfront and the beach."

"That's great advice. Thank you."

"Enjoy your stay," he tells me with a smile, and the gates roll open.

"I sure hope to." I drive off and follow his advice, taking the right side of the split. It's a long oval, but it does mislead them a little bit, so maybe they'll lose interest. One can only hope.

I pull into the garage and begin to unload the car as my cell phone pings.

Sara: I'm on my way. See, I could leave before 3.

My stomach flutters and I'm excited to see her. I rib her a little bit because it's 2:59.

Me: Just barely before 3.

Me: It's crazy getting through Mount Tamalpais. Be careful. I'll have dinner ready for you when you arrive. I hope you like seared ahi.

Sara: Sounds perfect. See you soon.

SARA

*A*s I raise my arm to move back the crepe drape of my blouse, my bangles cascade further down my arm than they would have only a week ago. In the muted evening light, I feel like I should be on my way home, not heading to the beach house. What was I thinking, reaching out to Trey?

As I descend and drive past the throng of gift shops and a small market that make up Stinson Beach, my anxiety increases. I grip the steering wheel tighter. I don't know how I'll explain why I pulled back. Why I need to protect myself.

When the house comes into view, I stop dead, my heart thumping.

I'll just have to make him understand.

As I park the car, Trey greets me with a glass containing a heavy pour of white wine.

"I thought you could use a drink after that drive."

"You know me so well. It's getting dark, and it was already a white-knuckle drive. Thank you." I smile, grateful to see him.

He's dressed in a baggy pair of khaki pants with the bottoms rolled up, a hint of sand on the top of his bare feet. His sweater is pushed up on his arms, and his dark hair is full of the curls he usually hides. He seems happy I'm here, but he also appears fragile, and I see the dark circles under his eyes.

I hug him, and he holds me tight. I know right at this moment that placing distance between us was a mistake. There's always the possibility that opening myself up will leave me vulnerable, but I might find something wonderful, too. Trey may one day break my heart, but I want to try. I'll keep a few walls up, but I like him. And I want people to know that his sex video, his last name and all the craziness that comes with it doesn't bother me.

He helps me with my bag, and I'm stunned to find a nice romantic table setting. He tells me that dinner's almost ready, and I sigh. "I could come home to this every day."

Smiling at me, he says, "Why don't you get changed into something more relaxing and join me by the fireplace."

I kiss him on the cheek. "Good idea."

I leave my messenger bag with my computer in the living room, pick up my overnight bag and walk back to my room to change. It's chilly out, so I put on a baggy pair of khakis and pull a UCLA Law sweatshirt on. I finally feel like I'm ready to explain my distance and take whatever he needs to say to me.

I wander back into the living room, finding Trey lying on the couch by the fire. He's drifted off to sleep. He looks so peaceful, and I don't want to disturb him, so I pull a blanket from the back of the couch and cover him. Moving into the kitchen, I glance over what he's prepared for dinner and wrap it up, snacking on the bread and an amazing olive oil dip he prepared.

Who needs anything more than good wine and good bread dipped in olive oil? Pure heaven.

Trey still hasn't woken, and I don't want to disturb him, so I get my computer out and work a bit more before calling it a night. I leave him a note that I'm looking forward to his world-famous French toast and a long walk along the beach.

FULL OF NERVOUS ENERGY, I wake early and get into the shower. Today's the day I've been dreading. I can't hide in my room forever, so I've showered, blown out my hair and applied my makeup. Everything hinges on what I say, and once done, it can never be undone. Today could be the difference between walking away with my heart torn in so many pieces it can't be put back together, or the first day of the rest of my life.

I gaze into the mirror and nod. *Okay, enough stalling.*

I walk into the kitchen and find Trey dancing to music from his iPhone, surrounded by a huge stack of French toast, bacon cooking on the stove and coffee—the nectar of the gods—ready to drink. "Good morning," I announce.

His gyrations stop and he stares at me, starting to turn red, as if embarrassed, but then a smile spreads across his face. He opens his arms as he walks toward me. "Hey. I'm sorry about last night. Not very romantic or even thankful for providing me shelter."

I laugh. "You were tired. I can only imagine how difficult it must be to deal with this mess. How are your parents managing? It's not like any parent wants to acknowledge their children are sexually active."

"I know! My mom's first concern was if I wore a condom. And even though CeCe and I have told my parents that someone voiced over the tape, I'm not sure they believe us."

I laugh harder. "That is awful."

We sit at the bar in the kitchen, catching up. He knows everything about what's going on at SHN, and I share my perspective. "I wish we could figure out why they felt it necessary to share our work. It doesn't make sense. Do you think the PR blitz is working?"

Sympathizing, he says, "I think it's made people understand how the venture capital world works. But it sucks that Dillon is a brilliant financial analyst of start-ups and his work is out for others to emulate."

I stand and clear our dishes from the table. "Ready to go for a walk?"

"Absolutely," I say with maybe a little too much enthusiasm.

We put our coats on and walk out past the dunes to the beach. The morning clouds dominate the sky, and though they're mostly white, there's a hint of grayness, a suggestion that rain may play a part in the day to come. The waves roll along the coastline in long white-fringed rows. Our feet are bare, and the sand is moist. It's cushiony, and we walk hand in hand, letting the sand ooze over our feet and between our toes. This moment is perfect.

We walk in silence. It's awkward at first, but I finally get up the nerve and admit, "I've missed you."

Squeezing my hand tighter, he asks, "Why did you go? I won't break, you know, if you tell me what's happening. I can't change everything about my life, but I might be able to make some adjustments that could make it easier for us."

"Trey, it has nothing to do with all the attention you get. It's the mess of my own life." I pause, struggling to tell him what should be happy and glorious news but only brings me huge heartache. "It's the mess with Henry. And I found my biological mother."

He stops and turns to me. "Your biological mother? That's wonderful."

I take a big breath. *Now for the hard part.* "Not really. She lives in Seattle. She's married to my biological father, and they have four kids together."

In a clipped and angry voice, he asks, "What?"

Trying hard not to cry, I whimper, "I have four siblings, none of them know I exist, and she wants to forget I'm alive."

Closing his eyes, he reaches for me. "Oh, Sara. I'm sorry."

He pulls me in, and I cry on his shoulder. Not the cute three or four tears that cascade nicely down my cheeks, but tears that are big, ugly and unending. Tears that fall until I've drained every ounce of moisture in my body, our feet buried deep in the sand as the water curls at our toes.

His fingers beneath my chin are gentle as he lifts my face to his, meeting my lips in a kiss of wanting and warmth. His tongue darts out to taste me, the movement wrought with possession. As if emboldened by my flavor, he groans before pulling me closer with a hand behind my neck, his embrace crushing my arms against his chest. I can't move, but I feel the power I have over him in the urgency of his kiss, his hardness against my core.

I break the kiss, my teeth chattering as I say, "I'm freezing. Can we go in and start a fire?"

"Sounds like a great idea."

Trey's quiet as he leads the way through the dunes to the back door. He picks up a towel from the back I hadn't seen him set there earlier, then bends down and rubs the sand from my feet.

As he holds the door for me, he shares, "I know *TMZ* makes my life a mess, and the sex video is out there, but I've missed you. Do you think you can accept my crazy life? At least for a little while. I'm not perfect, but I promise I'm faithful. All I've ever wanted was the courtesy of being treated with respect by a person I care about, another human I can relate to, and that is you."

I nod, and we curl under a blanket while the fire rages on. I'm happy I could share my heartbreak and rejection with Trey. He's as angry with Catherine as I am, and there's comfort in that knowledge.

I've polished off an entire bottle of pinot noir with him, and I'm feeling bolder than ever, coasting in a fog of wine. Nothing too strong to inhibit me, but enough to set me free of stress and guilt.

I kiss him, hard and feral, my tongue aggressive and forceful. Trey responds with equal passion.

We're made for each other.

TREY

THE HEAT WARMS OUR BARE SKIN as we lie spooning in front of the fire. Inching my nose a little nearer to her neck, I breathe in her scent. I can recognize the perfume she uses—one of my favorites—intermingling with the outlandish aroma of our wine, pâté, cheeses and crackers. She rests peacefully in my arms, and I caress her soft skin, the curve of her hips and the swell of her breasts.

Sara is perfect in every way, and I have an inner peace when I'm with her. I'm still angry about how Henry took advantage of her. Plus it kills me what Catherine's done, particularly when she wouldn't give up her parental rights. I'm making a mental note to do a bit of research. Something's a little fishy with that whole situation.

We lie there for hours, dozing by the fire, naked, and making love. I want to please her in every way I can. She opens her legs to me, allowing access. She has the most beautiful pussy, bare, smooth and wet with anticipation as it glistens between the slit. I inhale deeply at her scent and spread her lips, running my tongue along the side of her clit. Opening her wide, I want to taste her pink pussy.

Clawing at the blanket we're on top of, Sara grabs at the floor, like it can give her leverage—and I know her orgasm is building. She gasps as I continue to eat that sweet little pussy. I know I should prolong it, but she pushes into my face and I can't take it anymore. She tastes so fucking sweet that I have to get deep in there, and before I know it, I eat her harder and faster, sucking her clit and open-mouth kissing her tight pussy, the pussy that was made for me. She's so sexy as she moans out her pleasure and screams my name.

Removing a foil package from the side table, I sheath my hard and anxious cock. Watching her lick her lips makes me harder and she spreads her long legs wide.

"Please! Please, I can't take this torture," she begs.

Leaning down, I suckle each of her nipples, teasing them with my tongue and mouth. Her hips move beneath me involuntarily, seeking my hard cock. I find her wetness and just barely brush my thumb over the swollen nub. She moans at the contact, and I can't take her need and wanting anymore. I thrust hard into her and we both gasp. It's so tight, and I can tell by her eyes that there's a small tinge of pain as I split her open. Then her legs wrap around me, adding weight to every thrust.

I hold her hips to pull her hard on me while she rubs her clit. Her pussy holds my cock like a vice as she climaxes, and I can't take it any longer, shooting my load before she's come down. After sliding the condom off my flaccid cock, I wrap it in a tissue from the table. I don't want to leave her, even for a moment.

This feels right.

WE SPEND what's left of the weekend enjoying each other, sleeping and not caring about anything outside of the world we've created.

As we walk the beach after breakfast Sunday morning, she asks, "I need to go to the partners meeting at your parents' tonight. Are you coming?"

"No. My dad is still angry with me, and I don't want to be a distraction."

"Not one person in that room would see you as a distraction."

"SHN is dealing with its own public relations disaster."

"With Greer's guidance, I think Mason, Dillon and Cameron have managed to get out of the woods, but I understand you not wanting to go." Eyeing me, she asks, "With *TMZ* staking out your work, your place in The City and your family, where will you go?"

I peer at her, debating. Finally, I get the nerve. "Do you think Jim and Carol would mind if I stayed here? I'm happy to pay a generous rent. I just need to stay off the radar for a few weeks."

"It isn't the time of year that they come up here, so we may be fine. I don't know. Let's call them."

"Wait, what have you told them about me?"

Laughing, she says, "Nothing. They're wonderful people, and if I tell them you're my friend, we'll be fine. It comes down to if they're planning on using the house any time soon, that's all." She picks up her phone and places the call.

"Hello, lovely," a cheerful voice answers.

"Hey, Carol. I have my friend Trey here on speaker, and we're up in Stinson."

"Hello, Trey. Nice to meet you," she says warmly.

"Hi. You have a beautiful house here."

"You're very sweet. It needs a lot of work. That salt air is not good for all the wood."

I laugh. "Salt air isn't good for metal or concrete either."

"So true. Sara's dad is a structural engineer, and he could talk your ear off on that subject."

"Well, I hope one day I'll get the chance. I was wondering, are you planning on coming up here this month?"

"We were, but nothing's written in stone. What are you thinking?"

"Carol, Trey is somewhat famous," Sara interjects. "His last name is Arnault."

"Are you related to Charles and Margo?"

"Yes, they're my parents," I confirm. "I'm Charles Michael Arnault the third. I go by Trey since my grandfather was Charlie and my father is Charles."

"Wonderful. Now, what's going on?"

"Well, I have the tabloid press stalking me over a video someone secretly recorded and doctored. Would it be possible to rent the beach house for the month? I'll pay you five thousand a week. I can wire you the money today."

"Let me talk to Jim, but I don't think it'll be a problem if you stay. What number can I call you back at?"

I rattle off my cell phone number, and Sara picks up the phone and walks into the other room for a bit of privacy to continue the conversation. I hope she can work her magic so I can stay here this month. It would be a godsend to hide here.

Sara returns to the kitchen. "Jim came back while I was talking to Carol. He's fine with you staying. They don't want you to pay any rent, but I told them you could make sure that the deck was repaired and that the house was ready for the season."

"That's easy. Great. Thank you." I bring Sara in for a kiss. "I can't tell you how much I appreciate this."

Blushing, she says, "Don't worry about it." She glances at her watch. "I think I need to go if I'm going to be in Hillsboro for dinner."

I'm not ready for her to leave. "When will you be back?"

"I don't know." She runs her hands through her hair. I can tell she's choosing her words carefully. "So much depends on what we learn tonight."

I'm disappointed, but I understand. "Please at least try to come back next Friday for the weekend." Desperately, I add, "And I want to talk to you every day. It'll be lonely here without you."

She laughs. "So you only want me for my body."

I nod. "And your beauty and brains, too."

"Let me know how easy it is to work from here."

"I'll get a lot done without the distractions, and I'll get the deck figured out and whatever else might need to be done here."

She leans in and kisses me. "You're amazing, you know that?"

"I miss you already."

We walk to her car and off she starts the drive back to The City.

SARA

$\mathcal{A}$ s I DRIVE THE TWO AND A HALF HOURS to my partners meeting, my mind drifts to our weekend. Being vulnerable and sharing my biological mother's rejection lifts a huge weight off my shoulders. I'm happy for the first time in a long time.

This feels good. *I* feel good.

I'm not last to arrive at the Arnaults', but almost. Greer comes in a few moments after I do. Dillon asks about Trey, and I decide now's as good a time as any to announce that we might be more than friends. "Trey is reachable by cell phone. He's staying at my foster parents' beach house in Stinson for the next month."

With her brows knitted, CeCe says, "We talked as I drove down. He didn't mention it was through you that he got the beach house, but thank you for arranging that."

Wanting the focus to not be on me, I simply say, "I'm glad I could help."

I wait for CeCe to ask other questions, but I get pulled into a conversation with Mason and Dillon about an upcoming sale.

As we settle into our seats for our meeting, my cell phone pings.

Trey: Thank you for telling everyone. Does this mean we have a relationship we're telling people about?

Me: I was going to call you on my drive home tonight. Who told you?

Trey: CeCe.

Me: Is she upset?

Trey: Are you kidding? She's warning me that if I hurt you, she's promised something much more disastrous than the video.

I glance up to find CeCe watching me closely, smiling broadly. I'm excited that she's so happy for us. I text him back: She's planning our wedding already.

Our meeting runs for two more hours, and we discuss a few client bids we're working on. Since our traces of the saboteur didn't work out, Charles has reached out to several of his contacts. They've been working things in the background, and now we'll begin moving things up. They're going to reach out to Perkins Klein, searching for funding of some of their ideas, and we'll see what they come up with. They'll help us garner information and, if we're lucky, help us locate the leak at SHN. I take notes and know my plate is going to be full for the days to come.

As we break to go home, CeCe links her arm with mine. "My brother is completely smitten with you. Please tell me you like him at least a little bit? He's really a great guy. The video was taped by a crazy without his knowledge ages ago, and it was all voiced over."

I'm silent as she rattles on and on, selling me on her brother.

Eyeing me when she finally pauses for a breath, she says, "Well?"

CeCe is definitely okay with our coupling. Trey and I talked about a dozen topics but have yet to talk about what we are. I'm smitten, but beyond admitting we're friends, that's all I want to share.

"CeCe, you're amazing. And I know the video was faked." She stares at me, probably expecting me to profess my love, but until we do that together, I want to keep it special and so I fudge the truth a bit. "I like your brother. I don't know what we are, or if we're anything more than friends, but we are exploring our options."

Jumping up and down in her excitement, she says, "Give it time. I always thought you'd be an amazing sister."

I text Trey when we finish, but he doesn't text or call me back. That could mean he fell asleep, or he left his phone in another part of the house and didn't hear the alert.

As I lie in bed, I think about CeCe's admission. A sister. She would be an amazing sister, and I do like Trey. Actually, I'm without a doubt in love with him. I really wouldn't mind if this were to go somewhere. He's mighty yummy. I mean, he always looks good, but when he's naked—yowza! And that tongue. Those fingers. Holy cow, he's the whole package.

I better watch myself.

TREY

C RAP, I MISSED HER TEXT LAST NIGHT. I give her a call, and the phone rings to voice mail. "Hey! Sorry I missed you last night. I fell asleep in front of the fire again. Call me back. I'll be working from the beach house all day and would welcome a break if you have time to call."

I settle down and spend the day working. It's amazing how much you can get done when you're working without a thousand interruptions. I also call a friend I went to high school with who does deck work and make plans for him to come by this afternoon. It's slow this time of year, but if I can get him now, he can rebuild the deck without disruptions.

I fell asleep on the couch thinking over what Sara shared about her mother. It really bothers me. I'm not sure I can do anything to affect the relationship, but I really would like to help Sara, so I call a private investigator in Seattle that I've used in the past, and I ask him to find Catherine. I know she lives locally to him, but that's all I can give him. I tell him I want information on her husband and their kids. He asks me a few questions—

some I can answer and some I can't. He ends by telling me he'll get back to me as soon as he has something.

I bounce from conference call to conference call all day, and it's three o'clock before I know it. I still haven't heard from Sara, so I text her: Hope your day is going well.

She calls as I begin to make my dinner. "Hey."

"Hey. How was your day?" I ask.

"It was good. We were swamped, but that's nothing new." There's a short, awkward pause. "Fell asleep by the fire again?"

"Well, I had this amazing woman who kept me up Saturday night. She was incredible."

She has the most beautiful and sexy /. "Really? What makes her incredible?"

"You mean her hot body, the fact that she's super smart and talented"—my voice softens—"and she's generous and kind. And she sees me for me, despite all the chaos and crap that I bring to any relationship. Yep, she's incredible."

"Wow, that's quite a list. I don't think I deserve all that, but so you know, I do think you're incredible yourself. But it's about what you do with your tongue, your hands and well, that third leg of yours."

"Third leg? You can call it a penis. Or if you prefer, dick. If you're feeling super adventurous, call it a cock."

She laughs hard. "I think I'd call it my toy."

Now I'm laughing along with her. "Okay then, your toy misses you. When will you be coming to see it again?"

"I guess I should figure that out. I thought I might be able to make it this weekend. though right now, I don't have anything on my calendar in person on Friday, so I could probably leave early."

"How about I drive in and pick you up at your place on Thursday night after work? That would prevent you from driving over in the dark. You can work from here on Friday, and then I get a bit more time with you."

"Let me think about it and see if I can make it work." Changing subjects, I ask, "So, what's going on with work?"

"We have the sale of a finance app coming up and it's busy. What about you?"

Warmth hits me at her question, at the ease of the conversation. It's the simple things that make me the happiest. Being with Sara, walking the beach or sharing our days brings a smile to my face and fills my heart with joy.

"It was mostly conference calls. This acquisition is challenging to say the least."

We talk for almost an hour, bouncing from one subject to the next like a pinball.

She tells me she needs to get a few things done before she can go home.

"Call me tomorrow?" I ask.

"I promise."

"Good night, sweetheart."

"Good night, handsome."

SARA

As I RIDE THE BUS INTO THE OFFICE, I'm reading the *Silicon Valley Business Journal.* Perkins Klein has won yet another prospect, one that never came to us. In the article, while not naming us particularly, they do say that they 'chose to go with Perkins Klein because, unlike their main competitor, Perkins Klein is interested in our company goals and our software, not just the money they'll make through their investment.' All while stressing how successful and revolutionary their software is going to be.

This is going to upset Mason. And I know it'll only further anger Dillon. Maybe I should head to Stinson for a month, too.

My admin texts me: Partner's meeting in thirty minutes in Mason's office.

Thanks. Let them know I'll be there in ten minutes.

I'm dreading the walk into the office, knowing everyone's bound to have read the same article. Greer rides up in the elevator with me. She has circles under her eyes, and she seems exhausted. It'll be a miracle if she doesn't quit before too long. This was definitely not what she signed up for.

When I arrive at my office, there's already a coffee on my desk. There's no note to let me know who the buyer is, yet one sniff tells me it's my favorite—hazelnut latte. I sink into my chair and peer around. Hardly anyone's here yet, and no one even glances my way or acknowledges me at all. I ask my admin if she saw who left it, and she tells me she didn't buy it, nor does she know who did.

I turn my attention back to the cup. It's a venti, frothy and still hot. I want to resist it until I know the giver, but without a conscious thought, it's in my hand, the first milky sip creeping over my taste buds and down my throat. After only a few minutes I'm bathing in the kick of the caffeine. The time for finding my benefactor has passed; the partners meeting is going to begin, and I can't be late. I carry my tablet in one hand and the cup in the other. Until it's drained, it's to be within easy arm's reach.

Dillon is pacing when I round the corner and I stop dead in my tracks, causing Emerson to run into me from behind. "Oh, sorry," she says.

"My fault. I was watching Dillon and wasn't sure if I wanted to go in."

"I was watching him pace, too. He's been angry all morning over his formulas being shared, yet his old professors at Stanford have asked him to come in and guest lecture on it. I knew when I read this morning's paper that he was going to lose it. And he has. I must love him if I put up with this." We both giggle.

"Is it you I can thank for my latte?" I ask hesitantly.

"No, it wasn't me. I wonder if you have a secret admirer."

I laugh. *No admirer's here.*

The meeting is rough. Greer receives marching orders to get Tom Sutterland to be interviewed for a puff piece about how we helped their business, improved his valuation when he went public and how well he's done. She's also booking interviews with the business editor at the *San Jose News* and the *New York Times*. We're quickly working our way through a PR blitz to counter all the negative press we seem to be getting.

When I return to my desk, I find a text from Trey. How are the partners doing with the latest in the SVBJ?

I pick up my phone and call him. "Hey. How's your morning going?"

"Mine's busy, but probably not as yours."

"We had a meeting, and Greer's going to be busy for a while."

"She loves this. Don't worry about her. How was your latte this morning?"

"You bought me my latte? How?"

Laughing, he says, "I have my sources."

"Well, you made my morning." I lower my voice. "I'll have to find a way to thank you the next time I see you."

"I hope I see you sooner rather than later. Any thoughts on meeting up on Thursday? I'd like a few things from my condo, and I thought I'd send CeCe in and meet up with her later."

"You don't think the paparazzi have your place still staked out?"

"I'm sure they do. She can borrow Hadlee's car and go into my garage, take the elevator up and get out with little attention. Even if they do spot her, they'll get tired of following her because they'll never know when she'll connect with me."

"I have another option for you to consider. They don't know

me. I could go in the front door and walk right out without the paparazzi noticing." He's silent for a moment, so I continue. "Of course, I could always get your stuff to CeCe for delivery."

"I love the idea of you doing it. You're right, they wouldn't know you weren't going to see someone else in the building. Are you sure you wouldn't mind?"

"Talk to CeCe and get her thoughts, and if she prefers to do it, not a worry."

As the day wears on, I've studied my schedule, and I think I can make leaving on Thursday work.

Emerson peeks her head in my office and asks, "Are you up for a drink tonight? I had an idea today and thought it might be fun to run it by you and get your thoughts."

"Sure. When were you thinking?"

"I'd like to walk out the door right now, but how about an hour?"

"I can make it in thirty, if you prefer?"

"You can? Awesome. Meet you at the elevators."

I begin shutting my computer down and packing up, then quickly text Trey: I'm heading out with Emerson for drinks and probably dinner. You going to be awake for a while?

Trey: Have fun. I'll be awake.

Emerson waits until we're in the elevator to fill me in. "I thought rather than go to our normal spot, we'd head over to Acquerello. I'm in the mood for good homemade pasta. It's not too loud and out of our regular routine, plus I think CeCe may join us, if you're okay with that?"

"Sure. I took Muni in today, but we can call a Lyft."

Her cell phone pings. Turning to wink at me, she says, "CeCe's downstairs. She just texted."

"Well that's easy."

Once we pile into CeCe's car, she turns to me. "Trey told me you were heading out with Emerson. Sorry to crash your party, but you're two of my favorite people, and I need to talk to both of you."

"It isn't my party. Emerson has something she wants to run by me, but we were probably going to gossip most of the night anyway." I giggle.

"We have time before our reservation. No worries," Emerson's quick to add.

We drive to Acquerello's, chatting and catching up. "CeCe, your dad didn't say last night, but is he upset with Trey?"

"He is, but not exclusively with Trey. We all agree that the girl recorded the video without his knowledge, but my parents are struggling with the audio, and honestly with the fact that he's sleeping with strange women."

I nod. "I get that."

"They do get that the audio is faked, though, don't they?" Emerson asks.

"They do," CeCe replies, "but only because Trey's been emphatic that the video is him, but the voice isn't his."

We head inside, sit and order, and then CeCe turns to me. "It took me until yesterday to realize you were the woman in the *TMZ* picture a few months ago."

I turn crimson from my toes to my ears. "Yes."

Emerson, who's sitting next to me, reaches over and hugs me. "He's staying at your foster parents' beach house. Does this mean...?"

I eye them both and say, "I've had a few things going on, between my affair with Henry becoming extremely public and my biological mother's rejection. I pulled away from Trey." I know how I feel, but he's not said anything. I've been hurt so much recently, I can't lay myself open to my friends. I need to protect something in myself. Peeking at CeCe, I tell her, "I don't know what we are. He's a heartbreaker, and he's out of my league."

CeCe's been playing with the table bread, but she stops and regards me. "I honestly don't know why you would think you're out of his league. If anything, he's out of your league." Gazing at Emerson, she says, "Emerson is the only person in my life who knows this, but Trey and I fully acknowledge that we got lucky in the family lottery. We were born into a family with two parents who love and adore us, and who are incredibly wealthy." She takes a sip of her wine. "Sara, I don't know the whole story about your biological mom, but I do know that you bounced from foster home to foster home. You put yourself through college and law school—at some impressive schools, no less. Then you landed a great job where you're listed as one of the most influential women in The Valley. You're a self-made billionaire. You did that on your own, not with a fancy last name and not with a trust fund as your safety net." Emerson's holding my hand, and CeCe reaches across the table, giving me a warm embrace. "You're out of his league. And don't ever forget that."

With the corner of my dinner napkin, I wipe tears from my eyes. "You win. You're officially the president of the Sara Elizabeth White fan club."

We all giggle, and she insists, "It's all true. He'd be lucky to have you—and by the way, I think you'd make a wonderful sister-in-law."

"Slow down," I urge.

"I think we need to get away as a group," Emerson suggests. "I understand your parents' place sleeps over a dozen people. Any chance you think they might let us do a partners retreat there? It's off the beaten track, and we'd have the opportunity to do a few things under the public radar."

"It isn't fancy at all. There are two rooms with beds that will sleep couples—I think they're both queen-size. And then there are two rooms that each have two bunk beds and a trundle—sleeping six people per room. It's definitely rustic. Right now, the back deck needs some repair, and the kitchen is tight. But I *can* say it's in a gated area on the beach in a great location."

"I think it's perfect. What do you think about having Sunday's meeting at the beach house?" CeCe asks.

"Stinson Beach is on the other side of Mount Tamalpais State Park, and it can be a tricky drive after dark. Maybe it might be a better idea if we met Saturday afternoon instead. Plus everyone can make a better decision in person. And it won't hurt my feelings if they aren't interested."

"Saturday sounds great. That way we don't have to rush back to The City."

We spend the remainder of our dinner together gossiping

about Hadlee's latest love interest and wedding planning for Emerson. I glance at my watch, then tell the girls, "It's after ten, and I need to do a few things at home before going to bed."

I call a ride share and text Trey: I'm in my Lyft heading home. I'll call as soon as I get there.

He responds: CeCe already texted me.

I walk in the door, change into my pajamas and wash my face before I FaceTime with Trey.

As soon as his face appears, he says, "The patio will be done by Friday, and if your folks are okay with all the people at the beach house, I think it's a great idea."

"Let's see how Saturday goes. We'll oversee dinner. I can get Carol's brisket recipe, and we can slow-cook that and have barbeque brisket sandwiches, coleslaw, chips and pick up some great desserts from the bakery in town."

"That works. I'll also have the barbeque up and working, if you want to go more basic with grilled chicken and steaks."

"I like that. Not everyone likes brisket, and maybe we can slow-cook some ribs. It'll be a nice mix of beef, pork and chicken."

"You're a woman after my own heart."

We talk for a short time, and I begin to doze off. Trey quickly realizes it and says, "I think I'm losing you. Talk to you tomorrow?"

"Okay. Good night, Trey."

"Good night, Sara."

TREY

I DID MANAGE A DECENT NIGHT SLEEP. I know I'd have slept better with Sara at my side, but we'll get there. I take a run down the deserted beach as the sun breaks on the horizon. With each step, I run through the list of things I need to do with work and get done personally. I know if I don't tackle the personal to-do list first, I'll get immersed in work and it won't get done.

Late yesterday, I met my friend from high school about the deck and told him I needed a complete deck remodel done this week. He'll make a full kitchen area within the deck, which is easy given there's an outdoor shower there already. I know they were only hoping for some repairs, but with some of the new materials on the market, I can get them a beautiful deck. That's the advantage of having deep pockets. I hope they won't mind. It's the least I can do for them allowing me to stay here far away from the press.

The demo guys are arriving first thing today. This is going to get done quickly. The hard part is the appliances.

I text CeCe a list of things she needs to get for me that I don't want Sara to pick up. She's been wonderful, and I want to do something special for her. Then I call Ginger, my neighbor of many years. She's approaching ninety and has enjoyed San Francisco through the decades. She's never married and always has a string of beaus and friends. Most importantly, she's always good at helping me throw off the paparazzi.

"Hey, Ginger."

"Trey, I hope you're far away."

I cringe. "Is it that bad?

"The worst yet. I saw the video that girl posted. I know that's not your voice. How stupid can they be?"

"Thanks, Ginger. The video itself is me, and I feel terrible for how that's affected my friends and family. I'm hiding up the coast, but I left in such a hurry that I missed a few things. My friend Sara has volunteered to stop by and pick some things up from my condo. They don't know who she is, so they won't hound her. Do you mind being her sponsor to get into the building?"

"You're getting crafty to not have your sister come." She laughs. "Happy to help. What's her name?"

I go through the details with her and feel confident in our plan. I then call a florist and have an extra-large bouquet of hydrangeas sent to Ginger for always being kind to me when she could sell me out for big bucks.

Finally settling down for work, I run through my four conference calls. We discuss the earnings report, and we should meet our numbers, which should calm our stock holders. That helps me a lot personally.

Before I know it, my stomach's growling, and I see it's almost three o'clock. I need to stretch my legs, so I decide to go into the small village area and check out what's available. I'm surprised that, despite it being fall and having few visitors, almost everything is open.

Window-shopping, I see a great trinket store and buy a beautiful green and blue sea glass bracelet with matching earrings. They'll compliment Sara's eyes beautifully. I find the bakery she mentioned and order desserts for ten people for Saturday, plus an amazing sandwich to go. I meet the owner, Mackenzie, a vivacious brunette with dimples who's very quick to smile. She and Sara are very old friends.

"Sara's coming up on Thursday night. I was thinking a romantic dinner for her on Friday. I'm only good at grilling, and I can't be sure the barbeque will be ready, so do you have any suggestions on where I should order a romantic dinner to either be delivered or that I pick up locally?"

"Well, I don't usually do much more than bakery items and soups and sandwiches, but I've known Sara since she was a gangly high schooler and know exactly what to make that she would love, and would also be romantic."

"Are you sure? I don't want to put you out."

"I insist. Sara's very important to me, and I can tell she's important to you, too. It'll be fun. How about I drop it by Friday night at six o'clock?"

"That sounds perfect. Thank you so much, Mackenzie. I know she'll love it."

As I head back to the beach house, I get excited about my weekend. Of course, it's only Tuesday. I'd had better pace myself.

I immerse myself in work once more, and it isn't until after eight that my phone rings, bringing me out of my stupor. It's Sara, and my heart beats faster and a smile emerges before I even hear her softly say, "How was your day?"

It's such a benign question, but it warms my heart to know that she honestly wants to know the answer. "I got quite a bit accomplished. How about you?"

"Well, there's this amazingly handsome man who keeps having my favorite hazelnut latte delivered each morning to my desk. He must want me fat."

Laughing, I tell her, "I'll be crazy about you no matter your size, but I think they're putting in the sugar-free hazelnut syrup."

"I was hoping, but they both taste alike so you never know." Her voice softens. "I've never had anyone spoil me like this before. Thank you. I can't tell you how much I appreciate it."

I'm stunned by her admission. "I find it hard to believe, but trust me when I tell you, this is only the beginning."

We talk for a short time. I share with her my wanderings into the stores in town, and that I made it to the bakery and ordered the desserts for Saturday.

"What a relief. I called the butcher in town and ordered the brisket. The grocery store delivers, so go ahead and order whatever you need and put it on our account. "

"I can do that. But right now, I'm enjoying the distraction of getting out of the house at least once a day."

"Well, without the paparazzi at every corner, now you have that option."

I laugh. I can just imagine the look on her face right now—a look of disgust mixed with a smile. "What are you doing now?"

"I'm making dinner. And you?"

"The same. We can eat dinner together but not together."

"I like that." We flip to FaceTime and cook for a while as we talk about our days. She's reheating lunch leftovers from earlier in the day, and I'm making a quick chicken stir-fry.

"I know I talk about being here for a month, but I'm not sure I'll be able to be alone all that time," I confess.

"You may need a break after I'm there, and then everyone shows up on Saturday afternoon. Plus, I think if everyone gives it a thumbs-up, we're going to do a partner weekend retreat at the house. If nothing else, you may want to find another place to hide to get away from all the chaos my company's going to bring to the beach house."

"Not a chance. I look forward to having everyone here. You've all become good friends to me." We both sit at our tables and eat. "Are you stopping by my place tomorrow?"

"Yes. CeCe gave me the information and your key. I'm going to the condo after work, but my goal is to be there by seven. I have your list, and I'll call when I get there so you can help me find everything and be sure I stay away from your diary, your lifetime supply of condoms, and all your porn mags."

"There are no porn mags or diary, but I'll point you straight to my lifetime supply of condoms for us to play with. Do you journal?"

"No, but I wish I did. I don't lead much of an exciting life. Certainly not exciting enough that I'd want to chronicle it. Do CeCe or your mom journal?"

"My mom did when she was pregnant with us. She wrote a lot about her dreams, and they were extremely crazy. Sitting in meetings with people who were green, yellow, orange, blue, etc., or another was her arguing with her dead grandmother over a pair of shoes. Really out in left field."

"Well, I guess when I think about it, I journal what I eat most days."

"Really? Why?"

"I gain weight easily, and honestly I hate to work out, so I watch what I eat instead."

"You don't like to work out?"

"Breathing heavy after sex is all I like to do."

"Well, I guess we'll have to have a lot of sex so we keep your heartbeat up."

Her laugh is like the melody of a song you know and love but can't quite place.

"It's getting late. Mason wants to meet tomorrow for breakfast at seven thirty, and I'm not a morning person anymore. I work too many late nights."

"Good night, sweetheart."

"Good night. Talk to you tomorrow."

I think about Sara as I lie in bed. She's all about simplicity, making things easy, helping those around her to relax and be happy with what they have. Perhaps that's why her skin glows so—it's her inner beauty that lights her eyes and softens her features. When she smiles and laughs, you can't help but smile along as well, even if it's on the inside. To be in her company is to feel that you are someone, that you're warm in summer rays regardless of the season.

I am, without a doubt, completely and totally in love with her.

SARA

*B*REAKFAST WITH THE PARTNERS is both fun but also our chance to meet with just the six of us. As we grow, that'll become harder. We talk about things we don't necessarily want to speak with Charles about. We aren't hiding anything, we just don't want to waste his valuable time. Something he gives to us freely and without issue.

Cameron starts. "I've found someone who has strong cloud server experience for my team. I'm still looking for someone with a particular development experience but can also dumb it down for the nontechnical." We all nod, understanding the importance and knowing that working for Cameron is a rare find.

While we look at some forecasts, Dillon suggests, "We have some big wins we want. It might be time to consider a strong business development person to come in and help us with selling to the more challenging companies we want to court for our portfolio." We discuss at what level we want to bring this person in and agree that Emerson will have her recruiting team begin the search.

Greer walks through all the public relations she's been tasked with. "Mason, Dillon and Cameron are heading to New York for a marketing piece on Anderson Cooper's show. I do believe we have one more hit piece coming at us. I can't be sure, but if history repeats itself we will, and the PR firm and I are ready."

Emerson doesn't have much to share. Her team is doing well, but very busy.

When they come to me, I admit, "We're closing on three different companies this month, and I'm overwhelmed." I take a breath and ask hesitantly, "I would like a junior associate. Annabel has approached me about moving from reception to be my admin, and I'd like you all to consider the move. I could use the full-time help."

Cameron glances at Dillon. "You owe me."

Dillon pops out his wallet. "We bet that you'd be asking for help. I guessed over a year ago. You do a great job, but you work too many hours."

"Sara, we've had it in your budget for the past two years," Mason says. "Whenever you find someone, hire them. And if you're comfortable with Annabel, then that would work great. Carrie has enough work with Emerson to keep her busy full-time."

Emerson speaks up at this point. "We may have someone. We completed a search for PeopleMover, and there were a few strong candidates that may work—of course, if they're still on the market and willing to work here in The City. We'll make a few phone calls. When do you want to see candidates? Friday?"

I almost agree, then remember my plans. "I was going to head up to Stinson on Thursday after work so I can prepare for your visit on Saturday. I'm making a brisket, and we're smoking pork ribs and grilling chicken. There will be enough food to feed an army, so be ready to eat. Trey tells me the deck will be finished, and the weather is reporting sunny but cool."

Mason grins. "Enjoy your Friday. I promise to come hungry on Saturday. Should we bring anything?"

"I'll text you if I need anything. I know it's less than sixty miles to Stinson, but it's a drive through Mount Tamalpais State Park, which is narrow and has a lot of switchbacks. Take your time and drive carefully. This isn't a fancy place. Please make sure you keep your expectations low. If it's a clear day, the view is spectacular, and the company will be the best."

"We do need to start to focus on several more companies to approach. I think we need to try again to allow the investigators another chance to find the mole. Charles has his friends working Perkins Klein directly, but I want your teams working deals up front and behind closed doors. Any thoughts on a few members of the team we can bring in to do some work?"

Each of the partners pulls a few names, and we discuss them and agree to a small team. It's time to get aggressive. We're ready to combat Perkins Klein and anyone else who wants a piece of our business.

Standing, Mason says, "I think we should each review the list Dillon's team has put together and make notes." He has packets for each of us and begins passing them out. "I've taken the top twenty that the team likes, and we need to figure out what might fit well."

The remainder of the day flies by, and it's after six before I know it. I call myself a Lyft and head over to Trey's, giving the doorman my name and letting him know I'm headed up to

Ginger's unit. He lets me pass and I take the elevator to the penthouse floor, calling Trey once I'm inside.

He answers the phone on the first ring. "Hey. I was getting worried that the doorman forgot."

"No, I got sidetracked at work. I'm going through your underwear. Nice black silk boxers. They're so soft."

"You're funny. My underwear is in the right top drawer. Cotton boxers. Nothing too exciting."

"I won't look. What do you need?"

He quickly sets me on the task of picking up better than two-dozen items.

As we're wrapping up, he says, "Go into my bathroom to the medicine cabinet. Throw the box of condoms in the bag. We'll try to use them all this month. I suppose we'll have to have the conversation about birth control and our plans."

"Plans?"

"Yes, our plans for dating and monogamy."

I can't help but be excited—and maybe a bit terrified—at the thought of a monogamous relationship with Trey. "Oh, plans. Okay. I don't sleep around, and I'm happy to be tested. I thought Henry and I were monogamous, so it's probably a good idea that I confirm I'm clean again after that debacle."

"It's been a while since I've been in a serious relationship, and I really don't sleep around. I've been tested and I'm clean, but I'm happy to test again. We can do it together, if you'd like."

I go to bed thinking about him and what he said. I know he isn't Henry, and I know he's had a series of long-term girlfriends. But I also know he's had one-night stands. I need to sit back, have fun and enjoy myself.

I don't want to focus on my past, and I don't want to worry about the future.

I just want to enjoy the present.

TREY

THE DECK IS COMING ALONG NICELY, which I'm proud of. I picked up some filets for dinner tonight, potatoes to bake with all the fixings and some asparagus to grill. We're nearing the end of my culinary capabilities, but I can always order in if all else fails.

Sara calls and I grab my phone. "Hey. I'm on the Golden Gate Bridge headed your way. I'm hoping to be there before three. Do you need me to stop for anything?"

"Nope, I think I have it covered. Your friend at the bakery is able to get me a few things that make hiding here very easy."

"I can't wait to hear all about it. What do you want to do for dinner tonight? I'm already hungry."

"Sara, did you remember to eat breakfast and lunch today?"

"I may have had my hazelnut latte for breakfast, and I skipped lunch so I could get to you faster."

I chuckle. "Okay, forgiveness today. But please don't skip meals. I need you well-nourished. I promise to have something for you to nibble on while I prepare dinner."

"You're cooking? Is that safe?" she giggles.

Remembering the ahi tuna last week, I scoff. "Of course it is! I've cooked for you before."

With a touch of sarcasm, she retorts, "Well, sort of."

"Oh, you're going to pay for that!" I laugh.

Slightly above a whisper, she says, "I can't wait. See you in a little over an hour."

My cock stirs in my pants with the anticipation of seeing her again. "See you then. Drive safe."

"I promise," she murmurs in a very sultry voice.

I quickly call Mackenzie and ask what she might have for the two of us this evening, and she offers a nice antipasti platter. Sounds amazing. "I'm on my way."

When I get back to the beach house, I pour two glasses of wine and listen for the garage door to open. When it does, I set the music to quiet jazz and walk out with the drinks in my hands. She looks beautiful with her big sunglasses and her hair piled high in a loose bun on her head. Walking over to the car door, I wait while she steps out and takes a glass, then gives me a hug and a deep kiss.

"Welcome to the beach house, my love."

"I'm glad to be here. I've missed seeing you in person," she tells me as I hold on to her tightly.

Giving me side eye, she says, "Are you trying to get me drunk?"

Holding my hand to my heart, I promise, "Never. I have food inside once we get you all unloaded."

"Food first. Unload second."

"Your wish is my command. Follow me."

She stops as she walks into the living room. "Oh my goodness. It looks amazing. What did you do?"

"I strung some white Christmas lights to give it a more muted appearance, and I lit some candles. Nothing much. Wait till you see the deck."

"The deck? I thought you were getting it repaired."

"Well, my deck guy came in and said to repair would cost as much as it would to replace with some new composite materials. Come see." I open the sliding glass doors, and we both walk outside. "I know you have some holes, which will be filled tomorrow." I point to each open spot. "This is where the smoker will go. The grill arrived today and is already in, and the propane tank can be moved inside to the garage when you aren't at the house. The stove top will arrive tomorrow, and it has a locking cover. And I added a sink and fridge."

She has a puzzled expression. *Crap. Was this too much?* "Is it okay?"

"It's amazing, but you didn't have to do all of this. This is easily a hundred-thousand-dollar renovation. I'll pay you back what this all cost, I promise. We thought you might spend five hundred dollars getting a few of the rotted boards fixed. I can't believe you did all of this, and within a week!"

Breathing a sigh of relief, I say, "It wasn't a big deal. I knew you wanted it ready for the partners meeting." Holding her by the arms, I peer into her eyes. "Besides, this will be a place for our kids one day, and I wanted it done how I thought it would work best for all of us."

She smiles. "Our kids? Putting the cart before the horse, don't you think?"

"Well maybe, but that was my reasoning. Please know that I'm completely and totally in love with you."

"You are?" She wraps her arms around my neck and kisses me. "I'm completely and totally in love with you, too."

I feel settled. I don't think I've ever been this happy. We sit down and enjoy the beach from the patio. "This is truly amazing. We can sit here and watch the sunset." Turning to me, she warms my heart when she says, "I love it," and kisses me deeply. "Can we eat out here tonight? I know you set a beautiful table, but this truly is a tremendous addition to the house. Jim and Carol are going to love it."

I'm satisfied and happy that she loves it as much as I hoped she would. "I was hoping you'd want to eat out here."

We unload her car and get things put away. Sara snacks as I make dinner, and we talk about our days, our jobs and our families. Jim and Carol sound amazing. I know they must be proud of her.

After we eat and clean up, Sara loops her arm into mine and walks with me down to the beachfront. As we walk along the beach, we hold hands and wander aimlessly, the tide lapping at our feet, the seagulls singing their songs as they fish for their evening dinners.

Only a few of the beach houses have lights on, but as we pass, Sara tells me about the people who live in each one.

"You met Mackenzie at the bakery?"

"I did."

"This is her parents' place. Like us, they were mostly summer residents, but we were inseparable growing up. I'm a little older, but we would ride our bikes into town for ice cream, talking about boys and our grand plans for our futures."

"Did they turn out like you thought?"

"Not in our wildest dreams. They turned out better."

When we make our way back to the beach house, I lead her inside, then close and lock the door behind me. Her mouth crashes into mine, and we cling to each other as if we hadn't spent the afternoon together.

I pull her into the living room after me, hungry for more. Swaying her hips to an invisible beat as she removes her clothes and exposes herself, she moans before I even touch her.

Breathing in her delicious scent, I whisper, "So beautiful," and press my tongue to the center of her wetness, lapping a few times before moving to suck her clit into my mouth. She jerks at my touch and releases my hand, moving hers above me and latching onto the couch behind her head as her moans start to pour from her lips. My tongue is thick and deliciously wet as I rhythmically drag it across her core. The slight pressure of my fingers against her entrance has her crying out.

"I want to hear my name when you come, Sara." I lick her and she glances down at me, the expression on her face shooting an arrow deep into the core of my desire.

"Anything you want. Just please don't stop." She reaches to me and grips the top of my head, pulling me back down. "Trey," she groans a couple minutes later, writhing beneath me.

I sit back on my heels and smile, licking my lips and cleaning my fingers with my tongue. "I want more."

"Me, too." She scoots forward and wraps me in a hug, pulling me flush against her as she presses her lips to my ear and licks softly. "I want all of you."

"I'm all yours, baby. Take anything you want." My cock nudges her, finding her slick and ready. I groan. "Always ready for me."

Removing a foil packet from my pocket, I quickly tear it open and sheath my throbbing cock. It's only moments before I'm inside her, opening her wide. Her mouth opens in a silent cry as I seat myself completely inside her.

We eventually move to the bedroom and continue to alternate between sleep and our lovemaking, moving from soft and slow to hard and fast and back.

My Friday morning wake-up call is my favorite kind. Sara is remarkable. Her mouth is perfect as she gets on her knees, stroking my hard and wanting member.

She pauses and murmurs, "I think it's bigger this morning," before taking it deep in her mouth, sucking up and down while staring right at me, flattening her tongue so she can take more of my length deep into her throat. When she pulls up, she flicks at the tip, an incredible sensation. At the same time, one of her hands cups my balls and plays with them while the other holds my cock steady at the base as she works it in and out of her delicate mouth. Fire spreads through my veins—pure, hot, unadulterated lust.

God help me, I want her.

It doesn't take long before I warn her that I'm going to come, but she doesn't stop. I shoot my load deep down her throat, and she keeps going, swallowing every last drop.

"Fuck, girl. You're incredible," I exclaim as she smiles and wipes her wet chin.

She cuddles in close and wraps her arms around me. "Well, good morning to you, too."

I reach beneath the sheets for her hard, pink nipples, rolling them between my thumb and forefinger and tugging. Gently, I suck her hard nub into the warmth of my mouth, losing myself in a sea of emotions as her head falls back and her hips move with the rhythm of my tongue. Applying pressure to her swollen nub, I circle it over and over as I insert a finger and rub at her G-spot. Her moans encouraging me to keep going, she grabs my hair in one hand and pulls on her precious nipples with the other. Moving her pussy as if she's fucking my face, she climaxes, releasing her delicious musky scent all over my face and tongue with a glorious moan.

Breathing heavy, she grins down at me. "Yep. That's my idea of a workout."

I laugh. "Agreed."

We finally get out of bed and work our way to the bathroom. "Too bad there isn't enough room in the shower for two," I tell her.

"I saw your bathroom, you know. I think we could put all the partners in that shower."

"You could be right, but I'm not sure I want to see Emerson naked. She's essentially my sister."

"She's the only one you don't want to see? I'm not sure I want to see any of my partners naked."

"I only have eyes for you."

Rolling her eyes, she tells me, "You're too slick, and that means trouble."

"And here I thought you were the troublemaker."

Eventually, we settle down at opposite ends of the dining room table to work. I make coffee for both of us, making sure to add a hazelnut-flavored creamer to her cup.

When I place a mug in front of her, she takes a deep smell and then a sip. "You're too good for me."

I kiss her forehead. "Anything for you."

We finally get going when the phone rings from the front gate, alerting us to our delivery. The deck is almost complete.

While they begin their installation, we move to the dining room to work. She settles into her seat, examining her e-mail and typing away. I have a conference call, though I wind up watching her while I talk to several members of my team. Never does she glance up and break her concentration. As she studies her computer screen, I see a crease between her brows that deepens at times. She's beautiful.

I admire everything about her, from the way the breeze blows her hair to the soft lilt to her voice. But what makes me fall head over heels for her is the way she deals with her clients and partners. She puts them at ease with her authority and confidence. They hang on her every word, and she always knows what to say.

Her phone rings and she steps out of the room to take the call. I hear her laugh as she joins me once more.

"You'll never guess what the partners wanted to do. They wanted to come tonight."

"Are they coming?" *Oh, please don't let that happen. I have plans for us.*

"God no! They can come over tomorrow. We aren't ready for guests, and... I want you a little longer to myself."

"Have I told you recently how much I love you?" I hug her tightly, kissing the top of her head.

I should tell her that I have a business trip to Seattle next week. I'll do my best to work it in, but I also want to assure her of my love for her. I know that she's had a tough few months dealing with her mother's rejection and I want her to know how much I love her.

TREY

*E*XCEPT TO GO TO THE BATHROOM or take an occasional call, Sara's hardly moved from the chair she sat in nine hours earlier. Dressed in yoga pants and a sweatshirt, she glances up to find me showered and dressed in pressed khaki pants and a dark blue gingham shirt.

Eyes wide, she says, "You're all dressed up." She looks at her computer, then flicks her gaze back to me. "Oh! I'm sorry. My day got away from me. I promise I can be showered and ready to go in a few minutes."

"Take your time. I've ordered dinner in, so we aren't going anywhere. I just wanted an excuse to not be in sweats all day."

She turns crimson. "I'm sorry. I have some nicer clothes. I'll get changed."

"Again, don't worry about it. You look good in everything." I leave her to her routine and set up a small table in front of the fireplace with a nice tablecloth I found in town. I place the box with the sea glass bracelet and earrings on the table. The doorbell rings at exactly six, and I open the door to Sara's friend.

"Mackenzie. Thank you for delivering this. You're making me look like a hero."

"No problem. I'm happy to help. I've included a few notes on prep, so I'll get out of your way."

"Wait! Don't you want to say something to Sara? Let me get her."

"Oh no, that isn't necessary. I'll talk to her tomorrow."

"I think she'll be disappointed to know you were here and didn't at least say hello." I walk back toward the bathroom. "Sara? Mackenzie's here. She delivered dinner, and I told her you'd be disappointed if you didn't speak to her before she left."

"Really? You talked Mackenzie into making dinner? She's an amazing chef, so we're in for a treat."

Sara walks into the living room with her arms extended. "Mackenzie! You cooked for us? What did he promise you?"

Mackenzie stretches out her arms to hug Sara. "Great to see you. Once he told me it was for you, I knew I had to get my old culinary skills out. I hope you like it."

"Are you kidding me? I know we'll love it. When are you in the bakery tomorrow?"

"I'll be there at 5:00 a.m."

"Well, I promise to come by for coffee, a blueberry scone and a few minutes of your time."

Mackenzie gives Sara another hug and, just above a whisper, says, "This one may be a keeper. And he's arm candy, too."

Sara stares at me. "Unfortunately he knows it." She winks at me and my heart races.

I plate the food, just finishing as Sara walks back in from seeing Mackenzie off. Her hair is down and full of soft curls around her face. She put on some makeup that nicely accents her eyes, and she's in a muted green pair of silk pants with a beautiful pastel yellow sweater that compliments her tan. She looks like a present. And then I see them. She's wearing beautiful high-heeled sandals that make me want to bend her over and unwrap her.

"You're staring."

"You look beautiful," I tell her earnestly.

She crosses her arms in front of herself. "You're embarrassing me."

"I plan on lavishing you with all sorts of compliments tonight," I say with a wicked smile.

She shakes her head, giggling. "Okay. What did Mackenzie make us for dinner?"

"We have oysters on the half shell, a mixed green salad, an abalone chowder, grilled halibut and for dessert—other than each other—a chocolate tart with homemade ice cream."

"You have no idea what a treat we're in for."

We sit down and Sara sees the box. "What's this?"

"I saw this and thought of you, and I wanted to thank you for setting me up with Jim and Carol to stay here."

"I didn't do that much."

"Open it." I watch as she removes the simple ribbon and opens the box. Her eyes light up and a big smile crosses her face.

"I love it! How did you know I love sea glass?"

"It reminds me of your eyes."

She gives me a warm embrace that quickly leads to a long and deep kiss. My erection becomes obvious and she pants, "If we don't stop, all of Mackenzie's hard work will be for nothing."

Sara's right, our meal is amazing. We spend dinner talking

about our life journeys and what we want out of life.

"You've made 'Sexiest Man' lists and 'Most Eligible' lists. What do you want?" she asks.

I'm surprised by her question. No one other than my family has ever asked that of me. "Well, I'm not sure I want to run the family business my whole life. I may not have a choice, but I know I want a family, and I want to live outside of the limelight."

"All the attention must be tough, but you must like all the girls swooning."

Thoughtfully, I share, "I did when I was younger. But I got my heart broken a few times."

"Wait! You got *your* heart broken?"

"Yes. Why is that so hard to believe?"

"Because you've always had a bevy of women chasing you."

"True, but I learned quickly that they wanted something from me. They weren't interested in *me*." Sara is visibly surprised by my admission. "Do you remember Jennifer Martin, the actress I dated?"

"Of course. I was in grad school and watched that like one would a train wreck."

"Well, I liked her. She was honest and vulnerable, or so I thought. In reality, she used me to up her profile and get parts in movies. Thankfully the movies were all flops, so I'm glad about karma."

"Okay, I buy that. You did date her for six years though, so there must've been something else for her than the notoriety."

I'm humiliated that she's pointed out my biggest embarrassment, so I steer the conversation away from Jennifer. "I can't deny that, over the years, I've slept with a lot of women. However,

I do have rules. Always wear a condom, never leave the condom behind, never bring her back to my place—or my parents', for that matter—never spend the night, never film, and most important, make sure she's satisfied."

She glances down and blushes. "You're very good at the satisfying. And we've always spent the nights together."

I reach across the table and grasp her hand. "Sara, you're different than anyone I've dated in a long time. You don't care about my family, you don't care about my checkbook, and you don't need anything from me."

"I don't know about that. I love your family. CeCe is the sister I never had and I love her, and I think I do want something from you. I want to be respected, valued and adored."

"I want to do all that."

Gazing at me through the candlelight, she whispers, "I believe that."

SARA

I WAKE BEFORE TREY and listen to his rhythmic breathing, thinking about our romantic night. I adore the sea glass bracelet and earrings. I'm sure I have several things I can wear them with.

Trey took wonderful care of me both mentally and physically. After dinner, we sat together by the fire and snuggled in close. I don't think I've ever been this happy in my life.

I want to stay in bed together with him all day, but I know the partners will be arriving early. Pulling on my yoga pants and a sweatshirt, I stop by the kitchen to start a large pot of coffee, then walk out to the new deck. Trey did an amazing job. He hid the patio kitchen well so people walking the public beach won't see it, but also managed to place the patio in such a way that it captures the waterfront view perfectly.

I hear the sliding glass door open behind me, and then his arms wrap around me. I feel safe and secure in his embrace. He brings me in tight and kisses the top of my head. "Good morning."

I hold his arms, and together we watch the daybreak. Sunlight fills the sky, pure scattered light ambitiously illuminating each crevice of the land. Sparrows chirp an explicit background melody. The trees shine as if they're wearing golden crowns, and the vast ocean is unable to absorb the bright sparks of the sun. The waves race among each other to reach the horizon from where the mighty sun appears.

Happiness fills my soul, and I turn and kiss him deeply. When our tongues touch, it feels as if I'm being zapped with a thousand watts of electricity. It's hot, raw and aggressive. My pulse increases as I arch my back and press my breasts into him, showing they're aching to be caressed, licked and sucked. I growl against his lips in appreciation of what my body is doing all on its own.

Pressing into him, I feel the rhythmic beat inside his chest. He fits so well with me, including his cock, which is nestled at the apex of my thighs. I'm under an attack of the most erotic kind. What we're doing is even more risqué, because people are beginning to walk the beach and we're essentially in public.

"If we don't stop, we'll be greeting the partners in our birthday suits," he murmurs.

"I know you're right, but"—pointing to his obvious erection, I tell him with a sultry smile—"someone thinks it doesn't matter."

He throws his head back in a deep and hearty laugh.

"Hopefully he can behave himself for the next twelve hours. If he can, he'll be happily rewarded."

We spend the morning preparing. The brisket's in the oven to slow-cook, the ribs are in the smoker with Trey's "secret dry rub," and we made the coleslaw. We make a quick run into town to hit the bakery for our order. The bell chimes as I walk in. "Hello?"

Mackenzie comes from the back, wiping her hands on a towel attached to her apron. "Hey! How was dinner last night?"

"You completely outdid yourself," I gush.

"Truly one of the best meals in my life," Trey adds.

"You're both very kind. I have your coffee and scones. Can you stay for a few?"

"Just a few. We have all the partners in my firm coming over for the afternoon, and I still need to get a few things done before they arrive." Glancing at Trey, I grin. "But I may be back next week."

He blanches as I say that. Something's up. I thought he wanted to tell me something last night, but he never did.

"Great. I love when you're in town and can visit."

We spend some time catching up, but then I see the time and tell her we have to go.

As we head out, I give her a tight hug, and she whispers in my ear, "He's a keeper. You deserve someone who adores you like he seems to."

I smile. "Give Paul a big hug for me and tell him to hurry up and make me an aunt." I wave goodbye as we head back to our car loaded with fresh rolls and desserts.

As Trey buckles his seat belt, he turns to me and says, "We're going to eat well this afternoon."

EMERSON, DILLON AND CECE are the first to arrive. Walking around, they admire the house and surrounding area and start planning the partner retreat.

"Be careful," I tell them. "The whole team may not agree. I've gotten the okay if we choose to meet, but you need to remember the beach house isn't that big, and it certainly isn't a five-star hotel and resort. It'll be a lot of work on our own."

"Are you kidding? This place is perfect. You and Trey can stay in the room you're in. Dillon and I will stay in the other adjoining room. CeCe and Greer will be in one of the bunkbed rooms, with Cameron and Mason in the other. If Charles and Margo want to stay here, Dillon and I will move into the bunkbed rooms. I know it's a lot of people, but we can do a few team-building events out on the beach or hike up at Mount Tamalpais State Park. This great outdoor kitchen area is perfect for cooking and eating. Plus, it's secluded, so we won't have to worry about anyone eavesdropping when we talk about sensitive matters. I think it's an easy sell to the team."

I've learned to not question Emerson and just roll with it. "You're probably right."

Cameron and Mason arrive with Charles and Margo right behind them. Everyone wanders around for a bit, then settles on the deck. Trey's made sure everyone has a drink as he grills the chicken, and we spend the time catching up. Margo is preening like a peacock over her son, and each time she sees me, she hugs me and gives me a compliment.

"I love your hair like that."

"Trey is so lucky."

"That green really brings out the green flecks in your eyes."

"We all love you."

There is so much hugging and touching, I'm struggling. I don't think I've had this much physical contact in a year.

Lunch is a success. Emerson takes an informal poll, and we all agree to have our partner meeting here late next month.

There'll be many more tourists by that point, but we'll have a lot of fun. We agree to leave early on a Friday morning and caravan over. The hope is that we'll have a new business development partner who can join us.

As we talk, we learn that Cameron, Dillon and Mason have been speaking to some candidates Emerson's identified for the position. It's down to a man and a woman, and they've set up time for me to talk to them later next week.

Charles has a report from the investigator regarding the mole. It isn't much, but it's agreed that they're behind the public relations nightmare.

After that, we spend the bulk of our time talking about prospective investments. The team is further along with their evaluations, and the hope is that by next week, some confidential information will be moving around the office and more vulnerable to being stolen.

Our meeting goes until after five, and we pick through what's left of lunch as we go along.

Eventually Trey stands and shares, "There's a great pizza place downtown. Shall I order in, or do we want to move this party over to the pizza place?"

Charles and Margo stand as well. "We're going to head out before it gets too hard to climb out of here in the dark." Winking at Trey, Margo continues, "Enjoy your time with your friends. Your dad and I are thrilled that you found a quiet spot and are able to enjoy yourself."

Trey gives them both a big hug, and he and his dad make plans to speak again next week. CeCe steps in and gives her parents a warm embrace. "I'll be by tomorrow. You both drive carefully. Love you."

I'm a bit envious. Jim and Carol know me and love me, and I love them, but I've never allowed them to hug me too often, and I struggle if they become too affectionate. I lean over to Emerson. "Do you think they'll have any problems with the drive home?"

She shakes her head. "I think they'll be fine. Mason said they actually led the way here."

Trey grasps my hand, squeezes it and leans over to me. "I think the rest of the team plan on staying the night."

Glancing around the room, I realize he's right. "I agree. Is that okay with you? This is technically your place this month, after all."

"I don't mind at all. I'd rather have time alone with you, but this group of people is probably the closest friends I have. I love the company."

I can't help but remember the look he had on his face when I referenced coming back next weekend. I think something's up, and it makes me nervous.

TREY

A FTER MY FOLKS HEAD HOME, the remaining team announces they're going to stay. I tell them, "I charge rent if you all are going to stay the night."

Cameron speaks up, "You're dating one of our favorite people, you owe us, my friend. Right now, you're in a rental situation, but when you decide to buy, the cost is significant."

We all laugh, but at the heart of it, I know that I'm only fully accepted by this group through Sara. Yet another reason to know that she's amazing. She has created a family that fiercely protects her. "I'm in the mood for pizza. Do we want to go into town or order delivery?"

We all agree to drive into town to get pizza after my parents leave, Emerson saying, "The more I can see here, the more I can plan for our retreat."

We're a little past the dinner hour, but they happily invite us in. Thankfully we're the only people in the restaurant, because we're loud and very rowdy. They bring us several pizzas that are house specialties, and we enjoy a local beer and laugh our way through our evening. I sit next to Sara and hold her hand under the table.

After we keep the restaurant open well beyond their typical hours, we pay for our pizzas, tip them extremely well for staying late, and then caravan back to the beach house. Sara and I weren't drinking, so we're the drivers.

When we return, we sit around the fire and hang out. Mason gets out a twenty-five-year old bottle of scotch he brought with him, and it's so smooth. CeCe brought wine from a new vineyard she, Greer, and Hadlee found and want to sample for Emerson and Dillon's wedding. Too much drinking and, not surprising, everyone packed an overnight bag.

As I lie in bed with Sara spooning in close, I press tight behind her, kiss her head and finally tell her, "I'm going to Seattle for a few weeks."

"A few weeks? When are you leaving?"

"Monday. We're trying to make sure we don't lose an acquisition we have in the works. I'm sorry. We decided late last Friday, and I wanted to tell you, but I didn't want to ruin our weekend."

Taking a big breath, she sighs. "I get it. Don't worry about me." She's quiet, and I don't know what to say. "Sara, I still want to be with you. I'm not breaking up with you. I'll have meetings that take me out of town at times, a downside to my job. But I'd love it if you flew up to Seattle to join me next weekend."

"I'm sorry, I don't mean to make a big deal of this. This is just all very new and exciting for me, and I'm very sensitive to all this. I only wish you would've told me earlier."

"We've had a great weekend. Let's focus on that."

I know she thinks I want away from her, but I do have the purchase of Cedar Pine Cypress Technologies to take care of. They're nervous to be selling to us after my sex video made the news. Paul Ellington is a conservative Christian and struggles to sell the company to what he sees as a giant conglomerate with a leader with no morals.

What I don't want Sara to know is that I have plans to meet Catherine and her husband to get a feel for what's going on. I'll go out of my way to talk to Sara at least once a day, and hopefully I can talk her into coming up to Seattle with me at some point.

FIFTY

SARA

T HE WEEKEND WAS FUN until he told me he's leaving. I understand it would've ruined our weekend, but he could've given me a warning: "Hey, Sara, the acquisition is heating up and I may have to go to Seattle. Just a heads-up." Would that have been so hard?

I think he was hoping to stay with me on Sunday night at my place in The City, but after we lock up the beach house, I give him a chaste kiss and tell him I'll talk to him later in the week.

I make the drive through the park and reflect on what he said, and I overthink it all. I realize I'm too raw from all the mess with Henry and my birth mother. Maybe that disappointment is why I'm taking the Seattle trip so hard. It's not his fault and I know I'm being ridiculous.

My cell phone pings, and it's Trey: Miss you already.

It makes me feel so much better. I know I'm being a jerk; he really is the perfect guy for me. I text him back: Miss you, too.

I'm relieved to be home, and I'm mad at myself for overreacting. I shouldn't be making a big deal of a slight change. We had fun, and I can't seem to focus on that. So I do what I always do and pour myself into my work, going until after midnight to catch up on missing out this weekend.

When I finally turn in for the night, I'm restless. I realize that I sleep better with Trey. I miss him.

I fall asleep thinking of the nice time we had this weekend, the beautiful bracelet and earrings, and the incredible deck he had built. I keep replaying our weekend and try to focus on the fun we had. He was clear that he wasn't breaking up with me, so I'm going to try to put all my negative thoughts out of my mind.

Rolling over before the alarm sounds, I check my phone as I finally get moving and see a text that came in from Trey at 5:00 a.m. I'm boarding my flight. Wish you were here. I'll let you know when I land.

I'm conflicted. I want to text back and tell him to have a safe flight, but he's probably close to landing at this point. Instead, I text him: Welcome to Seattle. Good luck, and I'll talk to you tonight if you have time.

I feel better about where we are, and it lifts my spirits.

When I finally arrive at the office, work is crazy busy, but he's never far from my thoughts. It seems to be one of those days where I don't even have time to go to the bathroom. When I see Trey calling on FaceTime, I glance at my wall clock and realize it's almost six.

"Hey."

His hair is frazzled, but he looks yummy. "Hi, beautiful. How was your day?"

"Very busy. Playing hooky on Friday has caught up with me."

"I'm sorry. You did work all day on Friday."

"I did, but there was an Adonis who kept distracting me."

"Wow. An Adonis? I'm flattered. But I had a beautiful woman who was distracting me nonstop all day."

I'm blushing from head to toe and need to change the subject, or we'll be having FaceTime sex—if that is such a thing. My office is all glass, so there's no way to hide what I'm doing. "What did you do today?"

"Mickey Johns met me at the airport, and we spent the morning preparing for our meeting with Cedar Pine Cypress Technologies."

"Their name is really Cedar Pine Cypress Technologies? As in the wood they believe made the cross for the crucifixion?"

"Wow, I'm impressed. Most people don't know that."

"I had a set of foster parents who were born again, and that's one thing I remember from their lectures."

"Their founder and CEO is a devout Christian. We met with the chief financial officer this afternoon, and tonight we're having dinner with the CEO, who owns the largest number of shares."

"What are you expecting?"

"Because of his faith, I've been warned that he's concerned about the videos."

"Oh crap!"

"Yeah, that's why I'm here. I need to assure him that I was secretly filmed and that I'm not searching for a lot of attention. I'm sure you'll come up in conversation often, and he most likely will want to meet you at some point."

"This is different than the mergers and acquisitions we usually do."

We talk for about twenty minutes more, sharing mindless activities and things we observed during the day. It's comforting to know we can talk about silly things.

He glances at his watch. "Okay, honey, I guess I should get downstairs to meet up with Mickey so we can meet our dinner guest. Can I call you later?"

"Of course."

"Good night, sweetheart."

"Good night."

I stare at the phone long after he's gone, then slowly realize I'm not productive sitting here in my office any longer. It's already been a fourteen-hour day.

Turning off my computer, I pack up and head out the door to catch the bus home, walking in the fresh air usually helping to clear my thoughts. I get to my bus stop and stare beyond the tall buildings at the stars—the great expanse of the sky makes me feel even smaller and more insignificant. It's times like this that I think of Catherine. Tears of rejection beg to be set free, but I won't give in to them.

I come to the realization that I'm more than her biological daughter. I have wonderful foster parents who truly care and love me. I have friends who've stuck by me when life's been difficult. And I have a man who, despite my pushing him away repeatedly, still seems to care about me. Life is good, and I need to embrace it.

TREY

*T*HINGS ARE FINALLY ON TRACK with Cedar Pine Cypress Technologies, so it's time to tackle the next reason I'm here in Seattle. The private investigator found Catherine, who her attorney is, and how he's sheltering her. I've contacted my attorney and set up a meeting at her attorney's office for today.

I arrive a few minutes late on purpose. I don't want to be sitting with her in a waiting room or conference room. We all shake hands and sit down.

"Mr. Arnault, you asked for this meeting, and it seems rather out of place. What can we do for you?" her lawyer asks.

Catherine's in a black pantsuit, cream blouse and a strand of pearls with matching earrings. She and Sara could be twins. "Well, my girlfriend is Sara White." She blanches at Sara's name and fidgets, obviously uncomfortable with my statement. "I don't know if you're aware, but your husband is CEO of a company that Sandy Systems is currently doing due diligence to purchase. This is not public knowledge, but our personal lives are about to collide."

"I'm confused," her attorney says. "Why would your personal lives collide?"

Deferring to Catherine, I ask, "Do you want to tell him?"

If looks could kill, I'd be dead. She remains quiet, and her attorney asks, "What do I need to know, Catherine?"

Since she's choosing to remain silent, I explain. "Sara White is Paul and Catherine's daughter, and she was abandoned by them when Sara was three years old." The room is silent. "It's my understanding that Paul doesn't know Sara exists, but once the announcement of this sale goes through, because of my notoriety, the press will be talking about her." Taking a picture of Sara from my pocket, I put it on the table. "People will most likely learn that Sara was abandoned at three years old at a Catholic church in San Francisco. As you can see, Sara and Catherine could be sisters."

Catherine stands. "How dare you blackmail me!"

Her lawyer reaches for her arm and says, "Catherine, sit down. Let's hear what Mr. Arnault wants."

"I know what he wants," she spits. "He wants me to acknowledge her existence so she can inherit my money."

I laugh. "Do you have any idea who Sara is? You're shameful. I've seen the letters she sent to you. She doesn't want anything from you. And by the way, she's richer than you and me combined. It's going to get out that you dumped your daughter with a priest in San Francisco, and how you've withheld that information from your husband and children. No, I'm not threatening you, Catherine. I'm warning you." I stand up and look her in the eye. "I began the acquisition of Cedar Pine Cypress Technologies long before I began dating Sara. I was surprised when I learned your husband was Sara's father. He's been all about holding a secretly recorded sex video against me in the negotiations. Let me be clear. I love Sara, and I won't let her be dragged through the mud and castigated by you. The world will know what you did."

Her lawyer speaks up at that. "Mr. Arnault, are you threatening to release information about Catherine and Paul Ellington?"

I laugh a deep belly laugh. "I don't have to. The press has already started to get wind of Sara, and enough people know her life story. She's been written about in the legal press, and it's no secret that she has a delightful rags-to-riches story. Once the press pulls together that your client dumped her daughter at a church, then proceeded to marry her father and have four more children with him, they're going to be a pack of rabid dogs. Not to mention, as you can see from the photo, Sara is the spitting image of her mother. No, I don't have to leak information. My notoriety will push the gossip press to find it themselves, and you won't be able to deny it."

Catherine stands once again. "I won't be blackmailed."

Her lawyer reaches for her arm, and as I walk out, I warn her, "I'm inviting Sara up this weekend. I'd suggest you let your family know by Saturday, because I plan on taking her to the ball to benefit the Museum of Flight. The press will be there, and I'm introducing Sara as my girlfriend, so it won't be a secret to anyone by Sunday morning. The press will know everything by this time next week. Listen to your lawyer. He knows I'm right."

SARA MAY NEVER KNOW what I did, but I do know that if I didn't, it would affect the negotiations of our purchase of Cedar

Pine Cypress Technologies. I'll do whatever I can to protect Sara. I won't let Catherine's actions affect her. My family adores Sara, and with the help of Jim and Carol, her partners at SHN and her friends, we'll all show her how loved she is.

Picking up my phone, I scroll through some of the pictures I've taken of her when we were together. I miss her, so I push the FaceTime app and call her. She answers, and I see her beautiful face on the screen. My heart beats faster with her subtle smile. "Hey, you. How was your day?"

She sits back in her seat and relaxes before she says, "Busy, but that's nothing new. How was yours?"

I share with her all the ins and outs of my day without mentioning my meeting with Catherine. "I have tickets to the hottest event in Seattle on Saturday night. Can you come with me? It's at the Museum of Flight. It should be a lot of fun."

She lights up. "I'm not sure I have anything to wear."

"Don't let that stop you. I know you can find a lot of options in San Francisco, or we can go shopping that morning here in Seattle. I'd love to help you pick something out," I tell her with a devilish grin.

"I can call someone at Nordstrom. Are you sure?"

"More than sure. I'll send you the flight information. Can you leave Thursday night?"

"I have an interview on Friday morning with a potential attorney. I could probably be at the San Francisco airport by one, if they have a flight."

"I'll get back to you." In a quiet voice, I add, "I've missed you this week."

SARA

I'VE SPOKEN WITH TREY at least once every day this week. I'm in love with him. I'm certain on that. He never leaves my mind, always with me mentally if not physically. It's incomprehensible. He's my one stable force, my rock in a world filled with chaos, and I desperately need that in my life. I can't believe I've only recently realized it.

It's strange—frightening, even—how you can go from someone being a complete stranger to then being completely infatuated with them. Wondering how it ever was that you were able to live without them because you sure as hell couldn't imagine being without them now. He's my best friend and, as cheesy as it sounds, he's my anchor.

My cell phone pings, and I see it's Henry: I'm coming over. Can you meet me at Starbucks for a cup of coffee? It pings again. I'll be there in 15 minutes.

Me: I'm very busy today. It's not a good time.

Henry: Please. It's urgent.

I absolutely resent being summoned by Henry. I've told him time and again that we are nothing more than work colleagues.

Besides, right now he's only the major shareholder of his company. He currently doesn't run it because of the lawsuit, so there's no reason why I should be dealing with him at all.

I tell Annabel on my way out, "Henry Sinclair has texted me that he's at Starbucks across the street and would like to meet me. Can you please tell Mason that he's welcome to join me?"

I walk down to Starbucks, bitter that Henry's essentially dropping by unannounced. I see him sitting in the corner, and he waves to me.

"Thank you for coming down. I picked up a drink for you."

I take a seat opposite him. "Thank you. What is it?"

"It's your regular drink—a nonfat latte," he replies, obviously proud of himself.

I'm too irritated to tell him that isn't my drink. "Thank you." I take a sip, missing the hazelnut flavoring that reduces the coffee bitterness. "What do you need?"

Henry reaches forward, grasps my hand and says, "Claudia has agreed to grant me a divorce. We can be together."

I almost choke on my drink. "Henry, let me be very clear. I'm involved with someone else. I'm not interested in you romantically. I'm not in a place to be able to be your friend. Please only e-mail and text me if you need something work-related, because moving forward, that'll be the only time we need to interact." I rise from the table, proud for standing up for myself, and leave him to walk back up to my office, stopping long enough to ask the barista, "Can you add three pumps of sugar-free hazelnut flavoring?"

As I walk out, Mason and Cameron approach me. "What did he want? Are you okay?" Mason asks.

"Thanks for walking over. Henry wanted to tell me he's divorcing his wife." Cameron and Mason both blanch, but I assure them, "Not to worry, he's getting his just desserts."

I HAD SPOKEN TO JENNIFER at Nordstrom this morning and explained about the fundraiser in Seattle. "Do you have anything that might work for me?"

"I have the perfect outfit for you. I can bring it over this afternoon. Do you have a time preference?"

Jennifer arrives a little after four thirty and brings with her a stunning Calvin Klein navy blue full-length sleeveless gown, a beautiful and sexy silver pump with a matching handbag, and a silver cashmere pashmina wrap. She includes matching LaPerla lingerie, and surprises me with a rental of a diamond necklace and matching cuff from Cartier.

Staring at the stunning shimmering jewels, I gush, "How did you manage the jewelry?"

"Well, I know the manager of the store, and I shared that you were headed to Seattle and most likely would be photographed wearing it. It didn't take much, but I did give him your Black Amex number in case it doesn't make it back or you decide to keep it."

I laugh and pull her in for a warm embrace. "You're a lifesaver. Thank you, Jennifer!"

"Have a great time. And when you get back, let's work on a spring wardrobe for you."

"Deal!"

I DIDN'T SLEEP WELL at all last night. I'm nervous to have all these diamonds in my possession, and I'm also excited to see Trey and spend a weekend with him in Seattle.

I arrive at the office early, and Annabel's there waiting for me. "Good morning."

"Good morning, Annabel. I certainly don't expect you to be here in the office so early."

"Oh, I don't mind. The learning curve is a bit steeper than I expected, so I'm putting in the extra hours to make sure I get caught up. Plus, I knew you were heading out early today and would probably need me. I'll head out a bit early myself if I'm done and you're good with it."

"Sounds good. Elizabeth Rollins will be coming in to interview for the attorney position about nine. Please let me know when she gets here."

My interview with Elizabeth goes well. I like her and set her to meet with the other partners so they can give their rubber stamp of approval. She went to Santa Clara for law school and realized the actual practice of law isn't for her, but she's outgoing enough to blend in with our company culture while also serious enough to get her work done.

I share, "My plan for the position is to help with all the due diligence and help to draft the sales contracts. You don't have any experience in this area, so it may take some time to get you up to speed. "

"I'd love the opportunity to learn from you and take as much off your plate as you're willing to give me."

Before leaving, I poke my head into Emerson's office. "I like

Elizabeth. If Mason, Cameron and Dillon like her, and her references work out, then I'm good with offering her a job.

"Great. You headed back to Stinson?"

"No. Trey is in Seattle, so I'm heading there." I wave and start for the elevators, my car service having alerted me that they're two minutes from arrival.

"Have fun. I want details on Monday," she yells after me.

As I exit the elevator, I see the car waiting for me, and he whisks me off to the airport and drops me at the departures area. I walk right through to security and make it just in time for boarding. Sitting in my first-class seat, I worry about having close to a million dollars in diamonds in my carry-on.

When I land and walk out to the arrivals area, I see him standing at the base of the escalators holding a sign with my name on it. Women are standing around and staring, and I see several taking photos with their cell phones. He's so sexy with his tie pulled down, the top button undone and his hair showing a bit of curl at the top.

Might as well lay claim to my man.

I walk up and give him a deep and passionate kiss, our tongues doing a delicate tango. "You look good enough to eat," I murmur.

"That sounds exciting. I think you can tell how much," he whispers as we pretend we don't hear the cameras clicking away. He takes my garment bag and drag bag and escorts me out to his waiting car.

Once we get settled in the back seat, his arm goes around me and I snuggle in close. "What's the plan?" I ask.

"We have dinner reservations downtown tonight, but first

we need to head into Bellevue and meet with a lawyer."

"Do you want me to wait in the car?"

"No, it's important you hear this. I'll want your perspective."

"No problem. Does it have anything to do with your acquisition?"

"Yes. Afterward, we'll head to the hotel and have dinner at the top of the Space Needle."

"Very touristy, but I love it."

Kissing me on the nose, he says with great affection, "I knew you would."

I pull out my carry-on and show him the Cartier boxes. "I don't know what to do with these, but I don't feel comfortable carrying them around."

"Wow. That's some serious ice."

"I know. I'm renting it to go with my dress tomorrow night. If you think it's too much, I can leave it in the hotel safe."

"I think it'll be perfect because you're wearing it."

It takes us almost an hour in traffic to get to Bellevue. We walk into the building elevator, and he lets the doors close before he turns to me and says, "Sara, I don't want this to be too big of a surprise. I want you to know that I love you very, very much. I'll explain everything over dinner." He pushes the button to the twenty-fourth floor, and we begin to rise.

"I love you, too, but you're making me nervous."

Kissing me, he assures me, "I love you. Remember that."

As we exit the elevator, a young woman is waiting for us. She walks us to a large conference room that overlooks the mountains and, in the distance, I can see Mount Rainier. She opens the door and asks if we'd like something to drink. We politely decline while a gentleman in his mid-fifties with sandy blond hair approaches. He watches me carefully.

He shakes hands with Trey and turns to me as Trey introduces him. "Sara, I'd like you to meet Paul Ellington."

My heart stops. Staring into his eyes, I see my own reflecting back. I know exactly who Paul Ellington is. He's my biological father.

He turns to a group of people behind him who look like him. "I know you've had some e-mail exchanges with my wife, Catherine." The woman next to him raises her trembling hand for a handshake. "And these are our children, Paul Junior, Michael, Grace and Mary."

I'm staring at replicas of me. I nod and murmur, "Hello. Very nice to meet you."

Paul continues, "Catherine has recently told us about you. I hate to admit this, but we're all in a bit of shock."

"I've had thirty-two years to deal with it, so I can only imagine." I feel the anger rising from within. Turning to Catherine, I spew, "You told me you wanted nothing to do with me."

"Sara, Catherine was young and confused. She didn't realize the repercussions her decision would have. She ran away from her parents and me when she learned she was pregnant. She didn't tell them, and she didn't tell me. In speaking with Father Tom, she thought by giving you to him, you would find a better family."

"Then why wouldn't she give up her parental rights when I asked her seventeen years ago?" Paul appears surprised, and Catherine gives me a look that could kill. "I spent my whole life waiting for you to come back. Never mind. It doesn't matter." I glance at Trey and find the courage. "This is the first time I've looked into anyone's eyes who's related to me. That's all I ever wanted." Staring at Catherine, I tell her, "You're the one who has to sleep every night knowing you left a three-year-old to the State of California and never looked back."

I can see how angry Catherine is becoming, but I'm not interested in any explanation she could give.

I look at Trey. "Do we need to do anything else?"

"No, sweetheart."

Paul implores, "Sara, this is very new to us. Catherine was young. She didn't know that leaving you behind with a priest would create so many problems for you." I'm stunned by this as he continues, his tone softening. "And I can see a bit of a surprise for you, too, right? We all want to get to know each other a bit better."

"I'm not sure I want that from you." Gazing around the room, I seethe, "From any of you, for that matter." Staring at Catherine and Paul, I assert, "I've essentially been on my own since I was three years old. If you didn't want me, you should've given me up for adoption rather than leaving me to hope that you were going to come get me one day."

Paul appears crestfallen. I hear his daughters sniff and cry. Catherine is fuming, and her boys are sitting stoically.

Looking at Trey, Paul inquires, "What are our next steps?"

"Know that it's going to get out what happened with Sara," Trey replies. "She's a big deal in the technology world and has been interviewed by several publications about her start in life. It took my private investigator less than a day to trace it to you. This is going to come out, and you need to prepare. I've lived in the limelight my entire life. It isn't easy. This is going to be hard on all of you."

"And when you want to blame me," I chime in, "remember that Catherine is the one who dumped me at a church and then refused to give up her parental rights when I was thirteen years old, so my loving foster parents weren't allowed to adopt me and protect me. And rather than welcome me, she's an ice-cold bitch. Blame her for the chaos that's about to rain down on you. Don't blame me. I'm the victim here. I lived in fourteen foster homes with creeps and abusers. People who only cared about a check they got for giving me a soiled bed."

At that, I turn and walk out to wait by the elevator. I want to cry but I don't, pinching my hand to distract me.

Trey stays behind a few more minutes and then meets me at the elevator. "Are you okay?" I nod and step into the waiting elevator. When the doors close, the dam releases and tears fall from my eyes. "I'm sorry. I didn't know until earlier this week that your father was the CEO of the company I'm buying. I knew it would get out in the tabloids, and I met with her to warn her the press would find out. Her lawyer spoke with her and Paul, and they agreed to tell the kids. Paul wanted to meet you. I'm sorry I didn't tell you this sooner, but I was afraid you'd refuse to go. The first time we talked, you shared that you wanted to meet the people who shared some of your genetic makeup, and I wanted to provide that."

I hug him tightly, still crying. "Thank you."

Dinner atop the Space Needle in the Sky City Restaurant is romantic yet also very touristy, and I love every minute of it. I won't let myself cry anymore. The look Catherine had when I mentioned the fourteen foster homes was a real surprise for her. I still don't understand why she's angry at me.

Trying to shake it off, I take in the splendor of the Puget Sound from the Space Needle's world-famous restaurant located five hundred feet above the ground. "Thank you for inviting me to Seattle. This is the first time I've been here. What a beautiful city. I don't want to rehash our afternoon. I hear Trey's cell phone ping repeatedly this evening, but he ignores it, so he can focus on me. "It's incredibly green compared to San Francisco. I can see why they call San Francisco a concrete jungle."

"They say it always rains here, but I haven't seen a drop."

The waiter hears Trey's comment and says, "It rains for nine months of the year here, which makes it gray and wet. But the other three months are spectacular, just like now."

Dinner is good, but I love the company better. Trey shares, "Tomorrow night, I'll be introducing you as my girlfriend. I've given the benefit your name. Normally I'd only list you as a guest, but I want you to be a part of my life for a very long time and not be a 'guest.' Because of that, the press will have your name, and you'll be in the tabloids for a while. I know we didn't discuss this upfront, but I wanted to control the story instead of them finding out who you were by digging through your trash. They're going to investigate you, and because you've done a few newspaper articles, they'll dig that up and ask you about it. It's a great story, and they'll run with it. Our life is going to be hectic for a few weeks, but I promise when something else happens, they'll move on. But I warn you, they're like roaches. Every time you feel you've killed them all, you'll realize there are five more hiding in the wall."

Giggling, I shake my head and exclaim, "That is gross."

"They're gross." He reaches for my hand across the table and gives me an assuring squeeze. Taking in the lights of The Sound, we watch the ferries shuttle people from Seattle to the various little islands.

Squeezing my hand tightly, I bring it to my mouth and softly kiss it. "What are you doing next weekend?"

"Well, I think I'll be able to come back to San Francisco on Friday. Do you want to go up to Stinson?"

"I'd like that. I'd also like you to meet Jim and Carol."

"I'd love to."

TREY

M Y WEEK DEALING with Cedar Pine Cypress Technologies is busy as we work through our agreement. As predicted, Sara is the bell of the tabloid media. They find the articles written in the *Law Journal,* and that blows up everywhere, so she goes into hiding in Stinson herself. It makes me smile to know we have a great place to hide out, at least until they figure it out.

Before I leave Seattle, Paul pulls me aside. "Catherine had a very difficult childhood. I know she made some very big mistakes with Sara, but she didn't do it out of malice. She feared how her lie would affect all of us. Please believe me, had I known about Sara, she would've been pulled from foster care and immediately come to live with us."

"She needs to hear that from you. Maybe not today, but one day."

He nods. "You can tell her that we're very proud of her. Her brothers and sisters would like to come down to San Francisco and spend some time with her. When she's ready. They're angry, but not with her. They feel like they've missed out on a big sister."

"Catherine has Sara's e-mail address, and I'd encourage them to reach out to her. I know she would love to get to know them."

"Was it as bad as she described?"

"I think it was worse. But when she was a teenager, she went to live with Jim and Carol. They were the first people who loved her. While they're not her legal parents, they've always been there for her. They got her into college with great scholarships and then to law school at UCLA."

He nods, and I see a bit of pride. "I hope to one day sit down and have some time with her."

"I hope for your sake that happens, too."

I'm happy for Sara. I know this is new and may make it awkward that my future father-in-law works for me, but together, Sara and I can do anything.

SARA MEETS ME AT THE AIRPORT when I return from Seattle, a few paparazzi hanging out around her. She's the flavor of the month. When I descend on the escalator, she opens a piece of paper just long enough for me to see that says 'Hot guy.' We laugh and embrace, and she kisses me while the camera bulbs pop.

As we drive to Stinson, I share with her what Paul said. She wipes a few tears away, then tells me, "I'd like to get to know my brothers and sisters. It wasn't their fault that our mom is a crazy bitch."

Laughing, I assure her, "All moms can be crazy bitches, you know."

"Not yours."

"Even CeCe would tell you she can be crazy. Don't be fooled."

"Well, you're going to meet Jim and Carol tonight. Are you nervous?"

"Terribly." I've been looking forward to meeting them, but I'm also nervous. What if they don't approve of all the attention I receive? What if they don't like me? I can only hope that they can see how much I love Sara and how much I want to take care of her.

"Good. You can be nervous. Carol was an inner-city school teacher. She knows some real thugs, and Jim, he's an engineer. He knows where all the fresh concrete is being poured, so he knows where to bury you."

"I guess it's a good thing the paparazzi are around every corner. Then again, it would be top ratings for them to get pictures of my dead body."

We laugh all the way to Stinson, and haven't been here long when Jim and Carol arrive. I love them immediately. I can see some of Sara's characteristics in Carol; I guess sometimes it isn't genetic.

When I walk them out to the deck, Jim and Carol are stunned.

"You did all of this?" Carol gushes.

"This is too much," Jim stammers.

"It's the least I can do."

We have drinks on the patio and enjoy the early spring evening, taking in the beautiful evening and the sunset. Sara reaches for me, and we hold hands while we talk. I see Carol spot our clasped hands, and she smiles bigger than she did when she saw the deck. She knows this is a big deal, too.

When Sara runs inside to get the chicken for the grill, Jim says, "Sara seems quite taken with you."

My stomach flips and my heart rate quickens. "Well, honestly I'm quite taken with her. As I've had the opportunity to get to know her well, I've come to realize that I am positively, completely and with all of my being in love with her. She's the woman who centers me and I'm hoping, with your permission, to ask her to marry me."

Staring me squarely in the eyes, he tells me, "You do realize that she will do whatever she wants."

Nodding, I reply, "I do. But I also know she's traditional, and while you may never tell her I asked for permission, I know that if she finds out, she'll be much happier to know that we've discussed this."

Slightly above a whisper, Carol says, "When she came to us when she was thirteen, she wouldn't let us touch her for the first year and a half. It took us a long time to break those walls down. Despite what this big lug says"—she pushes his shoulder—"I think it's a wonderful idea."

"You know, we may have you sign a prenuptial agreement," Jim states firmly.

"Jim!" Carol swears.

Turning to her, he contends, "Carol, Sara has earned her wealth, and I don't want some tabloid porn star to only be interested in her money."

Turning ashen, Carol reminds him, "Jim, I think Trey is doing okay financially, and Sara told us those sex videos were released by some crazy girl."

My heart warms that Jim and Carol are worried about her. I hold my hand up before Sara hears and figures out what I'm trying to do. Leaning in, I assure them, "Jim and Carol, I love Sara, and I want to be with her for the rest of my life. I don't believe in divorce. However, I do know that Sara most likely has much more money than I do. I have no problem whatsoever signing any agreement you or she wants, because I don't think it's anything we'll ever need."

Carol wipes a tear from her eyes and starts to say something when Sara appears and asks, "What's going on?"

"I'm just so overwhelmed by Trey's thoughtfulness with this patio," Carol tells her. "It's so lovely to sit here and enjoy the sunset."

I breathe a sigh of relief to know that she likes the patio, but also that she didn't give away my plans. "Is there anything I can do to help with our feast?"

Ruffling my hair, Sara says, "Mackenzie took very good care of us." She turns to Jim. "And she included your favorite—a berry cobbler with homemade cinnamon ice cream."

Carol pats him on the knee and grins. "Today is a good day."

After dinner, Carol and Sara go inside to talk about Emerson and Dillon's wedding, leaving Jim and me talking about the Giants' season and our lack of optimism for a World Series in their immediate future. Suddenly, Jim gets very serious and says, "Well, to answer your question from before dinner, you do know that isn't up to us, but I have to say I've never seen her so in love. When are you going to ask her?"

"I'm not sure, but probably soon."

He nods. "We'll be happy to have you as part of our family."

I'm over the moon. Now to plan how to make the proposal memorable.

THE CHAOS of Sara's biological family dies down in the tabloids, though Sara herself is in the gossip columns longer than expected, the publicity of her rags-to-riches story a real pull. She's the consummate professional when it comes to handling the media, working hard to take public transportation everywhere she goes with a string of photographers following her every move. She tells me she's often surprised when young women approach and ask for her autograph or to have their picture taken with her, but she's always gracious and does her best to accommodate.

Elizabeth and Annabel are happily taking work off her plate. She's down to working sixty-hour work weeks, which is still crazy, but at least when she's not working, she's all mine.

She's exchanging e-mails with her sisters, Grace and Mary, who'd like to come down and see her, but she's holding them back. "The paparazzi needs to die down a bit more so we can enjoy all that San Francisco has to offer without an audience."

Since the craziness has finally slowed down and we seem to be managing a bit of a private life again, I figure it's time.

It's Saturday night, and Sara has spent the day at the office. She's late, so I have the chance to introduce Jim and Carol to my parents. Carol confides to my mom, "That girl will be late to her own funeral. She'll want to do two more things and go to the bathroom before they close her casket."

Carol and my mom quickly bond over their children as my dad and Jim head out of sight so they can enjoy a drink and get to know each other. I hear CeCe telling Hadlee and Greer about a recent matchme.com date, something about him wearing an ankle monitor.

"No way," Greer exclaims. "He took you to McDonald's for dinner? Did he have a coupon, too?"

CeCe gazes at me, "It's no wonder why many of my friends are single in this city." Sitting beneath the stars in Del Popolo's whimsical garden patio situated next to a rustic, ivy-covered wall, we have one table for the two of us. I've booked the entire garden to enjoy a romantic evening. The engagement ring's in my pocket, and I'm nervous. Almost everyone knows tonight is the night. I thought Hadlee was going to accidentally share the secret, but with CeCe's help, they covered their tracks, and Sara's none the wiser.

Emerson texts me: She's finally leaving. She had to get dressed in something other than jeans and a sweater. We'll be behind her shortly. Good luck!

I scoot everyone to a different private room where they're having their own dinner that CeCe helped me order. I think she's more excited than I am. I pace while I wait for Sara to finally arrive.

She's a vision when she arrives, her hair up in a loose bun that goes well with her beautiful short brown dress with a simple gold drop necklace and long brown boots. My heart skips a beat when she comes into the garden and whispers, "It's so beautiful and romantic."

"I thought we could enjoy a night out paparazzi free."

"You and your camera-ready friends," she says with a sly smile.

I bring her into my arms. "I love you."

"I love you, too."

She's absolutely clueless, has no idea that everyone is outside waiting for the signal to come in. I keep checking my jacket pocket to make sure the ring is still there.

Sara stares at me concerned, "Trey are you okay? You keep grasping your heart. Should I call 9-1-1?"

"I'm fine." Reaching across the table, I take her hand as our dessert is delivered, then get down on one knee and ask, "Sara, from the moment I met you, I knew you were smart, sexy and beautiful on the inside and the outside. I also knew you were the one for me. Please make me the happiest man in the world and agree to marry me."

She nods and cries but doesn't speak. I finally ask, "Is that a yes?"

She laughs and says resoundingly, "Yes! I'll marry you! I love you with all my heart, and I want to share the rest of my life with you."

I slip an eighteen-carat oval sapphire circled in four carats of small diamonds set in a platinum band on her left hand.

We stand and fall into a deep and passionate kiss. I'm euphoric.

The waiter opens the door to the garden, and in flood our family and friends popping champagne bottles. The waitstaff fills the room with additional tables and a buffet of several desserts. Everyone is hugging us, and we're already fielding questions about the wedding date.

Sara is glowing, and I've never been so happy. She's talking to our friends and family, and nothing seems to faze her.

A spoon taps the side of a glass and CeCe says, "I'd like to say a toast to the newly engaged couple, please raise your glasses and join me." CeCe has a few items with her. Turning to us, she begins, "To my amazing twin brother, Charles Michael Arnault, the third and Sara Elizabeth White. I like to say a toast to the newly engaged couple. I offer you," and she lift a small bottle and hands it to me, "this jar of cinnamon to add spice to your life." Reaching for the next item, "I offer you this red paper lantern as a symbol that you will always find joy and good fortune." She hands it to us before reaching for a blue cashmere throw, "And, for this blanket to keep you warm." She shows a beautiful designed loaf of bread that looks much too good to eat. "This loaf of bread so that your home never knows hunger." Picking up the last item, "And, finally this glass to share not only a fine wine but also so that your home will have prosperity and happiness. May your future always be bright. I toast to Trey and Sara. Sara and Trey—we love you."

Everyone lifts a glass and we hear "Cheers" and "Here! Here!"

Sara takes the microphone from CeCe and says, "Thank you all for being here. I can't tell you how much this means to Trey and me. For a girl who really started with nothing—no parents, no family, no home and no safety net—glancing around this room and seeing so many people who've made such a difference in my life...." She starts to weep. "I've had so much, and I'm so grateful that you're here to celebrate with us."

I reach in and give her a tight hug. "I'll love you forever."

Thank you !

Thanks for reading Venture Capitalist: Promise. I do hope you enjoyed Trey and Sara's story and reading the second in the Venture Capitalist series. I appreciate your help in spreading the word, including telling a friend. Before you go, it would mean so much to me if you would take a few minutes to write a review and capture how you feel about what you've read so others may find my work. Reviews help readers find books. Please leave a review on your favorite book site.

Don't miss out on New Releases, Exclusive Giveaways and much more!

- Join Ainsley's **newsletter:**
  www.ainsleystclaire.com

- Like Ainsley St Claire on **Facebook:**
  https://www.facebook.com/ainsleystclaire/?notif_id=1513620809190446&notif_t=page_admin

- Join Ainsley's **reader group:**
  www.ainsleystclaire.com

- Follow Ainsley St Claire on **Twitter:**
  https://twitter.com/AinsleyStClaire

- Follow Ainsley St Claire on **Pinterest:**
  https://www.pinterest.ca/ainsleystclaire/

- Follow Ainsley St Claire on **Goodreads:**
  https://www.goodreads.com/author/show/
  16752271.Ainsley_St_Claire

- Follow Ainsley St Claire on **Reddit:**
  https://www.ainsleystclaire.com/www.reddit.
  com/user/ainsleystclaire

- Visit Ainsley's **website** for her current booklist:
  www.ainsleystclaire.com

I love to hear from you directly, too. Please feel free to **email** me at ainsley@ainsleystclaire.com or check out my **website** www.ainsleystclaire.com for updates.

Other Books
by Ainsley St Claire

If you loved *Venture Capitalist: Promise*, you may enjoy the other sensual, sexy and romantic stories and books she has published.

The Golf Lesson
(An Erotic Short Story)

In a Perfect World

Venture Capitalist: Forbidden Love

About
Ainsley

Ainsley St Claire is a contemporary romance author and adventurer on a lifelong mission to craft sultry story-lines and steamy love scenes that captivate her readers. To date, she's best known for her debut "naughty Nicholas Sparks" novel entitled In A Perfect World.

An avid reader since the age of four, Ainsley's love of books knew no genre. After reading came her love of writing, fully immersing herself in the colorful, impassioned world of contemporary romance.

Ainsley's passion immediately shifted to a vocation when, during a night of terrible insomnia, her first book came to her. Ultimately, this is what inspired her to take that next big step. The moment she wrote her first story, the rest was history.

Currently, Ainsley is in the midst of writing her Venture Capitalist series.

When she isn't being a bookworm or typing away her next story on her computer, Ainsley enjoys spending quality family time with her loved ones. She's happily married to her amazing soul mate and is a proud mother of two rambunctious boys. She is also a scotch aficionada and lover of good food (especially melt-in-your-mouth, velvety chocolate). Outside of books, family, and food, Ainsley is a professional sports spectator and an equally terrible golfer and tennis player.

Made in the USA
Coppell, TX
05 November 2020